Love by Night:

A Black Vampire Story

Love by Night:

A Black Vampire Story

Stina

www.urbanbooks.net

Urban Books, LLC
300 Farmingdale Road, NY-Route 109
Farmingdale, NY 11735

ISBN 13: 978-1-62286-675-5
ISBN 10: 1-62286-675-4

First Mass Market Printing February 2018
First Trade Paperback Printing September 2017
Printed in the United States of America

10 9 8 7 6 5 4 3 2 1

This is a work of fiction. Any references or similarities to actual events, real people, living or dead, or to real locales are intended to give the novel a sense of reality. Any similarity in other names, characters, places, and incidents is entirely coincidental.

Distributed by Kensington Publishing Corp.
Submit orders to:
Customer Service
400 Hahn Road
Westminster, MD 21157-4627
Phone: 1-800-733-3000
Fax: 1-800-659-243

Love by Night:

A Black Vampire Story

Stina

Prologue

"Do you love me?" Kesh asked, his gleaming white teeth like shining lightbulbs against the dark. He hovered over the pretty girl in his bed, his long, twisted locks of hair dangling around his face as he moved between her legs with a rhythm that left her speechless. "I asked you a question," he panted, swirling his hips faster and harder.

She groaned but didn't speak. He grabbed both of her hands and pinned them to the bed at the sides of her head.

"I asked you a question," he panted, swirling his hips faster and harder. "Look at me," he whispered. "Look into my eyes."

"Mmm." A low guttural moan was all the girl could manage.

"Look at me," Kesh demanded, grinding harder.

The girl's eyes fluttered open into slits, then widened with every thrust of his pelvis. She stared into Kesh's eyes, mesmerized.

He grinned, satisfied. He knew that between his powers, his thick, rock-hard love muscle, and the incense burning, her senses were scrambled. He could've gotten her to do anything in that moment. He'd already succeeded in taking over her mind, bending her to his every whim.

This was nothing new for Kesh: he could seduce any woman. He'd been doing it for so long, it was becoming too easy.

He looked down at the simple girl and thought, *No will. No desire. No strength.* Then he slammed into the girl without mercy, his swollen member more of a weapon than a source of pleasure. A low growl bubbled up from his core and escaped his lips. In that moment, he was one part man, one part monster.

The girl, finally aware of the pain, opened her mouth to scream, but Kesh quickly clamped his hand over her open lips. His body bucked against hers with ferocity. He had to get it out. He had to feed all his needs.

"I asked you a question. *Do* you love me?" he growled. His voice was deep and sinister. It made him sound how he felt, like a beast. A fire flashed in his eyes. He didn't want to do it—he needed to do it.

The girl stared up into Kesh's contorted face. The terror ripping through her body stretched her eyes to capacity. She whimpered against his smothering hand. She should have listened to her friend and stayed away from Kesh. But there was something about him that called to her, like she was under his control.

A lone tear leaked from each eye and pooled in her ears. She strained against his grip to move her head up and down—the only way she could say yes. Pain rippled across her face like the effect of a rock hitting a still pond.

"Good. I hope it's enough to die for." Kesh smiled, revealing the weapon that was about to take her life. He slowly lowered his head to her neck. He wanted to savor this meal. Kesh opened his mouth, exposing his long, sharp canines, and bit down on her carotid artery. The girl's legs moved like she was riding an invisible bicycle. Her pelvis bucked, but Kesh's weight was too much. She was at his mercy.

His eyes rolled into his head as he feasted. As he consumed her blood, he had an orgasm. When the girl finally stopped moving, Kesh loosened his grip. He finished his feast, then slid himself out of her. He liked to stay inside the women while he took their life. Kesh rolled off her and climbed off his tall black four-poster bed. He found his way out of the black mesh drapes that hung from each bedpost.

"Weakling," he mumbled, using his forearm to wipe the blood from his face and mouth. "Even tastes weak," he complained.

Kesh put on a pair of brown slacks before walking over to the antique glass-top bar in the far corner of his room. He scanned his choices. "Something strong," he said aloud to himself. He picked up a bottle of vintage scotch. "You'll do." He poured himself a double shot and took it straight to the head.

"Ah," Kesh said and winced, feeling the libation light up his chest and stomach. It still wasn't enough to soothe his longing. He was bored being king of his clan. He could have any woman of his kind that he wanted, but Kesh thought they were all weak. He wanted a challenge: someone strong and intriguing.

He walked over to his old platinum treasure chest, bent down in front of it, and opened it. In the dark room, the contents lit up like Christmas lights. Kesh reached down into the purple velvet-lined chest and picked up the tiny goosenecked bottle. He held it up to his face, examined the contents, and let out an exasperated breath. He'd had the elixir for years now, but what good was it? A tiny drop of the liquid had the power to take over the strongest mind. The rules said it could be used only on humans and not on others like him.

"I guess I'll never get to use it," he whispered. "They're all so easy without it. I haven't met a solid, strong one yet." Kesh sighed at the thought. Over the years, since his making, he'd watch women fight for the right to vote, fight for the right to work and get equal pay, fight for the right to have abortions, and lead an entire feminist movement, yet he couldn't find a woman who could challenge him enough to be his queen. Women swooned over him and competed for his time and attention. He wanted one who wouldn't be so easy, so boring.

A loud knock at the door interrupted Kesh's thoughts. He quickly put the bottle back into the chest and closed it.

"Who is it?" he called out.

"Me."

"Tiev? Come in."

Tiev, Kesh's best friend and second in command, entered the room and immediately shook his head.

"I thought you liked her?" Tiev asked, looking over at the limp, pale leg hanging off the side of the bed.

Kesh shook his head and shrugged. "I thought so too."

"It's been a hundred years, brother. When are you going to, as the mortals say, settle down with a companion? Is anyone going to be good enough?"

Kesh looked over at his beautiful victim and smirked. "I don't know, Tiev. I guess when I find *the one*."

"Well, hurry up. The longer you're without a mate, the easier it is for *them* to attack us again. Our fate depends on it," Tiev said seriously.

Kesh rubbed his chin, contemplating what his friend had said. Tiev was right. In their world, a true king had a mate. Although she carried muted powers and had limited control, the queen, they all knew, gave the king his strength. It was the queen who kept the king's needs fed and who stopped at nothing to protect him and his entire following. But that meant whoever was chosen to be queen had to be strong too. Kesh knew he hadn't yet found the one.

"Is everyone ready to move?" Kesh asked, changing the subject. He'd had this conversation with Tiev a million times.

"Yes. I told them all tonight. Have you decided where?"

Kesh turned toward Tiev. "We're going back to where it all started for me. North Carolina. Raleigh, North Carolina."

Chapter 1

Adirah sang along to Whitney Houston's "Greatest Love of All" as the engine in her beat-up 1999 Honda Accord sputtered and hissed across the North Carolina state line.

"Finally," Adirah yelled over the music. "I made it."

She had been driving for fifteen hours from New York City and had stopped only once to use the bathroom. Even that was a chance she'd taken, since she had had to run inside and leave the car running for fear that it wouldn't start up again. Adirah had pumped her fist when she returned to find her car still there.

"Beast mode," Adirah cheered, slapping the steering wheel to let the car know how much she appreciated her. "Lucinda, we made it. We made it. Two girls from the hood made it all the way down here to chase our dreams." Adirah laughed.

Nothing was going to stop Adirah from going to the college of her dreams. She was determined to make a difference in the lives of women who'd grown up under the same circumstances she had endured as a child.

"I can't wait to tell Mommy that I made it. And, Adol, I'm going to make you proud . . . ," Adirah said, her voice trailing off. She thought back to . . .

Brooklyn, New York
August 2007

"Shh." Adirah placed a shaky hand over her little brother, Addis's mouth. He continued to moan, despite her squeezing. She could feel his entire body trembling just like hers.

"Addis, be quiet, or he will hear you," Adirah whispered harshly in his little ear. It was all she could do to protect him from the danger lurking outside of their bedroom door.

Adolphis, her older brother by two years, sat across from them, his head down, his knees to his chest, and his fists curled at his sides. He rocked back and forth. Something Adirah had seen before—a sign that he was in distress.

"Please! No! No!"

Adirah jumped at the sound of her mother's pleading screams. She stared across the room at the door, silently praying it didn't burst open at any minute. Adirah's heart sank, and the gnawing disappointment of powerlessness settled inside of her. She couldn't do anything to save her mother.

"No! No!" her mother screamed some more.

Addis whimpered and curled his body closer to Adirah's. She tried to comfort him, but she could barely control her own shaking hands and pounding heart. Sweat beads ran a race down her back, and her throat was desert dry.

"It . . . it's o-okay," Adirah whispered, burying Addis's face in her stomach. "I'm going to protect you." But who was going to protect her? At ten years old, Adirah felt like she'd been left in the middle of barren lands with no food or water. She felt like a leaf left out in the sun.

Loud thumps and crashing glass resounded through their bedroom door. More screams from their mother cut through the silence of their room. Adirah's chest trembled as tears streaked her dark skin, leaving salty white lines down her cheeks. She listened as her father's booming voice got closer. He cursed her mother in Ibo—his native Nigerian language. Adirah was able to make out some of the words—whore, liar, slut. *She couldn't understand what evil thing had possessed her father, but it seemed to be coming more often. Almost every day.*

"Agh!" *Her mother let out another ear-shattering scream.*

This time, Adolphis got to his feet, his chest heaving. He stared at the door, ready to charge like a bull at the sight of a matador's red cape.

"No, Adol. You can't go. Stay here," *Adirah pleaded, her shaky voice coming out in raggedy, jagged breaths.*

"He is going to kill her this time. I have to help her," *Adolphis said, starting for the door.*

Adirah unhooked herself from Addis and scrambled to her feet. "No, Adol. Please. Let's just wait." *She had seen what her father was capable of in his fits of fury. Their mother had already suffered a broken nose, a broken eye socket, knocked-out teeth, broken ribs, and too many bruises to name. Adirah had been the one to care for her mother each time her father left her battered until she could barely move.*

"You're not big enough yet, Adol," *Adirah pleaded, blocking his path with her body. Adolphis pushed back. They struggled against each other. Adirah was desperate to keep her brother in the room.* "He will hurt you bad. You have to stay here, with us."

Just then, more screams cut through the door. Adirah startled, instinctively whipped her head around. The distraction lasted long enough for her brother Adolphis to push her aside and yank the door open.

"No! God, no!" her mother hollered, the sound amplified.

Adirah watched as Adolphis barreled forward with the force of a wrecking ball.

"Leave her alone!" Adolphis barked. Adirah cringed when Adolphis slammed into her father. "Leave her alone, I said! Let her go!"

Adirah watched in horror as her father released his grip on her mother's hair and, with a powerful shove, sent her mother's head slamming to the floor.

"You think you're a man now?" her father barked in Ibo. "You think you can stand up to me in my own house?" he said, turning his attention to Adolphis.

Adolphis did not back down. His feet were firmly planted on the floor, his chest was puffed out, and his shoulders were squared. He pointed at his father and said, "Don't touch her again. I will protect her from you. I won't let you hurt her again."

Adirah swallowed hard. Her father's laugh made her shiver like someone had pumped ice water into her veins. It was the same malevolent cackle he'd made right before he knocked her mother unconscious in their kitchen one time.

"You don't want me to touch my own whore of a wife?" her father snarled. He walked over to her mother, lifted his boot, and kicked her in the stomach.

Adirah winced and clamped her hands over her mouth to stifle the scream that bubbled up in her throat.

"What will you do about it?" Her father towered over both Adolphis and his wife; his eyes were flashing like a flame of malice.

"Argh!" Adolphis charged forward, his fists out in front of him.

Her father caught Adolphis by the throat with one hand. "You wanted this?" her father yelled, spit spewing from his lips. "You wanted to be treated like a man?" He clamped down on Adolphis's neck and lifted him off his feet. At twelve years old, Adolphis was no match for her father's six-foot-three-inch, 250-pound frame.

In Adirah's eyes, her father was a monster with seemingly superhuman strength. She had seen him in action before, but this time, his eyes seemed to glow orange and red, and his face scrunched into the shape of a beast's . . . a werewolf on attack, baring sharp teeth, drooling from the sides of his mouth. Adirah squeezed her eyes shut. She was experiencing a nightmare. She prayed that when she opened her eyes, everything would be normal and she would be in her bed. Her prayers weren't answered: the evil image of her father's face turned back into its human form, but the scene was just as violent.

As her father squeezed Adolphis's neck, Adirah heard something crack and crunch. Things had already gone too far, and there was no going back. Her mother screeched from the floor; blood leaked from her head. Addis screamed at Adirah's side. They all watched, horrified and terrified.

Adolphis's legs dangled as if he were hanging from a noose. His body bucked, and he clawed at his father's fingers. He let out a sickening gurgle, which made Adirah feel as if a thousand spiders were crawling over her skin.

"Please!" Adirah cried out, finally finding her voice. She watched her brother's face turn a shocking shade of burgundy, while his lips turned pale gray. White foam oozed from the left side of his mouth. "Daddy! Please!" Adirah begged. "He didn't mean it! Please, let him go!"

She fell to her knees. Her pleas fell on deaf ears. Adolphis's eyes rolled so far into the back of his head, all Adirah could see was white.

Her father cackled again. The sound rang in Adirah's ears over and over as she stood rooted to the floor, unable to take her eyes off Adolphis until he went limp.

Adirah watched the life leave his body. His legs stopped moving. His arms dangled at his sides, and urine dripped down his pant leg.

"Adol!" Adirah screamed so loud, the back of her throat itched. "No! Adol!"

Her father finally released his grip. Adolphis's body fell lifeless at Adirah's feet just before she passed out.

"I'm going to do it all for you, Adol," Adirah murmured, touching the sterling silver locket with her brother's picture inside that she wore around her neck. "You tried to save us once, but now it is my turn."

As Adirah drove her car onto the campus of historic Billet University, she inhaled and exhaled. This was the start of a new beginning. Her past was behind her; she was looking forward only from here on out.

"I'm going to make our entire family proud," she murmured. "And this is the place that is going to make it happen."

Adirah had done tons of research on the university and its rich legacy for people of color. Billet was one of the only schools founded by African Americans back in the 1800s. But the school's existence hadn't come without a struggle and, ultimately, some bloodshed. Adirah had read about the race war between blacks and whites that had happened right on the campus grounds. She'd been proud to learn that her people had prevailed, although hundreds had died. The school had since become one of the premier colleges for African-American students, although it boasted a legacy of complete diversity. Adirah had literally jumped for joy when she'd gotten her acceptance letter.

She parked her car in the visitors' building parking lot and got out. She stretched her body and took in her surroundings. The campus was more beautiful than she had imagined. Majestic trees, green grass, students milling about, smiling. A far cry from New York City. Her legs literally shook with anticipation and excitement. There would be no stopping Adirah—the daughter of Nigerian immigrants, whose father had committed suicide and whose mother had gone insane. She would not accept her fate as a forgotten orphan in the world. Adirah didn't want anyone to feel sorry for her. She never had. She wanted to make her own way. She'd already proven how resilient she was to everyone else; now she wanted to show herself.

She inhaled and smiled. The scent of old earth and red clay settled in the back of her throat until she could taste it. Even the air on the campus felt different . . . in some ways almost magical. The campus was more majestic than it was in the pictures she'd looked at over and over again in the brochure. The old Gothic-style buildings ringed by gargoyle protectors—perfectly lined up and perched along the roofs, with their mouths open in a battle cry—spoke of the school's old-world history. The one-hundred-year-old weeping willow trees that formed an archway down the center of the campus invited everyone in. And the faded gray statues of the school's brave founders sent a chill down Adirah's spine. She couldn't help but feel she had stepped back in time.

She'd read that the school had worked tirelessly to preserve all its old structures and spaces—even the sacred grounds where many had died during the race war. There were spirits on the campus, and Adirah could feel and hear them. For years Adirah had been connected to spirits. They had been reaching out to her and making contact since she was a little girl. Not wanting to believe that it was happening, Adirah would ignore the signs. It was her secret. Something about the aura of these spirits made Adirah uncomfortable. It sent a shiver down her spine. "Ignore them, Adirah," she whispered to herself.

Adirah went inside the building, got her dorm assignment, and drove around to Rothschild, the building she would be living in. She looked out of her windshield at the building's facade. The gargoyles seemed to be staring at Adirah, daring her to enter. It made her uneasy. Adirah ignored the lifelike gargoyles and focused on the building's history. Rothschild was one of the oldest dorms on campus and had housed only black women in the 1800s. This fact made Adirah more determined to live up to the history created by her ancestors, who'd fought so hard for equality.

"Well, baby girl, we made it all the way here." Adirah rubbed the surface of her car's cracked dashboard as she spoke. "Now we just have to stay focused and win at this. I promise you I will walk out of here a new person—a better, wiser person." She smiled and exited the car.

There was so much going on around her. Music played in the distance. It wasn't coming from a radio; it sounded more like an impromptu gathering of musicians on campus somewhere. Adirah pictured students gathered in a circle, each with their respective instrument, singing along to the chosen song. Sororities and fraternities had tables set out in different spots, with members standing and passing out fliers advertising their parties. Even from where she stood, Adirah noticed one particular fraternity's table. It had the biggest crowd, and all its members seemed to be gorgeous . . . almost perfect. She'd heard about sororities and fraternities choosing people based on certain beauty standards. She'd already decided she wasn't going to fall into that. There would be no time for frivolous activities. Schoolwork was all Adirah would be focused on.

The members of that popular fraternity were mesmerizing. Even though Adirah wasn't planning on joining a sorority, she still felt an urge to stare at all the tables. Adirah blinked a few times. "You can't be staring at people," she said under her breath. She turned her attention back to her surroundings. The Billet campus seemed to have a pulse of its own. People hustled up and down the green grounds around the Rothschild building, some alone, some in groups. Even the birds—tiny gray ones, whistling blue jays, and a murder of circling black crows—seemed to be buzzing around with move-in-day excitement.

Adirah went over to her trunk, opened it, and looked down into the stuffed crater. Bags of clothes, boxes of her most cherished belongings, and numerous trinkets filled the trunk, as well as the backseat of her car. It was a wonder that her car had been able to drive on all four wheels with all the extra weight crammed into the back of it. She put her hands on her hips and sighed. She had her work cut out for her. Reluctantly, she reached into the trunk and hefted the first of many boxes she'd have to unload. As she leaned up from digging in her trunk, she let out a long exasperated breath. It wasn't lost on her that she was alone. Her stomach clenched as she watched all the gushing parents proudly helping their college freshmen move into their new homes, lifting boxes of brand-new matching houseware items with smiles on their faces. She listened to parents and students share joyous laughter and watched each long embrace when it was time to part ways.

Adirah sat one of her bags down for a moment and placed her hand over her aching heart. She thought about her mother, something that always brought tears to her eyes. Her mother had once been so vibrant and happy. She'd sing Adirah and her brothers songs that she'd learned as a child in Nigeria. She'd dance and grab their hands to make them dance too. Her mother would cook meals, and they'd all sit around the pot and share from it—another tradition. Adirah missed that. She missed the sparkle that had faded from her mother's eyes over the years.

All her life, Adirah could see the yellow glow around her mother. As a child, Adirah hadn't understood why her father had a dark, almost black, shadow around him. As she got older, Adirah realized the glow she saw around people was the reading of their spirit. She couldn't always see a glow around everyone she met, but when she did, Adirah paid attention.

"Not now, Adirah," she whispered to herself, swiping roughly at the tears rimming her eyes. She wasn't going to allow herself to wallow in the suffering of her past. She'd promised her mother she would study hard and become the best psychotherapist alive so she could save families like her own. She had vowed not to dwell in the past but to learn from it.

After Adolphis's death, her mother had never recovered. "Mommy, do you like these flowers?" Adirah would say, holding up a bunch of yellow weeds she'd picked from the lot outside of their building. Her mother would just stare, her mouth slack. "Smell them, Mommy. That will help," Adirah would urge, her voice cracking with emotion. "Please." When Adirah didn't get any reaction from her mother, she would throw the flowers to the floor and crush them under her feet.

Weeks would pass, and her mother wouldn't speak or eat or bathe. Instead, she would stare ahead at nothing, barely blinking. Addis would cry and tug on his mother's arms, but all to no avail. Over the course of months, Adirah had fought to take care of her mother, herself, and her little brother. She'd forced soft food between her mother's lips, unsure if any was making it down to her stomach. Adirah had watched her mother begin to shrink, both physically and mentally. Some days Adirah couldn't stand to look at the bones jutting out of her mother's face, as if sharp objects had been inserted under her skin. Her mother's dark, sunken eyes made Adirah depressed.

Eventually, on the urging of Adirah's school, the city's child protective services showed up. Adirah tried desperately to pretend things were fine, but her efforts were of no use. Addis wouldn't stop screaming, and her mother was a complete zombie the entire time the caseworker was there. It wasn't a difficult decision for the caseworker: she had her mother committed to a mental institution, and Adirah and Addis were sent to foster care.

The foster-care experience proved devastating for her younger brother. He didn't have the mental strength that Adirah had. She did everything she could to comfort Addis and protect him, but he couldn't handle the upheaval in his life. He began fighting, stealing, and acting violently. Over time, Addis became a miniature version of their father.

Adirah shivered and shook her head now as she thought about the day Addis was sentenced to juvenile jail for beating a boy so badly, he left him in a coma. When the judge committed her little brother to a juvenile detention facility until the age of twenty-one, Adirah collapsed backward onto the hard wooden bench in the courtroom and sobbed. The reality had hit her then that she had lost her entire family. Now, just like then, Adirah was all alone, with one thing on her mind—survival.

Balancing two boxes out in front of her, Adirah used her foot to push open the door to her dorm room. Her entire body was slick with sweat, and her muscles screamed under the weight of her load.

"Aye, let me help you with all of that," a female voice called from somewhere behind the stack. Adirah couldn't see the source of the voice, but she was sure glad when one of the boxes was eased out of her hands.

"Thank you," Adirah huffed. "Those stairs are . . ."

"Something else," said the young woman who belonged to the voice, finishing Adirah's sentence. "I know. This is one of the oldest buildings on campus, and those are the original stairs. Tiny, winding, and impossible with boxes. I guess back then they weren't as needy as we are, with all our gadgets and fancy trappings," she noted. "I'm Lina. Glad you're here." She moved Adirah's box to her right hip and extended her free left hand toward Adirah.

"Adirah. Adirah Messa."

Lina laughed. "Okay, Adirah Messa, since we are giving out our entire government name, I am Lina Boyd. Your official college dorm mate. And soon I will probably be your resident pain in the ass too."

Adirah blushed, realizing she didn't know anything about introduction etiquette. "Sorry. I'm used to having to say my whole name when I first meet people."

"Why is that?" Lina asked.

"I'm a product of the foster system. That's just how they wanted it."

"Well, you've made it through, and now you're in college. Good for you. That tells me you've got drive."

Adirah smiled. "Thanks." She couldn't remember the last time someone had genuinely complimented her like that.

Adirah took in an eyeful of her new roommate. She thought Lina had a simple beauty about her—round doe eyes, tiny button nose, and full lips. But most importantly, Lina had a yellow glow around her. It set Adirah at ease, although she could already tell from the chunky silver jewelry layered around Lina's neck, and from her head-to-toe black clothes, that Lina was different, maybe even eccentric.

Adirah took note of how Lina's honey-colored skin showed up against her dark lipstick and how her glowing green eyes were like shiny jewels in the light. Adirah felt that this meeting was getting off to a good start. Lina seemed nice. But, as always, Adirah was wary of strangers. No matter how friendly they seemed.

"Ah, no worries," Lina said. "This is your side over here. Nice and quaint. I hate sleeping near windows, so"—Lina turned to the right and pointed—"she's all yours."

Adirah sat her box down and looked at the twin-size bed, the tiny desk, and the empty corner. She smiled. "At least it is all *mine*," she mumbled. No more sharing spaces with girls she was forced to call sister or with group-home girls who stole her belongings and terrorized her daily.

Adirah appreciated Lina's help with carrying the rest of her things up from the car, but she quickly noticed how much her roommate could talk. *Nonstop* was probably the best way to describe Lina's banter. She jumped from topic to topic like a frog in a lily pond. Adirah could barely keep up.

"So, you know all the history of Billet University?" Lina asked in the middle of her blabbing.

"I think I did a fair amount of research," Adirah replied, sticking her chest out a bit. "I know it is one of the best schools in North Carolina . . . or one of the best for *us*, anyways."

"That's all true, but do you know about the *other* history?" Lina asked, looking at Adirah with wide eyes. "The *real* history of everything that happened here?"

Adirah dropped her last trash bag full of clothes at the foot of her bed and flopped down, exhausted. "Other history? Real history?" Adirah repeated, her brows furrowed.

"You know . . . the school's dark side. The things that are unseen but that have happened and still happen to this day," Lina replied, dropping her voice to a mysterious whisper. "'Things that go bump in the night' type of stuff."

Adirah chuckled. "You look like a scary-movie narrator right now, girl. What in the world are you talking about?" Adirah was starting to have second thoughts about liking Lina. Was she going to turn out to be some conspiracy theory nut job? If there was one thing that Adirah did not go for, it was all this conspiracy theory mumbo jumbo.

"I'm telling you, Adirah, I did a lot of digging," Lina said. "I've been waiting to show this to somebody. C'mere. Look." Lina leaned over and pointed out of Adirah's window. "You see that spot over there at the side of the Freeman building?" Lina was pointing to a patch of discolored grass about the size of a basketball court.

Adirah climbed off the bed, glanced out the window, and shrugged. "Yeah. Okay?"

"Look at the ground there. Now look at the ground everywhere else. Do you see how different that spot is compared to all the plush green lawns and rich grassy spots around?" Lina pointed, moving her right pointer finger from side to side.

"Yeah, I see it. That spot looks kind of gray and dried up," Adirah answered, squinting and contemplating what she was being shown. "What about it?"

"Well, it has been said that that is where the fights happened . . . the killings back in the 1800s, at the end of slavery. You know, the war between black and white, good and evil. I've heard it was a freed slave revolt, but unlike others you've heard about, the slaves prevailed here. They fought to keep a school they had secretly erected to educate themselves. It stood right where the Freeman building stands now. Of course, the white masters back then didn't like it. School was supposed to be only for the whites," Lina lectured.

Adirah stared at the patch of dried grass. A vision appeared. She could see black men, women, and children—descendants from Africa—standing up for their right to learn. She could see blood on the ground and bodies. She could see a younger woman, no older than herself, stumbling and tripping over the long material of her tattered skirt as she tried to escape a white man's ax. Adirah let out a small gasp, and the vision disappeared. Adirah wasn't sure if she had imagined it or if she had really witnessed the historical battle.

"People say that the souls that died there never really died. That they still walk the campus at night, but by day they rest underground over there, so that is why nothing ever grows there. No life form can flourish in that spot because the undead inhabit that patch of earth. They live under the ground there during the day and come up from it at night, leaving the land too disturbed to grow anything on," Lina said spookily.

Adirah shook off the images and sucked her teeth. "Who believes in ghosts at our age?" Adirah replied. "That's got to be the silliest thing I've ever heard." But still, she stared out at the parched gray ground near the Freeman building, her eyes darting from that spot to the green earth of the rest of the campus. Lina was right. That spot was the only place on campus that didn't have healthy grass growing. It was, in fact, an eyesore. Suddenly goose bumps cropped up on Adirah's arms.

"Not ghosts . . . the undead," Lina replied almost breathlessly. She moved closer to Adirah, until she was almost right in her ear. "Ghosts can't be seen, just felt. The undead are like real people, except they live for hundreds of years, feasting on humans and expanding their groups."

Adirah laughed and took a few steps away from Lina. "Listen, if I never believed my mother when she talked about seeing spirits back in Nigeria, I will never believe that this campus is inhabited by the *undead* at night. What are the undead, anyway? You mean, like, vampires?" Adirah said.

Lina only raised her eyebrows in response.

"Vampires?" Adirah shook her head at her roommate. "You sure your major isn't fiction storytelling?"

Chapter 2

Adirah looked at herself one last time. The mirror standing in the corner of her dorm room reflected the image of a woman about to begin a new chapter in her journey. She had been fussing with her outfit and had changed several times already. She adjusted her head wrap and made sure her cardigan didn't have any lint on it. It was the first day of class; she had to look her best. Her mother would've been proud of how she looked—like a regal Nigerian girl, one focused on her studies. Adirah smiled at the thought. What the heck was a regal Nigerian, anyway? She'd always thought her mother's stories of living like a princess back in Nigeria were far-fetched.

In Brooklyn, her father had struggled as an underpaid cabdriver, his pride always getting the best of him. He had turned bitter and hadn't admitted to being helpless when he had to drag his family into public housing. Her mother had stayed at home, raising Adirah and her brothers, but she'd occasionally taken sewing jobs for a neighborhood African clothing shop to help out. She'd give all the money she made to Adirah's father, but nothing had ever seemed to be enough. Adirah didn't see anything regal about her childhood and the nights she'd gone hungry or the days she'd been teased about her homemade clothes.

Now Adirah contemplated snatching off her head wrap, but then she remembered that she hadn't twisted her natural hair, so it was a big, puffy mess underneath.

"Your outfit screams newbie," Lina said with a chuckle from her side of the room.

Adirah turned around, feeling self-conscious now. "Well, I don't own a wardrobe of all black," she shot back.

Lina stood up from her bed and began smoothing her hair back into a ponytail. "You think I wear all black because I want to?"

Adirah put her hands up and tilted her head. "Uh, well, most of us get dressed in what we want to wear. I didn't think we lived in a country where we were told to wear a certain color. So yes, I think you wear black because you want to."

"You're missing the point," Lina said, moving closer to Adirah. "I wear all black to protect my soul. My soul is pure, but if I dressed like you"—Lina moved her pointer finger in the air, starting at Adirah's head and moving to her feet—"the evils that lurk would be able to see that I am a pure soul. I would be a target. We are the ones they want . . . the pure, untouched souls. Don't you know anything?"

Adirah scoffed and rolled her eyes. "Oh, boy. Not this whole undead, spirits, ghosts, and goblins talk again. Who would want to snatch your soul?" Adirah waved at her and picked up her backpack.

"The undead want all our souls, Adirah. They're here. Trust me. You better protect yours too. They say that all black protects the things inside of you . . . your spirit, your soul."

Adirah laughed. "Really, Lina?"

"I'm sure you've seen them. They're the popular crowd. The biggest fraternity on campus. All good looking . . . no, gorgeous. Beautiful glowing skin. Perfect bodies. They're all charming. Everyone on campus wants to be with them . . . until it's too late," Lina said. "Until their souls are snatched and they are forced to join their coven."

"So now the popular students are the undead? A coven? As in, like, a coven of witches or a clan of vampires? Or maybe even a brood, you know, the vampires that don't come directly from the bloodline," Adirah said sarcastically, twisting her lips.

"Whatever they call their group, at Billet they pass themselves off as a fraternity. But . . . ," Lina replied.

"Oh, my God," Adirah shot back. "Every college has that one fraternity that girls go crazy for. Stop it."

"I'll show you later. You'll see," Lina said.

"Right. You'll show me the undead fraternity that snatches people's souls," Adirah replied sarcastically. "I'm starting to think that when I become a psychotherapist, you might be my first patient. Have a good first day of classes, Lina."

Adirah couldn't stop thinking about her crazy roommate's words as she navigated through the sea of bodies on campus. She entered one of the classroom buildings and couldn't believe how many people were in the hallways. There were students hustling and bustling in both directions, like traffic on busy thoroughfares during rush hour. Adirah got pushed out of the way more than once as she tried to walk and read the room numbers on her schedule at the same time. Lina had been right about one thing. Adirah stuck out on campus. She looked like a scared baby doe stuck in oncoming traffic in the middle of the highway.

"What?" Adirah murmured and stopped walking. She turned around. It felt like someone was behind her . . . close behind her. Adirah waved it off, but she still felt an eerie sensation on her neck. It happened again.

"Stop," Adirah grumbled. She could've sworn someone had whispered in her ear. She touched the back of her neck, trying to get the prickly hairs standing up back there to lie down. Although she'd always waved them off, the voices and the feeling that some invisible person was with her all the time were something she'd never gotten used to since her childhood. Adirah's mother had told her that communicating with the spirit world was her gift, but Adirah just thought it made her look and feel crazy.

Adirah rushed into her first class with her chest heaving. She stumbled forward, noticing that all eyes were on her. She was the last to come in and sat in one of the auditorium-style seats just two seconds before the professor closed the door, preventing latecomers from entering.

Adirah let out a long, relieved breath and wiped sweat from her forehead. College was definitely an entirely different world. She couldn't believe how big the campus was and how easy it was to get lost. She listened to the low hum of student chatter and looked around at all the faces. Back in Brooklyn there hadn't been this much diversity in her schools. Adirah touched her head wrap and adjusted her preppy sweater. She had certainly overdressed for class. Her cheeks flamed over.

Lina was right. You look silly. Definitely like a lame freshman.

There were girls there in jogging pants, pajamas, and jeans, and here Adirah was dressed like a prep school nerd. She folded her arms across her chest and sank down in her seat. Her entire look screamed "fresh meat freshman."

Adirah finally settled her thrumming heart and prepared to open her textbook, but the feeling that someone was right next to her came back.

Dira. Dira. Dira.

Adirah was startled, and her eyes went wide. This time the voice was calling out to her. She shifted in her seat, her body tense. She looked to her left and then to her right, her head whipping around in a frenzy. She waved her hands near her ears but then caught herself. Adirah knew that she couldn't afford to look crazy in class. There would be no talk about spirits following her or voices in her ear this time. That had backfired on her when she was in high school. She'd almost been committed for psychiatric treatment behind that.

As Adirah tried to get herself together, she turned one more time and made sure there was no one there. This time, she locked eyes with a stranger. He was staring straight at her, unflinching. Adirah held his gaze for several long seconds. Her heart immediately began pounding again. She didn't recognize the feeling. Could it be fear, or could it be excitement? Adirah squinted. She had seen this stranger before but couldn't place where.

Whoa. He is gorgeous.

She twitched in her chair, palms getting wet with sweat.

Why is he looking at me? He's too fine to be interested in me.

Adirah noticed that the guy's smooth brown skin seemed to glow, and he had the most gorgeous smile she'd seen on a man in her life. There was something about him that struck Adirah immediately. She felt her face get hot.

No. Stop it.

Adirah shook her head and broke eye contact with him. She turned around in her seat and shook her head. Why was he smiling at her like he knew her? Adirah touched her temple and closed her eyes for a few seconds.

You're not at school to meet guys. You're here to make something out of yourself. Now, shake it off.

After twenty minutes of daydreaming, Adirah finally focused on the lecture.

"And we also try to find the connection between what we perceive as psychiatric disorders and real telekinetic and telepathic abilities. Are we mistaking psychosis for what is a real ability to do what is considered superhuman?" the professor said.

Adirah had heard enough. She sucked her teeth and raised her hand.

"Yes. Young lady down in the center," the professor said and pointed at her.

"I am not sure that an entire psychology class can be dedicated to what might amount to no more than fiction and is not fact," Adirah said, shaking her head.

"How so?" the professor asked, walking forward with his arms folded.

"Well, telekinesis, as you should know, isn't real. You're talking about human beings saying they can move inanimate objects with their minds. Isn't that a far reach and way too sci-fi, fantasy, and fictional for a college psychology class, which serious students like myself attend to earn a degree?" Adirah answered, frustration lacing her words.

The professor chuckled. "Well, that's the—"

"Telekinesis is not fiction," came a deep voice from Adirah's left.

The entire class turned toward the voice that had interrupted their professor. It was *him*! Adirah's heart sped up again. He stood up, and she was able to see his muscular chest pushing against the thin material of his black T-shirt. She noticed the shiny onyx emblem, with what appeared to be a four-point star and Greek letters, hanging on a braided leather necklace around his neck.

That's where I've seen him! The big crowd on move-in day. The popular fraternity . . . he is one of the members.

"Or is it?" the gorgeous stranger went on, rising from his seat and taking a few steps toward her. His smile was almost infectious. Adirah caught herself wanting to smile back at him, although he was grandstanding on her point. "Aren't fact and fiction both about perception? I mean, if you believe only in things you can prove, then would you ever accomplish anything?" he said, getting closer now. Adirah swore she could smell him. It was a powerful masculine scent mixed with an earthy smoked-wood aroma. It was sexy.

He continued. "Isn't telekinesis part of every psyche? Telepathy too? Don't you tell yourself you're going to move forward in life, so you do? Just like if I tell myself I can make that door slam, it might. Or that if I can make a beautiful woman love me, she might," the stranger said, his eyes trained on Adirah with so much intensity, she had to shift in her seat.

He was speaking directly to her, as if everyone else in the class had suddenly fallen through the floor. His chestnut-brown eyes were like a hypnotist's gem, darting from side to side, trying to lull her mind. Adirah's insides warmed up. She exhaled and sat up straight in her seat and broke eye contact with him. No one would have that kind of power over her. Her jaw rocked. She was mad at herself for having that reaction to him.

"So, miss, do you think I can use my mind to do what I want?" the stranger asked Adirah. He smiled, mocking her.

Adirah swallowed hard, her nostrils flaring. She hated to be embarrassed. Now all eyes were on her for sure. Her face felt like it would burst into flames at any moment. The professor had a pleased grin on his face, unfazed by the gorgeous student who had taken over his class.

"I still stick to my argument. What does perception or fake powers have to do with my psychology degree? Psychology is about the human mind, not some fictional version of the human mind," Adirah argued. "And no. Only a beautiful woman can decide for *herself* if she loves someone." She slammed her thick psychology textbook closed and put her bag on her shoulder. She was done. "Psychology is about helping people," Adirah mumbled. "Not about hoaxes and tricks and mind games." She hated to lose an argument. She was seething inside.

Adirah spent the last few minutes of the class anxiously tapping her foot, praying for it to end. When it was over, she shot up from her seat and scrambled toward the door as quickly as she could. She wasn't fast enough. By the time she reached the door, her new nemesis had already made it there and was waiting, wearing that perfect smile.

"Hey," he said, pushing his long locks out of his face. "About earlier . . ."

Adirah refused to look into his eyes this time. Although she was sweating and her stomach

churned, she played tough, like he wasn't having
any effect on her. She put up her hand. "No
need to discuss it. You have your opinion. I have
mine."

With that, she went to brush past him. He
reached out and held on to her arm. Adirah
felt a jolt of electricity flash through her body.
Shocked, she stopped abruptly, her right hand
flying up to her neck. Her locket . . . She had
forgotten to put it back on. Adirah sucked in
her breath. She had never felt anything like that
before from a simple touch. She finally looked
up at the stranger, her eyebrows dipping low on
her face.

"What . . . what are you . . . ?" she stammered,
unable to find her words.

"Sorry," he said, snatching his hand from her
arm. "I . . . I didn't mean to grab you. It's just
that I couldn't let you slip away. I didn't get your
name." Adirah could hear a hint of desperation
in his voice.

"That's because I didn't give it to you," Adirah
snapped, squaring her shoulders and gathering
her composure. She wanted to leave, to run
away fast. But for some reason, she was stuck.
It was like her mind had suddenly slowed down
to a crawl and wouldn't control the rest of her
body. She wanted to keep looking into his eyes,

listening to his voice. There was a magnetic attraction, and Adirah had to fight hard to keep from being sucked in.

"I'm Kesh," he said, extending his hand. "And you are?"

Adirah snapped out of her trance again. She squinted at his hand like it was a poisonous snake. "I don't tell strangers my name. Especially strangers who try to embarrass me," she snarled. With that, she was finally able to stomp away. She moved so fast, she was almost jogging.

Adirah could feel his eyes on her as she left. The voices around her whispered in her ears.

Turn around. Look at him. Turn around.

Adirah wanted so badly to obey and turn around, but she resisted the urge. "No," she mumbled. "No."

In the end, she had come out the victor. Just how she liked it. But Adirah didn't know if she could resist the gorgeous stranger every time she had to see him in class, which was three days a week. There was something very irresistible about him.

Kesh grimaced as he made his way over to the Freeman building. His auditory senses were overwhelmed by the overlapping chatter of those conversing around him. The noise sounded like a vinyl record being played backward, and it rushed through his ears as if it were moving at the speed of light. The piercing laughter, the rustle of passersby's clothes as they moved, and the crunching of car wheels on gravel all seemed to stab at his eardrums. Kesh wanted to stop, cover his ears with his hands, and scream. The older Kesh got, the less tolerance he had for the life. The *alive* life.

"What's the matter with you?" Tiev asked as Kesh approached, wearing a frown.

"I don't know how anyone survives with all the noise during the day," Kesh complained. "I can hear every sound. Even people's whispers sound loud to me. I can hear the tiniest noises, like birds tearing up leaves to build nests, and field mice scratching to make new homes."

Tiev chuckled. "First of all, you have sharp animal senses. Remember that. That's your gift. And this is how life is supposed to sound. Noise. Voices. Laughter. Birds. Cars. You've gotten too used to living in the night, when all life forms settle down for their quick run through the afterlife . . . what the mortals, for some reason, call dreams. I thought by now you'd be used to living in the light. I mean, it's only been decades, Kesh." Tiev laughed again.

Kesh twisted the gold ring on his left ring finger, contemplating the whole "walk among the living" thing. Tiev was right. Kesh had learned to live in the light decades ago, but there were times when he'd taken a break and gone back to the night. Kesh sometimes craved the darkness, but he knew he'd never find a queen if he lived that way.

"Ah, don't even think about taking that off," Tiev said, nodding toward Kesh's ring. "We fought too hard for the ability to walk among them, to walk in the daylight. A lot of people died so you'd have that freedom," Tiev reminded.

Kesh looked down at his ring and shook his head. The huge onyx stone with its diamond center resembled a human eye. This version of the ring was reserved for the king of the clan. Kesh had taken it off the former king's finger right before he died at the hands of their rivals. When Kesh had learned that the ring had the power to protect him from the light of day, he'd begun walking during the day, banished no more to the darkness of night. Kesh knew walking during the day was the only way he'd find his queen. He also knew that time was running out. His rivals, the Malum Clan, would find him again, and soon. This time, Kesh wanted to be prepared.

"First day of school is always fun," Vila announced, rushing over to Kesh and Tiev, wearing
a huge smile.

Kesh smiled and raised one brow at her. "Uh-
oh. What trouble did you get into now? I know
that look."

Vila was always the life or death of every
party. Although she was really over sixty-four
years old, Vila looked eighteen and had adopted
the college kid way of dressing. Her smooth skin
and bright eyes were a sure benefit of being one
of the clan.

"I'll have you know, sir, that I've been very
good. I like this place," Vila said, whirling aro-
und until her skirt made a parachute around her
legs. "I think it's the best campus so far. It's so
much fun taking over people's minds to make
them believe I've been here and I'm a popular
girl." She giggled. "I guess if you can't be popular in the first life, the second time is a charm."

Tiev shook his head and laughed. "You're at
it again, huh? How many minds did you charm
today? Wait. . . . Let me guess." He laughed
again.

Vila laughed too. "Not many," she replied,
batting her eyes in mock innocence. "But
tomorrow and the next day and the next day . . ."
She shrugged. "There's no telling what trouble

I might find. Because this campus feels like home." Vila inhaled and exhaled. "Something about being here makes me feel . . . well . . . alive."

Kesh shook his head. "I agree with, Vila. This campus holds a rich history and has some of the most beautiful descendants of our ancestors walking around. I came back here to learn more about my ancestors, the ones that survived the Haitian Revolution, only to be brought here by white men for enslavement. It was us, their children, who fought. I guess revolt was in their blood. It was here that we had our start," Kesh said, breathing in deep and looking out at the expansive campus grounds with pride. "I wasn't going to come back. I didn't want to remember. But in my search for a queen, something pulled me back here."

"Don't go digging too deep. We are here for you to find a queen," Tiev said. "I know you feel nostalgic, but no one wants to be reminded of their making . . . of love lost and a time when we couldn't control our own destiny."

Kesh contemplated what Tiev had said. His jaw went stiff, and he closed his eyes. His thoughts whipped in his head like a tornado's eye. It was the first time in decades he'd thought back to the day he was turned.

Raleigh, North Carolina
December 1865

"We free! We free! Free! Free!"
The chants filtered through the tiny wooden shack. Keston lifted his head from the book he was reading by candlelight, opened his eyes wide, and listened.

"We free! Free! Free!"
There it went again. Keston thought he might've fallen to sleep and started dreaming, as often happened when he crouched in the corner of his quarters, secretly reading and teaching himself the ways of the world.

"We free! We free!"
The chants came again. This time Keston was sure he wasn't hearing things. He was definitely awake. Keston listened as the chants continued and increased in volume. They were getting closer. Keston closed his book and got up from his hiding place. He picked up the half-melted candle and used it to light his way.

"We free! We free!"
It was loud and clear now. Keston crumpled his brow and craned his neck to look through the murky window of his shack. He could see them, a group of fellow slaves, huddled together shoulder to shoulder, marching toward the Billet main house.

"What in the . . . ?" Keston huffed, his heart beating faster. He yanked back his wooden plank door and stepped out onto the dirt. The ground under his bare feet was moist; the dew had left a fine layer. The approaching angry mob was causing the earth to rumble. The air was thick with tension. He'd never seen the slaves all together like this unless they were summoned and forced to watch one of their own get punished for a perceived crime. Even then, it didn't seem like as many as there were now. Keston hadn't known there were so many slaves. To his surprise, there seemed to be more slaves than the white men who controlled them. *Why hadn't they gotten together like this before?* Keston thought. Eyes wide, Keston moved forward on shaky legs to get a better look at the jeering crowd.

"Free! Free! Free!" they called out and moved toward him like a swelling wave at high tide.

Keston stepped forward, his mouth hanging open. He wanted to see where they were going. His heart almost seized in his chest when he noticed Adie, a beautiful woman he'd admired, out in front of the crowd, with her arm locked with that of a slave named Seth. Keston's eyes hooded over, and his nostrils flared. He'd always known Seth to be a troublemaker. He'd been lashed so many times, it was a wonder he still had skin on his body. There were countless times when Keston thought for sure Seth would die from his injuries.

Seth was always quick to tell a tale. For some reason, Keston was usually his preferred audience. Seth always spoke about how Seth was his slave name and Gerard Pierre was his given name. Seth also spoke of his parents' days in Haiti and how they were kidnapped at the end of the Haitian Revolution and forced into slavery in America. Seth said he was born on the Billet plantation but a Haitian revolutionary lived inside of him, and he asserted that he was a Pierre, not a Billet. Seth didn't believe in the Christianity they were all taught on the plantation. He was a part of another religion. His Haitian roots were strong, and they manifested themselves in the voodoo he practiced when the slave owners were asleep. He was always trying to recruit Keston to take part in the midnight rituals, but Keston had decided long ago he didn't want to be part of Seth's secret group.

"Free! Free! Free!"

Keston's heart sank as he watched Adie's mouth say the word with so much venom that her usually beautiful face appeared marred. The usually quiet, obedient girl had transformed into a fierce revolutionary. Keston had watched Adie from afar as she waited on the Billets hand and foot. She was lucky to be in the house. Adie had pretty hazel eyes and soft caramel skin. When she smiled, every single one of her teeth showed.

Keston would find an excuse to work near the house just to get a glimpse of Adie as she moved about inside or on the huge porch. When they'd lock eyes and hold each other's gaze, Keston felt things move inside of him that he didn't know existed. He'd loved Adie from afar for years.

Keston reached out his hand, his lips in position to say her name. Adie turned and saw him. There was something in her eyes. A fire or anger? He shivered, but he could not stop staring at her. A gunshot finally broke Keston's trance. He threw his hands over his head and shrank down to the ground, something he'd learned to do when the white men sent a warning shot into the air.

Adie and the group stopped moving. They were defiant in their stance. They didn't run, scream, or quit chanting. They certainly didn't drop to the ground in submission. There was an empowered energy running through the crowd.

"Free! Free! We free!" they barked out in defiance.

"Now, look here. This here is my land. You can't take over. Just cus' they said y'all free, that don't mean nothin'," Master Billet shouted, brandishing his rifle as a growing crowd of white men swelled behind him. "Get back to your quarters 'fore someone gets themselves killed."

"We wants to share in this land. We worked it since we was babies. 'Tis ours jus' as much as yours," Seth announced, the veins in his neck cording against his skin. "We want what's ours, what was built off the backs of our free parents!"

"You niggers ain't got no rights to no land in this here country," shouted a fat white man with a grossly protruding gut. He held a silver pistol. "Now, get back to your quarters. Y'all can't win 'gainst no white men, and you knows it."

"We already won. We free, and we want this bit of land! We free now!" Adie shouted in response.

The fat white man charged forward and backhanded Adie so hard, her head snapped to the left and blood and spit shot from her lips. "Don't you sass me, nigger gal. You ain't nobody free."

Adie didn't fall. Instead, she turned her face back to the white man, and with blood leaking from her left nostril, she spat in the white man's face. The man went to lift his hand to hit her again, and a sea of black men and women behind her charged forward, screaming.

Keston watched in horror as gunshots dropped several of the slaves. White men shrieked as axes were taken to their limbs. Blood spurted from guts and spilled from head wounds. The carnage kept him frozen where he stood. He wanted to run but felt paralyzed by the scene playing out before his eyes. He was trembling while witnessing the chaotic scene. He frantically scanned the tangle of bodies for Adie. The battle was so furious and violent that he was having trouble focusing on anyone. It was a swarm of violence.

Keston looked to his left and saw a white man holding Adie by the throat against a tree, his gun pressed to her head. She was wildly clawing at the man, but her efforts had no effect.

The veins in her forehead were bulging, and her face was flushed from lack of oxygen. Without hesitation, Keston took off running. Seeing Adie in distress had finally spurred him into action.

Running at full speed, Keston slammed his fist into the side of the white man's head. The unexpected blow caused him to release his grip on Adie, and she collapsed at the base of the tree.

"You dirty nigger," the white man snarled, turning his gun on Keston.

He fired a shot into Keston's chest, and it sent him flying backward onto the dirt. Keston felt like someone had lit his chest on fire. Keston lay there, stunned and struggling to breathe. The fire in his chest was quickly replaced by a freezing chill throughout his body.

"No! No!" Adie screamed.

"You're next, you dirty nigger," the white man hissed.

"No!" Adie screamed again.

She turned her body away from the man to shield herself from the onslaught about to befall her. As the man got closer, Adie spun around, leaped up from the ground, and slammed a huge rock into the man's skull. The contact left a huge crack across the left side of his head. He fell sideways, his gun skittering out of his hand.

Keston struggled for breath. Adie rushed to his side. Bodies fell all around them. She held on to him, sobbing.

"Save me," Keston gurgled, blood spilling from his mouth.

The hole in his chest was draining blood quickly, the dark crimson staining his shirt and the dirt surrounding him.

"There's only one way," Adie said, lowering her mouth to his neck. Keston screamed out in agony from the pain, and his legs bucked against the dirt. Adie lifted her head and reared her head back, his blood painting her mouth and chin. Keston's eyes shot open, stretched to their capacity, and his mouth formed a perfect O. "You will live forever now, as Kesh. You're one of us now, the Sefu—the sword, the protectors."

"I thought we were here to party. To feast on the fresh and young," Vila interjected, snapping Kesh out of his memories.

Kesh was startled and snapped back to the present. He looked around, almost forgetting where he was. Several members of his clan had gathered. They were all abuzz about the big parties they wanted to throw and the beautiful mortals who lived on campus. They all loved the first days of school. It was the beginning of the hunt. The first time they laid eyes on their potential prey. Kesh didn't stop them, but he didn't add to the conversation, either. He moved over to a bench and sat on the back of it, distant.

"What is it?" Tiev asked, moving to Kesh's side. "It can't just be the noise that's still bothering you."

Kesh didn't know if it was the right time to tell Tiev or his clan about the beautiful, feisty, intelligent girl he'd met earlier. It had shocked Kesh that the girl could deny him. As hard as he'd tried to lure her with his eyes, his smile, and his charm, she'd been able to resist. That was unheard of. Kesh had never met a woman who was able to resist him like that. Usually, all it took was one look into his eyes and he would have them in any way he wanted. Kesh thought about how the girl had been able to fight it with an inner strength he hadn't witnessed before, a fire he hadn't seen since before his making. He had seen the struggle happening within her, but still she had prevailed. He was intrigued and stricken by her at the same time.

What is different about this one? Who is she? he thought.

"Hel-lo?" Vila waved her hand in Kesh's face. She frowned and looked at Tiev with her eyebrows raised. "What is going on with him?"

Tiev shrugged. "I've been trying to figure it out."

"I'm fine," Kesh lied. "It's just different being in the very place our ancestors walked. Back on hallowed grounds."

Vila twisted her lips. She studied Kesh's face. "I know you better than that. You aren't just my king. You're my maker, remember. There's more to it."

Kesh shook his head. He'd turned Vila decades ago, and she'd been in love with him ever since. Vila was his most loyal follower, but she was also hardheaded. Vila leaned in to kiss Kesh, but he moved his head, looking past her. His eyes suddenly lit up. Vila followed his line of sight. Kesh moved Vila aside and stood up. He stared ahead. It was her, the beautiful, strong-willed girl from class. She rested against a huge oak tree and read a book.

Tiev and Vila walked up and flanked Kesh on either side. They both stared ahead for a few seconds.

"Who is she?" Vila broke their silence.

Kesh, suddenly embarrassed, shook his head. "Who . . . ? I . . . I don't know her."

Vila growled low in her throat and stepped back. She was jealous. Kesh was going to need to keep Vila in line. She always did what he commanded, but Kesh had a bad feeling in his stomach.

"What is it about her?" Tiev asked, jerking his chin forward.

"I don't know. I want to find out," Kesh replied barely above a whisper. "I have to know as soon as possible." There was an urgency in his voice that even Kesh himself hadn't heard before.

"Vila," Kesh said, summoning her. Vila rushed back to Kesh's side. "I want her at the big party. Befriend her. Make sure she's there," he instructed.

Vila's jaw rocked, and she swallowed the lump that had suddenly formed in her throat. "Yes, master," she grumbled through clenched teeth. She went to walk away, but Kesh grabbed her arm.

"Vila, I have counted every hair on the girl's head, so I'll know if you harm even one. Be nice. That's a direct order," he said.

Vila snatched her arm away, snorted, and disappeared.

Kesh noticed Tiev's scathing look. "We've already had this conversation, Tiev. Vila can't be my queen, so stop looking at me that way. She will continue to serve me, and when I find a queen, she will serve her too."

Chapter 3

Adirah woke in a fit from her sleep. The over-size T-shirt she wore as a nightgown clung to her curves. Her body was covered in sweat. She clutched her chest, feeling her heart racing. She whipped her head around frantically and inhaled deeply. "Oh, my God," she huffed, touching herself all over. "That dream seemed so real."

Adirah looked across the room at her roommate. Lina still slept soundly. It was a dream, Adirah told herself. Her room was not filled with spirits, and there was no old woman with long dark hair hovering over her face, trying to snatch her breath.

Adirah tossed her comforter back and threw her legs over the side of her bed. She sat there for a few moments to gather herself. The dream felt too real. Her heart needed some time to begin beating at a normal pace, and her breathing needed to readjust. Fresh air was needed. There was no way she would get back to sleep after that nightmare.

She stood up and shrugged into a hoodie and slipped her feet into a pair of fluffy slippers. Adirah took one last look around the room to make sure no one but Lina was there. Although the room was empty but for Lina, Adirah still shivered before she left it. Back in Brooklyn it was easier for Adirah to ignore the feeling of a presence around her, but for some reason, since she'd arrived at Billet, the feeling was much stronger. It was almost impossible to ignore. She was growing tired of feeling like there was a constant presence around her. Adirah would give anything to be free from this persistent company.

Once outside, Adirah inhaled the night air. She took a seat on the front steps of her dorm and ran her hands over her face and tried to get her thoughts together. Lately, she'd been thinking about her mother and brothers a lot. Maybe that was what the nightmares were about. Adirah wished she could've done more before and after Adolphis's death. She wanted to fight harder for all of them. She closed her eyes.

Brooklyn, New York
January 2008
"Agh!"

Adirah jumped out of her sleep to the sounds of Addis's screams. She rushed across the room to his bed and scooped him into her arms.

"Shh, Addis. Shhh," Adirah whispered, comforting. Her baby brother kept screaming. Adirah put her hand over his mouth. "Shh. You'll upset her. It's okay. It's okay. I'm here. I'm here." She forced his head against her chest and rocked him. Adirah worked hard to slow her own rapid breathing. Her head pounded from being snatched out of her sleep.

After a few seconds Addis calmed down and relaxed against Adirah's chest. She slowed the rocking until she was almost still. Her eyes darted around the darkened room, searching for any signs of the cause of Addis's discomfort. When Addis fell back to sleep, she gently released him onto the bed and stood up. She took a few steps into the middle of the room.

"Adol, stop coming here. He is just a baby. He doesn't understand it," Adirah rasped, folding her arms across her stomach, trembling. She jumped and whirled around when the small jewelry box on her dresser slammed shut by itself.

"Just stop it. It's not our fault. Leave Mama alone too. We need her," Adirah whispered harshly, tears racing down her face. "We love

you, Adol. We will always love you. But we need to be free. We need to try to move on. We can't keep being scared. People think she's crazy, and me too," Adirah whispered, her words barely audible. *"You can't keep coming here. We didn't do it. We can't suffer anymore. We need to be free."*

The jewelry box flew off the dresser. Adirah's earrings and bracelets were dumped onto the floor. Adirah fell to her knees, sobbing. She'd always been able to feel spirits around her, but knowing her brother's spirit wasn't resting easy upset her. "Please, Adol, try to rest in peace," she whimpered.

Suddenly a breeze whipped over her face, and the sheer curtains at her bedroom window shifted. Adirah sucked in her breath and squeezed herself tighter. Everything went still. Adirah felt a calm she hadn't felt since the incident.

"I thought *I* was the only one who hung out on campus in the middle of the night."

Adirah, startled, was drawn out of her trance at the sound of the familiar voice. Her face immediately folded into a frown, but that didn't change the pounding of her heart. "So you're just everywhere, huh?" she grumbled, bunching her toes in the slippers.

"I could say the same thing about you." Kesh smiled. "May I?" he asked, pointing to the space on the steps next to her.

"It's a free country," Adirah replied, looking at the empty spot. She was trying to play hard, but the sexy stranger from class had awakened something inside of her. She'd waved it off the first time, but this time, she acknowledged the knots in her stomach and the tiny sweat beads cropping up under her head scarf.

Kesh sat down next to her. His scent—the same masculine, earthy, wood scent she'd detected in class—wafted up to her nose. Adirah squeezed her knees together. It was all she could do to stop the tingling that had suddenly started in places below her navel.

"I like the solitude of the night. The silence of things that are alive, but dead to the world, is refreshing," Kesh said, looking up at the dark sky.

Adirah looked over at him, kind of amused. "Not that I asked you," she said, still trying to play hard. She eased the scowl out of her facial expression. "But I will say, nighttime is usually when I can get my thoughts together. There is serenity in the air, the sky, everywhere. I think

I am at my best at night," she replied, inhaling. "No noise. No people talking to me. No demands. No distractions at all. Just my thoughts, the darkness, and me. I never understood why people are afraid of the dark."

"That's funny. I feel the same way. I am definitely my best at night," Kesh said. "Maybe we have more in common than we let on earlier. That's a good thing, right?" Kesh reached over and boldly patted her knee.

Adirah felt something warm explode in the center of her chest. The feeling made her so uncomfortable, she jumped. Kesh acted nonchalantly, like he hadn't noticed her reaction.

Kesh was too perfect, with his neatly twisted locks; his smooth, blemish-free skin; his straight white teeth. Kesh's bone structure was distinct in an Idris Elba kind of way, and Adirah could see the outlines of his thick biceps even through his black leather jacket. She didn't think she'd ever be attracted to someone like Kesh, but this man was gorgeous. When she realized that she'd let her guard down too easily, she broke eye contact. She couldn't afford to trust anyone. Especially not with her feelings.

She closed her eyes and folded her lips in. "I better go." She stood up abruptly.

Her sudden dismissal and movement seemed to shock Kesh. He bolted to his feet too, but not before Adirah had quickly darted up the steps to the Rothschild building. "Wait," Kesh called after her, his tone anxious. He held his hands up, "Please wait. I never got your name."

Adirah looked over her shoulder, fighting the urge to stare into his eyes. "That's because I never gave it to you," she snapped, repeating what she'd said to him in class the first time they'd met. "And it's too late for me to be out here with a strange man like this. Besides, I have an early start tomorrow, don't you?" she called over her shoulder. With that she was gone.

Kesh's shoulders slumped with disappointment as he watched her through the glass doors until she disappeared. His hands curled into fists, and his jaw locked. He had never worked this hard for a woman's attention.

Why won't she let me get to know her?

"So, this is where you snuck off to," Tiev said, rudely interrupting Kesh's thoughts.

Kesh rolled his eyes. "I wish you would stop following me . . . and popping up on me like this," he snapped, rounding on Tiev, scowling and baring his extended canine teeth.

"My job is to be your right hand. So where you go, I go," Tiev replied. "Now, don't try to change the subject. Tell me about her."

Kesh shook his head. "I can't understand why she doesn't find me attractive and alluring, like all the others. Why can't I get into her mind? No matter how hard I stare into her eyes, she doesn't budge. I have no power when it comes to her," Kesh said, pinching the bridge of his nose. "It's like . . . like . . . solving a riddle every time I'm around her. There is something mysterious about her, and it's got me." He gritted his teeth, punched his left fist into his right palm. "Urgh. I can't stop thinking about her. I'm supposed to take over her mind, not the other way around." Kesh started pacing. He was a king. No one treated him this way.

"Maybe this is all a good thing." Tiev put his hand on Kesh's shoulder, halting his movement. "Remember, all the ones who were too easy, you didn't want them," Tiev reminded him.

"How'd you know she was out here?" Vila asked, approaching from behind and interrupting their conversation.

Kesh turned his head slightly, but not enough to see Vila. "I followed you into her dream. You were supposed to be nice," Kesh admonished.

"So, you didn't trust me?" Vila asked.

"I don't *have* to trust you. I know you. Do better next time. Our time is running out," Kesh said with finality. He didn't have to look at Vila to know she was fuming.

Woodstock
Bethel, New York
August 1969

Kesh noticed her before she saw him. He was struck by her beauty—smooth skin; long, straight black hair; round innocent eyes; and a model's shape—long legs, short torso, full breasts. He could tell she was young, way younger than him. Suddenly he felt self-conscious about the full mustache and the long furry Elvis sideburns he'd let grow on his face. He'd done it to fit in with the times. Kesh had grown tired of changing his appearance with every new trend over the decades, but it was necessary for his survival. If he simply dressed like the era he was from, he would stick out too much. That level of attention was not what he needed or wanted. Kesh had to float through each new era, participating in the trends but keeping a distance from the population.

He eyed the girl as she twirled around and danced to the live music. The moment Kesh heard of the huge music festival, he knew it was going to be a perfect place to feed. Hundreds of thousands of young concertgoers partaking in the music and drug culture would have their guards down. It was going to be easy pickings.

The huge muddy field was crowded with people, yet she laughed like she was in her own world. There was no discernible music close by, so she was dancing to her own beat. A group of twenty to thirty people had gathered, and they were all dancing together. Kesh figured they were under the influence of one of the many illegal drugs that were making their way around the festival grounds. The girl's fluid movements were erotic, and Kesh was turned on. He watched her take a joint from another girl, put it to her lips, and take a long pull. Kesh's assumption was correct; they were all getting high. Even the way she locked her mouth around the tiny white homemade cigarette was sexy.

Kesh moved closer. He could smell her from where he stood. Marijuana, hemp oil, dead roses, and coconut were what she smelled like. Fresh blood. He felt his nature rise and had to turn away for a few seconds before anyone noticed. Having heightened senses was one of the things about being transformed that Kesh was still getting used to, even after a century of being a vampire. He could see, hear, taste, and smell better than any animal alive. When he turned back around, the beautiful girl was closer to him. Almost in his face. Her closeness caught him off guard, and he stumbled back a few steps.

"I saw you watching me," she said, giggling and moving her head around fluidly, like it wasn't fully connected to her neck. Up close, she was even prettier than she appeared from a distance. Kesh was entranced by her beauty. There was an aura surrounding her. Her smell was intoxicating. Her chestnut-brown eyes were bright, and the homemade headband of flowers that wrapped around her forehead contrasted beautifully with her skin and made her look ethereal, like a fairy.

"You're beautiful," Kesh said, grabbing her hand and kissing its top. "I had to stop and stare at your beauty." He looked into her eyes. "And your smell is delicious."

"Oh, my God," she gushed. "No man has ever done that to me before . . . kissed my hand like a real gentleman." Kesh could see her cheeks get rosy at his touch.

"Let me be your first for more than just that," Kesh said, pulling her closer to him and wrapping her in his arms. The freshness of her scent and the purity of her soul were driving him wild. He buried his face between her shoulder and neck to inhale her sweet scent. He had to bite down on his own lip to keep his animal instincts at rest. It was all he could do to keep from feasting on her supple neck.

"You're so strong," she said, her words floating on light breaths. "I want to touch your muscles." She squeezed his defined biceps. A quiet moan escaped from her lips.

Within minutes Kesh had her in his tent. The flicker of the candles on either side of the enclosed space cast a glow over the girl.

"What's your name?" he asked as he moved her long strands of hair behind her shoulders. He stared into her eyes and smiled.

"Ve . . . Veron . . . Veronica," she said, barely able to speak.

"You're beautiful, but I think I want to call you Vila," Kesh said, pulling one strap of her crop top down until it hung hear the crook of her arm. He ran his hand down her shoulder and over her breast.

"Vila," she repeated, entranced. "Ooh . . . okay." She moaned softly as Kesh circled the rigid skin of her areola with his finger.

"With me, your name can be no longer than four letters. A letter for each point on the Sefu symbol," Kesh replied, knowing that the girl would have no idea what he was speaking about. She shook her head up and down in agreement, anyway. She was entranced by this mysterious man who had seemingly floated into her life. Kesh pulled the other side of her top down until both breasts were exposed. He lowered his head to her left nipple and sucked it gently.

"Vi-la," she repeated again, dragging out each syllable on a hot breath.

"Yes," Kesh hissed. "Vila." He circled her, inhaling every bit of her essence. He stood behind her, taking deep breaths of her scent. He slowly pulled her shorts over her hips.

"What are you doing?" Vila giggled.

"Taking it all in," Kesh replied.

He put his hand on her waist and turned her toward him. She let out a hot breath as he drew her face to his and forced his tongue between her lips. Vila moaned. Kesh moved his *face from hers and trailed his tongue down the left side of her neck. He let out a low growl and gently guided her down to the floor. As she lay on her back, Kesh propped himself on his knees between her legs.*

"Touch yourself," he panted. "Let me watch."

Vila gave him a lazy grin and slowly moved her hand between her legs. Kesh touched his bulge as he watched her rub her swollen clitoris with one hand and pinch one nipple with the other hand.

"You're gorgeous," he said as they lay on the pallet of blankets covering the floor inside the tent. "I can't resist you," he told her. He used his knee to part her thighs and wedged himself between them. Kesh wanted to take special care with her. He kissed every inch of her body, and she didn't protest. She couldn't. Kesh had successfully seduced her.

Kesh started at her mouth, then moved his tongue over her neck and couldn't help but emit another low, hungry growl. He could feel the rush of blood and adrenaline through her skin. His urge was to feast right then, but he wanted this to last. He made his way down to her breasts and gently licked each one, sucking gently when he got to the dark, rigid circle of her areola. His body shook as he fought the impulse to bite the soft, delicate skin.

Vila moaned and panted through her mouth. She touched the top of his head, urging him on. Kesh continued down, taking his time, planting kisses on her flat stomach, the edge of her pelvic bone, her inner thighs. He inhaled like an animal on the hunt, sniffing out her fear and excitement. When he reached the fuzzy mound of her womanhood, the scent of her lady musk drove him insane. Kesh could tell she was different than the women who threw themselves at him and let him fall into them right after another man had just had them. She was pure of heart and soul. She was worth saving before the ways of the world corrupted her, he told himself. He might want to have her over and over for a long time.

Kesh extended his long tongue and flicked it over her clitoris, groaning in ecstasy, tasting her essence. He lowered his mouth and eased his tongue into her wet center. Vila yelled out her pleasure as he darted his tongue in and out, in and out. Kesh couldn't control the fire raging inside of him anymore. He drank up her juices like he needed them to live. Vila's thighs trembled. She was ready. Kesh leaned up and looked down into her face. He continued to watch as he entered her, gently at first, but with more vigor as his longing grew. Feeling his girth, Vila bit down on her bottom lip until she drew blood.

"Oww," she wailed as he moved deeper into her virginal opening.

"Are you a . . . Are you a virgin?" Kesh gasped, unable to get his own breathing under control. She felt so good. Her insides pulsed and grabbed him, pulling him deeper and deeper.

Vila shook her head no, but Kesh didn't believe her. The tightness, the pain, even the smell of blood coming from her busted lip was raw and pure, like that of a virgin. Kesh put his mouth on hers and tasted her blood. The sweet taste drove him wild. He moved in and out of her slippery opening carefully, but with enough vigor to make him want to explode. He couldn't let her go. He wanted her . . . forever.

Vila dug her nails into the flesh on Kesh's back. Her way of letting him know she was feeling every single one of his moves. Kesh rode a wave of ecstasy that he didn't want to stop. He reared his head back and growled, his canines extending on their own. He was at *that point. Vila looked up and saw the shine of his long teeth. Terror cropped up on her face, but Kesh didn't give her a chance to scream before he sank his teeth into her.*

"You're mine, Vila. I will keep you with me forever," he panted.

Chapter 4

"Adirah!" Lina screamed, bursting into their dorm room in a flurry. "Adirah!"

Adirah looked up from her textbook with wide eyes. "What? What's the matter?"

"No. Nothing is wrong," Lina replied, wheezing, her chest moving up and down like she'd been running a race.

Adirah looked from Lina to the girl standing next to her and back again at Lina.

"This is Vila," Lina said, introducing her, smiling like she was showing Adirah a prized possession.

Adirah's eyebrows went up. "Okay?" Adirah replied, baffled. She examined the pretty girl standing with Lina and thought the girl resembled a young Native American CoverGirl model—smooth skin; clear eyes; thick, long hair.

"Ugh. I forgot you don't know anything about campus life. Vila is a member of Sigma Gamma Phi," Lina said, still wearing a goofy smile.

This meant nothing to Adirah. She scratched her head and eyed both girls like they were aliens. It had been a week and a half with Lina, and every day was a new adventure or some new weird thing to learn. It was getting tiresome. Adirah just wanted to keep her head down, study, make the dean's list, and graduate.

"It's the sorority that is the sister organization to Sigma Rho, the most popular fraternity on campus. The hottest guys on campus too. The best parties on campus, the place everyone who is someone wants to be," Lina explained, the excitement in her voice confusing Adirah to no end.

"Um . . . the same fraternity that just a week ago you said snatched souls?" Adirah asked, crumpling her eyebrows.

"Oh . . . ha! That, um, that was just a joke," Lina said, looking over at Vila nervously. "My roommate is always joking." Lina shifted her weight back and forth like she had something itchy in her pants. Adirah's mouth hung open slightly. She would've never believed she'd see Lina behave like some coquettish groupie. Not the militant Lina. Not the Lina who wore all black to protect her soul and preached about the ills of falling too far into campus life.

"Hi, Adirah. I'm Vila," the girl said, stepping forward with her hand out. Adirah unenthusiastically took Vila's hand and shook it. The moment their hands touched, Adirah felt the same jolt she'd felt from the sexy stranger in her class the other day. Adirah quickly snatched her hand back and gave a halfhearted smile.

"Hi . . . I guess. I didn't know Lina was friends with any sorority girls." Adirah widened her eyes and shot Lina an arched brow and a tilted-head glare that said, "What the heck is going on here?"

Lina laughed way too hard and way too loud. "Adirah is so silly! Of course I'm friends with sorority girls. Vila and I have known each other forever," Lina said. "I thought I told you about my good friend Vila. We met at . . . um . . ."

"Freshmen orientation," Vila said, filling in the blank, laughing nervously. "Lina and I go way back. I can't believe she never told you about me."

"Right! I know I told you about Vila. I had to have," Lina said, then stepped up and slapped Adirah on the shoulder a little too hard.

Adirah couldn't help but frown. Lina's behavior was beyond strange. It was like she was on some drug that had her completely wired. Of course she hadn't mentioned being friends with any popular sorority girls. In fact, Lina had preached almost daily, for forty minutes straight, about how Adirah should stay away from the party crowd and the snatched souls and the undead.

"Vila invited us to an exclusive party tonight. It is invitation only," Lina announced with too much eagerness in her voice.

Adirah nodded. "That's nice of you, Vila, but I—"

"She has to find an outfit!" Lina yelled, cutting Adirah off in midsentence. "That's what she was about to say . . . an outfit. *But* she needs the perfect outfit. We will be there, but . . . but she has to get that outfit. You know how freshmen are . . . always trying to impress," Lina said, rambling as she stepped between Vila and Adirah.

"So I'll see you ladies there?" Vila asked, craning to see Adirah around Lina.

Adirah said, "Well—"

"Yes! We will be there," Lina asserted, interrupting again. This time she pushed Vila toward their door.

"I'll be looking for you. You'll love our group. We really know how to show everyone a good time," Vila said, smiling. "We are all about a good, good time."

"Great. That's great. Yes, we will be ready." Lina kept shoving Vila toward the door.

"Adirah," Vila called over her shoulder as she went to cross the doorsill, "I love that name. I think it is fit for a queen."

Adirah put up her hand and smiled weakly. "Um . . . thanks. I guess," she replied. She folded her arms across her chest and tapped her left foot, waiting.

As soon as Vila was gone and Lina returned, Adirah rounded on her like a lioness on prey. "What the heck, Lina? What was that all about?"

"Adirah, do you know how big this is? We have been asked to come to an invitation-only party, not just invitation only, but the most sought-after party on campus," Lina said, flopping down on her bed, kicking her legs in the air like she was living her wildest dream.

"B-but," Adirah stuttered, trying to find the words. This sudden change in Lina had Adirah confused. One minute she was a walking warning sign, counseling Adirah on the secrets of the campus and cautioning her not to get caught up in the social scene. And now she was diving headfirst into the shallow end of the pool with no life jacket and was pressuring Adirah to go to a party hosted by the one fraternity that she had warned Adirah about.

"But nothing! Let's put on our best outfits and go," Lina said, jumping up and shaking Adirah's shoulders. "We are here to learn and to have fun. We can do both," Lina cheered.

Adirah shook her head. "You don't even sound like the same person. If I didn't know any better, I'd think someone snatched your mind . . . not your soul."

As promised, the Sigma Rho party was packed, inside and outside. The way students were lined up trying to get in, Adirah thought they might be giving away free money inside. It also didn't feel too exclusive with the amount of people attending. Lina held on to Adirah's arm and pulled her along as they pushed their way through the crowd of students outside who were trying to get in without a personal invitation. It looked like a New York City nightclub on a Saturday night, with the masses waiting outside for the doorman to deem them worthy of entering, while the select beautiful people waltzed through the velvet rope. Adirah couldn't lie to herself. She felt a bit superior by being able to bypass the peons in line, go right up to the door, and be welcomed inside like a VIP.

"Whoa," Lina gasped when they walked in.

Adirah's eyebrows shot up into arches. She felt like she was looking at a scene from a movie.

The Sigma Rho frat party was everything she'd seen on television and read about in corny college kid novels. There were endless kegs of beer lined up on a tall counter that extended from the kitchen, straight through the living room, and into the adjoining room. One keg had a shirtless guy crouched under it, with his head back and his mouth open, while people took turns flipping the keg spout to control the amount of beer that flowed into his mouth. *I thought only white people did that*? Adirah thought.

Her eyes darted over to three half-dressed blondes dancing off beat in the middle of the floor to Lil Wayne and Drake, while dudes dressed in their fraternity T-shirts groped them and threw dollars at them. Adirah shook her head. Men could be so disrespectful. There were two groups in a seating area off the foyer, both a mix of guys and girls, and they were huddled around big, colorful bongs and were taking turns sucking in the smoke that swirled around inside the glass belly. A haze of smoke hovered above their heads. Now that Adirah was aware of the smoke, she began smelling the weed. It was something that she was not interested in trying. No need for her to get to know anyone in either of those groups. As Adirah made her way farther into the party, she saw couples making out in corners. Adirah thought they should get a room. Not that she was jealous; she just wasn't big on public displays of affection. When it came to getting physical, her motto was, "Keep it to yourself."

Adirah tried to relax and let the sound of Drake ease the edginess in her nerves. She would never admit it to Lina, but Adirah was glad she'd decided to loosen up a bit and come enjoy the party. Maybe a change of scenery from her dorm room and classes was what she needed.

"This is where it is at!" Lina shouted in Adirah's ear. "And we look hotter than any of these corny, overdressed, doing-too-much girls up in here."

Adirah laughed but agreed with Lina. She'd chosen a distressed jean skirt, a royal blue Jimi Hendrix T-shirt tied at the stomach, a black motorcycle jacket that Lina had loaned her, and her burgundy Doc Martens boots. Adirah felt comfortable but chic and didn't come across as trying too hard, like all the girls wearing freakum dresses and heels so high, they could barely walk, much less dance in them. It was a house party, for goodness' sake, not a fancy gala at the Four Seasons Hotel. Of course, Lina had on her usual head-to-toe black, but the one-piece T-shirt dress and over-the-knee boots she wore, and the way she'd twisted her natural hair up into a top bun, gave her a sophisticated appearance.

Adirah scanned the room and sucked in her breath when she spotted the sexy stranger from class. Her pulse quickened as she watched him. He had his dreads gathered into a black band and pulled back from his face. Adirah had a clear view of his chiseled chin and defined bone structure. She remembered thinking before that he was handsome, but she hadn't fully realized how perfect his bone structure was. Adirah had the urge to squeeze his square shoulders and sculpted biceps, which were visible through his black fraternity T-shirt. He reminded Adirah of an African warrior she'd seen in a painting at the Metropolitan Museum of Art. She would spend hours walking through the halls of that museum, soaking in the inspiration from artists of the past. There had been days when Adirah wished she could sleep at the museum, instead of having to go back to the foster home she was living in.

Adirah squinted as she looked at two girls hanging all over him. One had her hands planted on his chest and was giggling in his face, and the other had her eyes closed and was whispering in his ear. Adirah felt a flash of heat flit through her belly. Jealousy? She folded her bottom lip between her teeth and shook her head in disgust. She would never compete for a man's attention like that, no matter how gorgeous he was.

"He's like all the rest," she mumbled.

"What'd you say?" Lina yelled over the music, moving her body to the beat.

"Nothing," Adirah replied.

"Oh, I see Vila! Let's go!" Lina grabbed Adirah's arm and pulled her. Just as she moved, Adirah locked eyes with the stranger. He had finally looked up from his harem long enough to see her. Adirah stared at him long enough to see a mixture of shock and angst flicker over his facial features. She pursed her lips and shook her head at him before turning away.

Lina stopped tugging Adirah and grabbed her by the shoulders. "Okay, Adirah. Be cool," Lina warned right before they approached Vila. "We want them to like us."

Adirah sucked her teeth and looked over at Vila. She was surrounded by guys and girls who, from Adirah's standpoint, should've been walking a runway or been featured as centerfolds in some popular fashion magazine. They all looked perfect. All were tall, and all had perfect bodies and perfect bone structure. Vila looked hot too. Adirah was starting to think that being exceptionally gorgeous, with perfect features, flawless skin, and beautiful hair, was a requirement for membership in Sigma Gamma Phi and Sigma Rho. Adirah suddenly felt self-conscious about her amateur makeup job and the small pimple that had popped up on her forehead hours before the party.

"Ah, Lina," Vila greeted, flashing her picture-worthy smile. "I was starting to think you ladies had stood me up."

"No way. We are so excited to be here. This party is so lit," Lina gushed. "Right, Adirah? Aren't we having a ball?" Lina nudged Adirah with her elbow.

Adirah gave a fake smile and shook her head. She was still distracted by her thoughts of the sexy stranger.

"Let me introduce you ladies to my friends," Vila said. She turned to the group. "Hey, everyone, these are my friends Lina and *Adirah*," Vila announced, putting a weird emphasis on Adirah's name.

Adirah lifted her left eyebrow but didn't say anything. The emphasis on her name made her a bit uncomfortable. What was that supposed to mean?

"Hello, everyone," Lina said, cheerfully waving like she was meeting her favorite celebrity for the first time.

"Adirah, it's nice to meet you—" a tall, slim guy said, his hand moving slowly toward her, but he was interrupted.

"So, we meet again," said the sexy stranger from class, stepping between Adirah and the tall guy before they could shake hands.

Adirah dropped her hand and twisted her lips at him. "Broke away from your fans, I see."

Kesh chuckled. "Do you care, *Adirah*?"

She shivered when she heard him say her name. "Not really," she grumbled.

"So, I finally know your name," Kesh said and chuckled.

Adirah rolled her eyes. "Well, I . . ."

"I know." Kesh put up his hand. "You didn't give it to me, and I didn''t give you mine. I'm Kesh."

Adirah's cheeks got red. *Kesh. What an interesting name*, thought Adirah. *Is it short for something, a nickname?* Adirah wanted to know everything about this man.

"I'm glad you came out. We love to entertain, as you can see."

"Oh, I can see that *you* love to entertain, for sure," Adirah replied sarcastically.

Kesh laughed. "It's all in good fun. Harmless." He winked at her. "Can I get you a drink?" he asked.

"I don't—"

Before Adirah could finish, screams resounded through the room and sent the rest of Adirah's words tumbling back down her throat. Loud bangs and more screams sent the party into a frenzy. Adirah whirled around, but not before a fleeing partygoer plowed into her, sending her crashing to the floor.

"Ow!" she exclaimed and winced, grabbing for her ankle. From where she'd landed, Adirah heard the rapid footfalls of the crowd rushing toward her. She looked up in time to see Vila and the group rushing to Kesh's side.

"Kesh! They've come! We have to get you out of here now!" Adirah heard one of the guys announce. The others flanked Kesh on either side and whisked him away.

Adirah smelled the fire before she actually saw the raging flames and the hood of thick black smoke moving across the floor like the Grim Reaper. This was definitely not the same weed smoke Adirah had seen before. This smoke had death running through it.

"Oh, my God," she gasped, barely able to breathe. It had happened so fast. Adirah knew if she stayed there, she'd burn up or die of smoke inhalation. "Ah," she cried from the pain radiating through her ankle. It shot all the way up her leg. It was like a hot poker had been administered to her ankle. Or maybe it was the heat from the fire. She couldn't know for sure, but what she did know was that her ankle had to be broken. She also knew she had to get up fast.

The entire house was in chaos—girls screaming, feet thundering all around, loud banging, glass shattering, furniture cracking, fire crackling, and doors slamming. Adirah didn't see Lina anywhere. With her eyes, she desperately searched the last place she had seen Lina, but it was too difficult to make any sense out of the commotion. The smoke was getting thicker, and Adirah was having more difficulty breathing. She had to save herself.

Adirah coughed uncontrollably, her lungs quickly filling with smoke. Still, she planted the palms of her hands on the floor and tried to force herself up. As soon as she got her left leg under her, she was knocked back down.

"Agh!" Adirah hollered after falling flat on her stomach. The pain in her ankle was unbearable. A stampede of people rushed toward her. She curled up into a ball to protect herself from being crushed. Within seconds, Adirah was completely underfoot. She threw her arms over her head to protect it from kicks, stomps, and the merciless thumps of trampling feet on her body. When the sounds stopped, Adirah lifted her head and opened her mouth to scream for help, but she never got the words out. Something slammed into the side of her head with so much force, her world went black.

"Let me go," Kesh growled, wrestling his arm away from Tiev. "I have to go back. I have to know she's all right . . . that she got out with the crowd. What if she's still inside?"

"You can't!" Vila yelled at him. "The Malum are here. It's too risky, Kesh. Did you see how fast they destroyed the house? They've come for you, but they won't reveal themselves yet. They want to launch a sneak attack on us again, like before."

"I don't care what you all say. I can't know Adirah's in danger and just leave her. I've already told you . . . there is something about her," Kesh barked.

"You will risk everyone's safety for one mortal girl?" Tiev asked, holding on to Kesh's arm. "There will be more just like her. The Malum will have their spies following you. It's too risky, Kesh!"

"She's not just a mortal girl. She is my future queen," Kesh proclaimed. "We will stand and fight if we have to, but right now, I have to go save Adirah. She is the one." With that, Kesh took off, using his gift of speed to return to the frat house. He was a blur as he ran across campus, his feet barely touching the ground, almost like he was suspended just above the earth. He knew his entire clan would follow, but he'd get there first.

"Whoa! Whoa! Where do you think you're going?" a uniformed first responder asked, stepping up and blocking Kesh's path to the frat house door. Red, white, and blue lights lit up the night, and sirens screeched. There were over twenty vehicles parked haphazardly on the frat house lawn and the path leading to it. The fire was a full inferno at this point. Kesh could feel the heat emanating from the flames. The crackling of the burning wood was at a roar. Embers of burnt wood were falling all around, singeing the frat house lawn.

"My friend, sh-she's . . . in there, I think," Kesh stammered, moving to the left to try to get around the uniformed officer.

"It's too dangerous. Firefighters can't even get this blaze under control all the way. If your friend wasn't pulled out already, then . . . I'm sorry. I don't think anyone can survive that."

Kesh bit down on his lip. "I have to get inside. Please. I have to know if she's been saved. I have a feeling she's still in there," he pleaded, attempting to sidestep the officer again.

"Listen, guy. I already told you it's—"

Kesh grabbed the officer by the throat and forced him to stare into his eyes. "You're going to let me inside. You will move aside, and I'm going to walk right in," Kesh said, his voice stern. "I have to save my queen."

The officer shook his head up and down vigorously, unable to break eye contact with Kesh.

Kesh let him go and rushed up the steps and through the doors. He shrank back at first, the heat from the flames taking him aback. The firefighters had managed some of the blaze, but flames billowed out of the kitchen and ripped through some of the back rooms of the house with fury. Fire wasn't exactly his kind's favorite thing, but Kesh was on a mission. He covered his mouth and kicked through fallen debris and smoldering furniture. He whirled around and finally spotted tangles of bodies in different places on the floor. He ran over to the first person he saw. It was a guy. He was definitely dead. Kesh ran around him.

"Ay! What're you doing in here?" a firefighter in full gear yelled at Kesh through his mask.

Kesh ignored him and continued his search for Adirah.

"I found a live one here!" another firefighter called out. He was kneeling, with his hand on her jugular. "I got a faint pulse. I need aid stat!"

Kesh ran over to this firefighter, who was in the same spot that Kesh had last seen Adirah. His heart started jamming against his chest when he realized the man was tending to Adirah.

"Adirah!" Kesh shouted, rushing to her side.

"Hey! Get out of here! It's too dangerous for you in here!" the firefighter scolded.

Kesh forced Adirah out of the man's hands.

"Hey! Help! I need help over here!" the firefighter screamed.

Kesh hoisted Adirah over his left shoulder and used his right hand to push the firefighter so hard, he flew clear across the room. Kesh pulled Adirah into his arms until her head hung over his right arm and her legs hung over his left arm. He stared down at her, his heart breaking. The were burns on her face, neck, and hands. The flesh was charred, and Kesh could see parts of the subcutaneous fat. The fire had burned her down to the last layer of skin in places. His body trembled as he lifted her up so that her head was close to his face. Kesh heard faint breaths escaping her lips. He knew he didn't have much time. Fire raged to his left and his right now. He was distracted by the loud voices invading his sensitive ears and the heat of hell from the blaze. He couldn't let that distract him.

"I have to save her," Kesh wheezed. His lungs were filling with smoke. He needed to get out of there, or they both would perish. He lifted his right wrist and bit down on it until he drew blood. He shifted Adirah's body over so that he could put the blood from his leaking wrist to Adirah's lips. He rubbed it across her mouth, hoping.

"Drink," Kesh whispered. "Please."

The blood from his wrist dripped over Adirah's partially open mouth and painted her lips and teeth red. Kesh hoped that enough got into her system to save her. Just then, he heard the ceiling beams creak and knew what that meant. Kesh held on to her and ran toward the door. Just before the entire ceiling collapsed into the middle of the floor, Kesh leapt through the front door and onto the lawn.

"Hey. Put her here. She needs attention," an EMT screamed at Kesh.

Confused, Kesh looked down at Adirah's badly burned body, back over at the waving EMT, and then up at the sky.

"Ay! I said bring her over here! We can proba-bly save her," the EMT yelled again.

Kesh stared into the night sky and didn't see one sparkling star. The smoke hung over the house like a black cloud of death. He could feel his enemies circling. He sniffed out their evil intentions. Kesh knew what they wanted, just like the first time they'd attacked. He'd long since defected from the rules of their vampire council. He wanted a different life for himself, his clan too.

Kesh looked down at Adirah one last time. If he didn't let her go, he knew he'd be risking too much. The enemy was close, too close. He needed to take cover, regroup, and live to fight another day. At least he had gotten her out in time. He had no choice but to go stand with his clan and fight. He walked over and gently placed Adirah down on the gurney. The EMTs sprang into action. Kesh went to walk away, but not before he heard Adirah cough and suck in her breath. He smiled. In her condition, Kesh knew that it could only be the sip of his blood that had saved her.

Kesh returned to his clan, covered in black soot and sweat. They were huddled together on the sacred grounds next to the Freeman building. When he approached, they instinctively moved apart, opening up a path for him to pass.

"How bad was it?" Kesh asked, noticing the solemn looks on their faces.

"Zane and Torg didn't make it out," Tiev answered, his voice cracking. "They were stabbed in the heart, and they burned while we were getting you out of there. This was what they were waiting for . . . our guards to be down."

"It was a direct attack. According to the Council, we can attack right back," Vila said angrily. "We have to attack them back. We look weak every time they do this and we don't do it back to them. I'm tired of looking weak, Kesh." Tears ran a race down Vila's face, and her hands were curled so tight into fists, veins popped up on their tops.

Kesh put up his hand. "Let's be calm and think. We can't be like them . . . killing others senselessly. The whole reason I defected from the Council was so that we could be defenders and try to make a life among the living."

"No. We've been thinking too long. You said that last time, and we lost five people during that attack, Kesh. We can't keep letting them attack us like this. Don't you understand? We thrive off the living. . . . Killing is what we do to survive. There's no way around it," Vila replied adamantly. Her statement elicited grumbles of approval from the clan.

Kesh shoved his hands into his pants pockets and lowered his head, thinking. After he was turned, he had learned that Adie, his maker, was a direct descendant of the king of the Sefu Clan. No one had made her; instead, she was one of the few vampires who had been born that way. Once Adie turned him, Kesh had quickly become the most powerful of all his kind, because his maker had never been a mortal. Kesh had learned later that he was one of the only vampires who could reproduce like mortals did, but he never had and he had never told anyone. He never wanted to have offspring who would have to live the life he lived . . . walking the earth forever, never able to know that one day he'd rest in peace. It wasn't that he was weak; he was just tired. He wanted to find love and give up being king. He wanted to stop running from the Malum. His mind raced. . . .

Atlanta, Georgia
August 1900

Kesh sat with Tiev, discussing their next move. "It is not easy defecting from the Council, Tiev," Kesh said, his head in his hands. "There will be repercussions—"

His words were cut short when the door to his room splintered open with a crash. Kesh and Tiev swiveled their heads around at the same time. Kesh's face immediately folded into a frown.

"Tiba! How dare you enter my space like this . . . unannounced!" Kesh chastised.

Tiba, a warrior who'd been with him since he left the Council, could barely control her breathing. Her eyes were as round as dinner plates. Kesh's entire clan, especially Tiba, knew never to enter his room unannounced unless there was an emergency.

"Wait. What is it, Tiba? Why do you look so frightened?" he asked, having finally noticed her flaring nostrils and quivering cheeks.

"Th-they've found us. The Malum are coming now. I think the Council sent them," she huffed, her lips white with fear.

"We have to go!" Tiev grabbed Kesh by the arm. "Get dressed. We have to move!"

Kesh shook his head. "No, we have to stay and fight! We can't run forever."

"No, Kesh," Tiba told him. "They want you. It is you that they have always wanted. We cannot risk it. Without you, there is no clan. We are all prepared to die for you, but if you die for us, we will no longer have a purpose."

"She is right, Kesh," Tiev said. "We must go."

Tiba ducked and spun around at the booming sound of an explosion. She drew her sword with shaky hands. The entire room shook, and the sound of glass shattering cut through the air. Screams and shouting let Kesh know that the Malum had made their way inside. Kesh could hear the voices of his clan members in battle cry.

"I will not let my clan die defending a leader who runs away from battle. Go round up the others! Get them out of here!" Kesh commanded, barreling past Tiev and Tiba.

Kesh jumped the entire flight of stairs and landed so hard that his feet cracked the marble floor below. His chest heaved until it swelled up to his neck. Adrenaline coursed though his veins. His senses were heightened. He could smell fear and anger, and he could hear the pounding of the Malum Clan's feet, and their desperate breaths, as they rushed toward Kesh and his clan.

The members of the Malum Clan were descendants of ancient Europeans who had come to America to pillage and loot. Their leader, Tulum, had been made by a white man . . . a slave owner. Kesh had known Tulum for decades, but when they were both handled by the Council, it forbade Tulum from exacting revenge against

Kesh. When Kesh defected from the Council, the rules changed. It didn't help that Kesh was so much stronger and faster than Tulum, who secretly thirsted for the same power. When Kesh took a clan of defectors and became king of the Sefu Clan, deciding not to follow the most violent vampire tenants, Kesh's defiance infuriated Tulum and the Council. After all, in their eyes, Kesh was a black man. . . . He had no right to rise up. Kesh was open to attack. Although vampire law stipulated that a vampire was not to kill another vampire, Tulum didn't care. He had the blessing of the Council to go after Kesh, and that was all he needed.

Kesh followed his clan's battle cries until finally he entered the large living area. He ducked as one of his own men went flying through the air, narrowly missing Kesh's head. Bodies were tangled in combat, fists flew, sharp fangs were bared, and a vicious battle played out before his eyes. Kesh's stomach churned at the sight of the bloodshed. This was not what he wanted. His decision to leave the Council had been a personal one. He hadn't intended for there to be bloodshed. In fact, he had hoped for the opposite.

He moved with purpose, his fists curled, as he eyed the lifeless bodies of some of his clan members. His canines instantly extended into animal fangs; and his fingernails, into sharp claws.

"There!" one of the Malum yelled out. "There is their king!"

The other dozen vampires turned toward Kesh and dropped into low battle stances.

"You want me?" Kesh barked angrily. "You'll have to show me how badly you do!"

With that, Kesh moved with supernatural speed, advancing on his rivals instantly. The rival closest to him was a woman; she was the oldest of all of them. Kesh could smell the age seeping from her skin like death and burnt earth. Kesh backed off a few steps. Out of respect, he momentarily stopped his advancement. His admiration for his elders had been ingrained in him in childhood.

Although Kesh had stopped his progress, she kept advancing, with a wild look in her eye. Kesh's reverence for his elders was replaced with a desire for survival. Kesh thrust his left hand forward. Instead of ripping her heart out of her chest, he ripped her throat from her neck and shoved it into the mouth of the male Malum Clan member beside her.

"Argh!" Kesh let out a ferocious cry as he plowed into the others effortlessly.

They tried to stand their ground, but Kesh was just too fast and powerful for them. He easily overwhelmed them. Kesh threw two of them through the air. They hit the wall behind them so hard that Kesh heard their skulls crack. Their bodies slid to the ground and joined the other ten whom he'd defeated. There was only one left. Kesh walked slowly toward him. After witnessing the awesome power that Kesh possessed, the man was paralyzed with fear. He stood wide-eyed, with his mouth agape. Kesh wrapped his bloody hand around the intruder's neck, then hoisted him up in the air like a rag doll.

"What do they call you?" Kesh barked.

"I—" The rival choked from trying to speak. Kesh didn't loosen his grip. "I am Orlum . . . aide to King Tulum," he croaked out.

"King?" Kesh scoffed. "That is what he is calling himself these days? Where is he now?"

"He—he stayed behind," Orlum rasped. "We were to weaken you."

"Coward! And you call him King? He who will not fight me at full strength?"

Orlum surprised Kesh by laughing. It sounded more like a cough, but the smirk let Kesh know that the vampire in his clutches found something amusing.

"Tulum is no coward," Orlum said. "He just knows that your weakness is, and has always been, this clan of misfits. Look around you, King. You have grown so used to running that you have not even trained your followers to fight! Your numbers have dropped to half in a single night because of your benevolence. King Tulum did not send us to harm you physically. What we have done is far . . . far worse. . . . We want to watch your slow demise. Tulum is coming. And even you aren't man enough to face him and an entire army alone."

The words were like an openhanded slap to Kesh's face. His jaw went stiff. His anger turned to fury, and his growl turned beastly. Kesh brought Orlum's body down so that he could put his mouth by his ear.

"One thing you need to know about your king . . . he cares about nobody but himself. He sent you here to kill, but he also sent you here to die!"

With that, Kesh was done speaking. He placed a hand on Orlum's shoulder to get a grip on him and, with one swift tug, decapitated him. The black vampire blood, the blood of the dead, spurted on Kesh's face and chest. He hadn't wanted to do it, but he had to. Tulum had turned this into an all-out battle, and there would be only one winner. If Kesh hadn't killed

Orlum, it would have shown that his clan was weak. Orlum had been right about one thing: Kesh's clan was not prepared for the bloody war that lay ahead. He had to lead by example.

Kesh collapsed to the ground. His fangs retreated, along with his nails. His chest pumped up and down, getting slower with each passing minute. He wanted nothing more than to go find Tulum and end him. The cries of sorrow from his clan grew louder and louder in his head. He closed his eyes and squeezed his skull, hoping to drown out the screams of his clan. Kesh gathered his resolve, pushed past the doubts, and regained his authority. He finally drew himself up from the floor and made his way back to the stairs.

"My king!"

Kesh turned to the sound of Tiev's voice. He noticed Tiev standing there, holding a shirt, socks, and a pair of boots.

"Everyone is ready to move! We must go now, before the Malum return," Tiev told him. "So far they have been defeated, but we cannot withstand another battle tonight. We lost many Sefu. Too many of us have been killed. We will lose if we stay here."

Kesh nodded his head but still went toward the stairs. There was something he had to get.

"Your chest? Tiba has it. It is safe," Tiev called out.

Kesh stopped in his tracks. He nodded his head and turned, then made his way to Tiev. He thanked his friend and dressed in the clothes he held. The blood that was still on him instantly stained the fabric of the shirt.

"Brother," Kesh said, placing his hand on Tiev's shoulder, *"I have been negligent in thinking that I could protect them all. I was wrong."*

"What are you saying, Kesh?"

"I am saying that the Sefu must learn to fight again. Like we did so long ago. During the revolution and during our fight for freedom. I have to build a strong empire."

"Well, well, well . . ."

The words yanked Kesh back to reality. Gasps rose and fell over the group as they all turned at the sound of the voice and the crunching gravel underfoot. Kesh lifted his head. His chest swelled and he squinted his eyes into slits at the sight of his biggest enemy, Tulum.

"If it isn't Keston Priolou, leader of the defectors," Tulum announced viciously. "The king of the rejects. The weakest of our kind." Tulum laughed raucously at his own jokes, his long black leather jacket flapping behind him.

Kesh's jaw rocked at the sound of his birth name. "What do you want, Tulum? Why are you here? Why are you following me? Nothing else to do . . . ? Are there not enough mortals for you to kill? You have to go after other vampires? All these years later and you're not satisfied?"

It had been decades since the war between the two clans had ended. Or so Kesh had thought. For a hundred years Kesh and his clan had been traveling the world, untouched and left alone. A truce had been called, and each clan had gone its separate way. It had been agreed that it was better for the survival of their race if they ended their battle.

Tulum threw his head back and cackled some more, his pale face turning bright pink. "Why am I here? Oh, c'mon, Keston. You always know why I am here." Tulum walked closer to Kesh and lowered his voice into a sinister baritone. "I want to see you suffer, Keston. Why else would I be here? I am the defender of my ancestry, just like you're the defender of yours. I want to destroy you piece by piece, bit by bit. Black against white. We are the only pure breed, and we will work until eternity to make sure that you don't have a legacy." Evil flashed in his dark, dead eyes.

"This rivalry is stupid. The war was over one hundred years ago. I just want peace," Kesh said. "And about your brother . . . he was stupid to attack me when he knew he couldn't win. He brought it on himself. He tried to kill me, and I defended myself. I didn't seek him out to kill him. I can't understand hate based on skin color . . . because understand something, Tulum. We are all vampires."

Tulum lifted his hand and jerked it backward and forward. His powers picked Kesh up off his feet and sent him flying backward into the air. Kesh landed on his back with so much force that something cracked at the base of his skull and the air in his lungs involuntarily escaped his mouth in a loud rush. Kesh groaned, dazed from the impact of the fall.

Gasps and groans rose up among Kesh's clan. Several members rushed over to help him up. Tiev drew his silver-tipped sword and put it to Tulum's throat. The other Malum Clan members moved in close to their king, and the Sefu members came up behind Tiev.

Tulum laughed. "Well, I guess this is what it looked like back then . . . right here on the grounds of the Billet plantation. Whites versus blacks, good versus evil, in a heated standoff," he said, glaring at Tiev.

Tiev growled, his lip trembling, and his eyes hooded over. "Leave. Now."

"I could destroy you all right now, but I've been having too much fun keeping you on the run and picking you all off one by one," Tulum replied, smiling like they were all a joke.

Tiev pushed his sword forward slightly, the vein in his left temple thumping against the surface of his skin. "I said leave."

"I'll leave, but I want you to know one thing. Your clan will never survive. You'll all be done. Your king is weak, and I will never let him have a queen," Tulum snarled. "He can't change our entire culture because he wants to be good all of a sudden. A good vampire? What an oxymoron. He's stupid for even thinking he could pull this off. The Council and other clans are not happy. Not happy at all. I know why Keston wants a queen. . . . I know why he wants a certain queen too. I've seen her. I've smelled her. I know all about her gifts. She'll never be queen. There will never be a better queen than mine." Tulum held out his hand, and his queen, Calum, stepped closer to him.

He went on. "Keston will never change how vampires exist. I won't let that happen, and the Council is backing me. They want me to destroy him. With my queen by my side, I will remain more powerful than Keston or Kesh, or whatever you call him. My queen can't be stopped." Tulum moved his hand to Calum's ass. She licked her lips hungrily, kissed his cheek, and trailed her tongue down the side of his face. "You'll never have a queen. We will see to it that you don't," Calum hissed.

Chapter 5

"Take my hand, Dira. I missed you," Adolphis chimed, giving her that heartwarming smile that had always gotten him out of trouble when they were little.

Adirah moved her head from side to side and opened her mouth to say something, but the words wouldn't come out. It was as if someone had stolen her voice.

"C'mon, I can take you to see him. He can save your life," Adolphis said, smiling cheerfully. "Just take my hand, Dira. You have to take my hand so you can come with me. We can be together . . . forever. You'll like it here with me. I promise. Just take my hand." He extended his hand out to her and wiggled his little fingers. He looked the same as she remembered him. He hadn't grown up at all.

Adirah smiled at her brother, but she still couldn't speak. She'd missed Adolphis. The way they would play tag and hide-and-seek.

The times they were supposed to be doing a daily prayer but would giggle behind their mother's back. She really missed him. He was right. They could be together. Adirah extended her hand toward her brother, but she couldn't reach him.

"Take my hand, Dira. Please," Adolphis pleaded now, but some unknown force was pulling her farther away from him. "Dira! Hurry! Take my hand!"

Adirah was trying desperately to reach him, but she was failing. She couldn't speak to ask what was happening.

"Dira! Don't go!" Adolphis screamed at her, wide-eyed desperation playing across his face.

Adolphis was fading away, but she could still hear his cries echoing in her head.

"Come back, Dira! Take my hand, please! Don't leave me here all alone again! Dira! Dira!"

Adirah wanted to scream her brother's name, but again, she couldn't speak. She stretched her arm farther. But the more she reached, the farther away he moved. Tears sprang to her eyes, and her mouth opened into an O. She stretched and stretched, but she couldn't reach him. He was still fading away, but she could still hear him calling her.

"Dira! Dira! Dira!"

Adirah's eyes shot open, and she sucked in her breath until her throat made a loud noise. She tried to sit up, but some unknown force held her down. Her chest heaved and her head throbbed with every slam of her heart. Loud ringing came from her right. The sound of people shuffling around her came from her left.

"Dira? Dira?" Kesh's voice called out from afar.

"Sir, I'm going to have to ask you to move." Adirah opened her eyes in time to see a nurse pushing Kesh away. The nurse turned back to Adirah. "Calm down, honey," the nurse's soothing voice sang. "Calm down, or you'll make yourself worse."

Adirah took command of her body and shifted her head. She squinted against the lights, and finally the nurse—a chubby-faced woman in pink scrubs—came into focus.

"I'm Angie, your nurse. It's okay. You've been out of it for a little while, but you're alive . . . and that's a good thing," Angie soothed. "I'm going to get you another sedative so you're not in pain. You were in pretty bad shape, but I'm happy to see you awake."

Adirah closed her eyes again. She couldn't remember anything that had happened or why she was in the hospital. Her mind was fuzzy with sleep, but she was aware that he was there with her.

"Dira?" Kesh walked over. "How are you?"

Adirah groaned and shook her head. Her eyes darted around the room, from Kesh to Vila to the tall guy from the party. What were they doing there? Where was Lina? What happened? Adirah's head pounded, and her entire body ached, even in places she didn't know could hurt. She couldn't think straight. There were so many questions swirling around in her aching head, but she was too tired to figure things out. Adirah closed her eyes for a few seconds, and before she could reopen them, Angie was back. The nurse moved about like she couldn't see Kesh, Vila, and their friend, but Adirah could hear them whispering to one another somewhere across the room. Was she hallucinating? Had she really seen the sexy guy from her psychology class and the crazy girl Lina had brought to their dorm room?

"I'm going to give you something for the pain and check those burns," Angie told Adirah. "I'm just happy to see you opening those little eyes of yours. I wasn't so sure about you, young lady. I didn't think we would have you here with us right now. It was pretty touch and go. You're so lucky to be alive. That fire took many lives."

Adirah cracked her eyes open again and watched Angie plunge a syringe filled with clear liquid into the intravenous bag. Still, it was as if Angie couldn't see Kesh and his friends or hear the voices.

"There. That should make it all better," Angie said, smiling down at Adirah. "Now, get some rest. You have a long road ahead. Besides, as soon as I give the green light, there will be some important people coming to see you. You're the lone survivor of that terrible tragedy. God must have a pretty special plan for your life."

Adirah's head lulled to the side, but she could feel the nurse loosening the bandages on her right arm.

"What in the world? This is impossible," Angie gasped, her hands starting to shake right away. "There is no way. I know I am not crazy."

Adirah could hear the distress and shock in Angie's voice as she frantically removed more bandages. Adirah fought to stay awake. She wanted to know what was happening.

"I . . . I . . . can't believe this. Maybe I've been working too many hours. I have to go get someone," Angie said, flustered. "There's no way. I . . . I've never seen anything like this before in all my years," she mumbled as she scrambled toward the door like she'd seen a ghost.

Adirah closed her eyes again, still struggling to stay awake against the medication. She didn't want to be out of it. She had to find out what had happened to her. Why was the nurse so up in arms?

"Dira? Dira, I am here."

Adirah groaned and tried to move her head in the direction of the familiar voice.

"Dira, my queen. We have to get out of here before they figure it out. I have to take you with me," Kesh said, taking her hand in his. "I'm going to make sure I protect you. I'll never let you get hurt again."

Adirah groaned, but she couldn't hold on any longer. Sleep snatched her away again.

"Kesh, are you crazy? You can't just kidnap her, a mortal girl, from a crowded hospital. Everyone knows about the fire and the victims. I mean, she's the only person who survived, thanks to you. Should I call you the *mysterious hero*, since that's what they've been calling you on the news? She has a nurse, and they'll be sounding the alarms and looking for her, for crying out loud," Vila lectured as she paced on the far right side of Adirah's hospital room.

"I have to take her back and take care of her," Kesh said, struggling with his decision. "I know the risks, but I can't let the Malum get to her.

Just like we have clan members planted in regular places, they might have someone planted here at the hospital, just waiting for one of us to slip up. I can't leave her here. Period."

"King, Vila might be right," Tiev interjected, keeping his voice level. "If we remove her from here by using our gifts, it will be all over the news. Their cameras are outside, and you won't show up on their recordings. Can you imagine what they'll see when they play the videos back? Her body levitating down the street by itself." He shook his head. "You think that would be wise? We'd have more than just the Malum to worry about. We'd have vampire hunters flocking to North Carolina and trying to find her and then us," he said pleadingly. "We have to be smart about this."

"We can put her in a disguise and let her walk out," Kesh offered.

Tiev shook his head again. "That's not a good idea, either. It doesn't matter what idea you come up with. Everyone will be looking for her. That nurse will return here any minute with a crowd of doctors. She knows what she saw under those bandages, and she knows what is supposed to be there. Obviously, Adirah is having a miraculous recovery and is healing because she drank from you, and now the mortals are confused. Did you see the look on that nurse's face when she noticed that Adirah doesn't have any burns or scars on that arm? It won't be long before every burn on her body is gone. Or what about when she starts to feel different? Have new gifts and strength? This could spell disaster for us. It would be too much attention, which would be a perfect chance for the Malum to attack, this time directly. This time—"

Kesh put up his hand. "Enough. I already know everything you both are telling me. Stop talking and fix it. Vila, go take that nurse's mind. Charm her. Make her think she discharged this patient after a full recovery. Tiev, you do the same for the doctors. I don't care if you have to do it to the entire hospital, and to the reporters too. I don't care what has to be done. I'm taking Dira with me," Kesh commanded, his jaw set and his nostrils flaring.

Vila and Tiev had no choice but to obey, whether they agreed or not. Kesh was their king. They both bowed their heads and left the room to carry out Kesh's orders.

When he was finally alone with Adirah, Kesh walked over to her bedside and trailed his hand over her forehead. He felt a surge that jolted his body. He knew their connection was real. He loved her already, and he didn't even know why.

"The Malum are looking for you," he whispered to her. "There's something special about you. There's a reason they don't want me to have you as my queen, Dira. That's my new name for you, Dira. My queen. Dira, queen of the Sefu Clan."

Adirah awoke with a start. She bolted upright and tossed the black comforter off her body. She looked down at her naked body. "What the . . . ?" she murmured. She searched around for something to put on to cover her nakedness. There was nothing in sight. She reached back and wrapped the comforter around her. She touched her face and felt no pain. The headache she had been experiencing before was gone.

Adirah remembered being in a hospital but wasn't quite sure if it was a dream or not, because clearly she was not in a hospital now. The room was dark; the only light was from the flickering of a few candles that had been placed strategically around the perimeter and from a fire burning in the fireplace. There were two leather club chairs facing each other off to the left of the bed. Adirah was in a bed but was unsure if she was in an actually bedroom. The room had elements of a lounge or a living room, as well as a bedroom. There was a dresser, but there was also an oak bookshelf filled with classic literature. There was an oriental rug that looked to be about three hundred years old lying in front of a large brick fireplace. It had deep reds and blacks woven in an intricate pattern.

"I'm happy to see that you're doing better," a deep voice said from across the room.

Adirah jumped out of the strange bed in one leap and tried in vain to cover her breasts and private parts with her hands. "Where am I? What did you do to me?" she said, panicked.

"Shh." Kesh got up from the chair and walked toward her with his hands out in front of him. She could barely make out his shape in the dim lighting.

"Why am I here!" Adirah shouted, so loud her throat itched. She started coughing.

"It's okay. You're fine. You were out of it for a while, but you're better," Kesh said in a low, comforting tone. "No one hurt you. I took care of you." He saw that she was in distress, so he ended his advance toward her. He stood with his right hand extended to her.

"Don't touch me." Adirah jumped back. "Why . . . why am I here? Why am I . . . n-naked?" she quizzed, carefully retreating from Kesh. "What did you do to me? Did you give me some drug and take advantage of me?"

"No. No. Nothing like that. It's a long story, but first, you have to calm down. You don't want to make yourself sick again," Kesh said, reaching over and gingerly pulling a plush black terry-cloth robe off the bedpost. "Here. Take this to cover yourself." He held the robe out to her.

Adirah was trembling all over. She was so confused. One minute she was at a party, enjoying her life, then possibly at a hospital, and then she was waking up, naked, in a strange room. Adirah knew she shouldn't have gone to that party. Getting involved in the university's social life and not focusing on her studies was not her plan, and now she was paying the price.

She reached out and snatched the robe and attempted to put it on. She shook so badly, she couldn't get the sleeves of the heavy material to cooperate. She flipped the robe three times and still couldn't get it on.

Kesh stepped closer. "Let me help you," he said. He grabbed the back of the robe and helped her into it.

Once she was covered, Adirah quickly moved away from Kesh and stood in front of the fireplace. The brightness of the fire enveloped her in a warm glow. She wrapped her arms around her stomach and hugged herself. "I want to know why I am here," she repeated, her chest swelling with every word. She looked around the dimly lit room. "What place is this? What did you do to me? Did you . . . did you . . ."

"No." Kesh shook his head vigorously and reached out for her. "I already told you. I was the one that saved you. Let me talk to you . . . tell you everything."

Adirah stumbled backward away from him, her fists raised defensively. "Don't touch me."

"You don't understand. I saved your life. I took you out of the fire and nursed you back to health," Kesh said. "I am here for you." He slowly got closer to her. He could feel Adirah's reluctance start to ease.

Adirah's hands fell to her sides. She was exhausted. She had been fighting her entire life, and she was finished. Kesh grabbed both of her hands and pulled her into him. Adirah wanted to resist him, and she desperately tried, but for some reason, she couldn't. The glow surrounding him felt like it was sucking her in. She let him hold her, and it felt better than anything she had felt in years. Adirah closed her eyes, melted against him, and inhaled his scent. All her trembling stopped. She remembered this feeling as a child, when she got hugs from her mother. It was like being wrapped in a warm blanket during a cold storm. All her worries were melting away.

"Tell me," she whispered. "The truth about what happened to me. The truth about what you did to me. The truth about who you are. Tell me the truth . . . please."

Kesh started to say something, but loud pounding on the door caused him to pause. Adirah jumped and shook her head.

"Oh, my God," she gasped. "I have to go. I can't be here."

"No, Dira. Wait. Let me get rid of whoever it is," Kesh said, with urgency in his voice.

"Why are you calling me what my family called me?" she asked, her face crumpled in confusion.

"That's . . . that's my name for you," he said.

The loud pounding started again and interrupted their conversation.

"Just relax. I'll be right back," Kesh told her, putting both of his hands up to emphasize that he wanted her to stay put. He rushed to the door and yanked it open, wearing a frown. "What?" he muttered after finding Tiev and Vila on the other side.

"We need to speak to you right now," Vila whispered harshly. "Alone." Her eyes roved over his shoulder into the bedroom.

"I'm busy," Kesh said, stepping into the hallway and pulling the door behind him.

"Well, you're in *my* room, and I am asking for a minute of your precious time away from your precious mortal girl," Vila snapped.

Kesh contemplated this. He had taken over Vila's room since the frat house where he had a room had burned down. He certainly couldn't take Dira to their underground sleeping place, so he'd commanded Vila to give up her room. "What is it?" Kesh asked, annoyed.

"I can't believe you were about to reveal yourself to her, Kesh," Vila said through her teeth, pointing in his face. "She's a mortal. Or did you forget that? She has your blood in her now, but that doesn't make her one of *us*. I have never seen you act like this over a stupid girl."

Kesh exhaled loudly. "I am the king of this clan. I call the shots. I can do what I want with her."

"But there are laws, Kesh," Vila said, raising her voice. "Or did you forget them now that you're so in love with a strange mortal girl, who, for all you know, could be a vampire killer?"

Kesh scoffed and shook his head. "This jealousy has to stop, Vila."

"She's right, Kesh," Tiev said, stepping in.

Kesh's eyebrows shot up into arches at his best friend's betrayal. "You too?"

"If you reveal your true self to her, she will have to die or be turned. You know that. There's no other way to handle it. You'll have to turn her," Tiev insisted.

"Listen, she still doesn't know what or who I am. I didn't give her enough of my blood to turn her . . . only enough to save her. She won't have the benefits of my blood forever, and I won't turn her. She has gifts, and if I turn her, she'll lose them. I need her to be the way she is," Kesh told them. "She has to be my queen. That's the end of the discussion."

"She'll never be *my* queen, and if you reveal yourself to her, she can't live. I'll make sure of that," Vila replied.

Kesh rushed into Vila with superhuman speed and knocked her back. He pinned her against the wall by her throat and squeezed until Vila gagged.

"You let your jealousy show on your face and spew from your lips all the time," Kesh snarled, his mouth against Vila's left ear. "But you have no power to question me. I am the king. I know the rules, and I make and break them as I see fit. Now . . . you will never touch her, or you will die a slow, painful death, never to return for another life," Kesh said with feeling.

He released his grip. Vila threw her hands up to her neck and coughed uncontrollably. She shot Kesh a hooded eye glare.

"You don't know what you just did," she rasped.

"Now, both of you need to be strategizing about our preparation for the next visit from our enemies, and not standing here, questioning me. Get out of my sight," Kesh said, dismissing them.

Chapter 6

Adirah had barely made it through the door of her dorm room when Lina rushed into her so hard and fast, she almost fell backward.

"Oh, my God! I can't believe you're here," Lina cried, pulling Adirah into a tight embrace. "This feels like a miracle." Lina pulled away from Adirah and started touching Adirah's face and hair like she couldn't believe she was standing there. "I just knew you were . . . I . . . I didn't know," Lina sobbed, shaking her head.

"It's okay, Lina. I'm alive and well. I'm here and fine as can be," Adirah said to comfort Lina, patting her shoulder.

"But . . . but how?" Lina asked, her palms up in front of her. "After I got out of the frat house and they herded us down the street and cordoned it off, I watched it burn to the ground. Even the firefighters had to run out of there. One even perished in the fire. They had said there were no survivors. I scoured the hospitals, asking and searching for you," Lina said, still shaking her head in disbelief. "When I didn't find you, I just . . . I . . . I thought you were—"

"I was able to get out, Lina," Adirah said, cutting in. "I remember everyone running in all different directions. I got lost in the crowd, but I was never left in the fire," Adirah lied, repeating the words Kesh had planted in her head. "There was never a reason for you to worry about me. I was fine the whole time. I hung around for a few days, but I was always perfectly perfect," Adirah continued, smiling.

Lina squinted at her and looked her up and down. "What's different about you, Adirah?"

"Nothing. Nothing at all," Adirah said, then giggled. "Why'd you ask?"

"Your skin . . . it's glowing," Lina reached out to touch Adirah's face.

Adirah moved her head aside. "It's always been like this."

Lina shook her head, her mouth hanging open slightly. "No . . . Even your eyes are so bright and clear. It's like you've been changed into one of the beautiful ones on campus. I'd know that look." Lina said, her voice trailing off.

"Don't be silly, Lina. I've always been gorgeous. Maybe you just never noticed," Adirah joked, winking.

She snatched her hair down from the ponytail she was wearing, and it fell around her shoulders. She walked over to the mirror on her side of the room and looked at her reflection. She smiled. She was gorgeous and glowing. It looked like she had on a full face of professionally applied makeup when she didn't have on any. Adirah touched her own face and moved closer to the mirror. Lina was right. There was definitely something different about her. She was radiant without even trying. Not only did she look great, but she also felt more alive than she ever had.

"Are you going to class?" Lina asked.

"Today I have a date," Adirah said, turning around so Lina could see her wide, cheesy grin. Adirah licked her lips seductively.

"A date over class? After being missing for over a week?" Lina replied. "Oh, you're definitely different, Adirah."

"You only thought I was missing. I've always been right here," Adirah said cryptically. "Now if you'll excuse me, I have to be ready in an hour." She winked at Lina.

Lina gathered up her books and shook her head. "Strange things just keep happening. I will get to the bottom of it sooner or later," she grumbled. "I know what I saw."

***

Adirah sauntered down the steps of the Rothschild building with a confidence she hadn't felt before. She had a new sense of self-assurance and felt oddly sexy. She had even chosen to wear a pair of formfitting jeans and a low-cut black bodysuit, an outfit that she had worn once to a party and that had gotten way too much attention, so she'd vowed never to wear again. Adirah had topped her outfit off with a pair of wedge booties that made her already slender form look leaner and longer, like a model's. She had accented her outfit with a hint of mascara to extend her natural lashes and with bright red lipstick on her plump, heart-shaped lips. The combination stood out against her dark skin and gave her a sophisticated look.

Adirah immediately felt like all eyes were on her. She smiled, her newfound confidence seemingly seeping through her pores. As she walked, it felt like time stood still around her, given the way people paused to get a glimpse of her. They couldn't help themselves. It seemed like she had cast a spell on them. Adirah whirled around, watching everyone in amazement. People she didn't know were stopping to greet her. Some even knew her name. Something was going on. A guy stopped in front of her and started saying something to her. Adirah watched his mouth move, but she could not hear his voice; instead, she could hear only blood rushing through his body and the pounding of his heart.

"What? What's happening?" Adirah moved quickly down the campus, but it happened again. People ogled her and mouthed words to her, but she couldn't hear them. She could hear only things going on inside of them, like the sound of them swallowing, the rhythm of their hearts pumping, their stomachs growling, and blood rushing through their bodies. Adirah shook her head, trying to see if she was dreaming again. The voices had also returned.

Dira. Dira. I'm here, Dira.

Adirah fanned her hands around her ears, trying to get the sounds to stop. She turned around in a circle, thinking someone was behind her. She stumbled forward in her heels and fell right into someone.

"Ah," she gasped, her body going stiff.

"I got you," Kesh said. "I got you." He held on to her. He seemed to be everywhere.

Adirah shivered with electric pulses at his touch. "Some . . . something is happening to me," she stammered. "I can hear things, and people are stopping to stare at me." She shook her head. "And I feel . . . I feel different." She pushed away from him and held out her hands and looked at

them. The scar she had on her right pointer finger from a childhood injury was gone. "I . . . I
used to have an old scar here. And, my face . . .
I used to have acne," she said, touching her face
in a panic. "It's all gone. I never had this glow
to my skin, and my stomach wasn't this flat. It's
like I became perfect overnight."

"Why don't we walk and talk?" Kesh said. "I
think it might just be some medications you took
at the hospital that are making you feel like this."

Adirah walked with him. "I remember being
with you at that house," she said. "But I can't
remember everything."

Kesh took her hand. "Dira, you've always
been perfect. I am not sure why you feel like
you weren't." He paused and turned toward
her. She faced him and stared into his eyes.
"You've always been perfect to me," Kesh said.
He lowered his head and kissed her lips. Adirah
felt an explosion like fireworks in her loins. She
opened her mouth and allowed Kesh's tongue
inside. She'd forgotten they were standing in the
middle of campus until someone walked by and
whistled at them.

"Oh, my goodness," Adirah said, pulling away
and looking around. "I never do stuff like this."
She turned beet red. So much for her aversion
to public displays of affection. *What is this guy
doing to me*? Adirah thought.

Kesh smiled at her. "Let's go someplace private and talk about everything."

Once inside her dormitory, Kesh couldn't keep his hands off Adirah. She didn't know why, but she felt the same way. They stumbled into her dorm room, and their hands roamed all over each other as he walked her backward toward her bed. Kesh's body was on fire. The chemistry he felt with Adirah was unheard of; never in all his years had he met a woman who lit this kind of fire inside of him. For once, Kesh wasn't thinking about what the blood tasted like; instead, he was preoccupied with what the jewel between her legs was like, how sweet it was. Kesh could hear the pounding of Adirah's heart. She seemed to come into her own sexuality with an aggressiveness he admired.

"Come here," Adirah said through labored breaths. "I want you."

She grabbed Kesh's head and pulled him close to her face as she eased herself back onto her bed. He followed her lead and put his hot mouth over hers. Adirah opened her mouth and allowed his tongue between her lips. She let out a soft song of moans as she sucked Kesh's tongue. He could feel his manhood pressing hard against his pants. The sound of his blood rushing filled his ears. He moved his mouth from Adirah's and trailed his long, wet tongue down the ladder of her throat.

She cried out, "Take me." Kesh felt her squeeze her thighs together. He knew that meant she was trying to control the fierce pulsing of her pussy.

"You're so beautiful," Kesh whispered as he moved down, unzipping her pants as he went. Adirah let out a soft moan and squirmed against him, urging him on. She lifted her bottom and helped him take off her jeans. Then she reached down and undid the snaps on her bodysuit. Kesh ran his hands up her stomach until the bodysuit was around her breasts. He sucked in his breath at how soft her skin was against his hands. Like a pro, he had her bra loosened in a flash, freeing her perky, round breasts from their captivity.

"I've never seen anything so gorgeous," Kesh panted. He passed over her nipples with his tongue; they were so erect, they felt rigid against his lips. Adirah winced in a good way as he gently sucked each one. Kesh had to keep his animal instincts at bay. He wanted to growl and let his fangs out, but he fought against it. He was sure Adirah could feel his iron-stiff erection pressing against the top of her pelvis.

"I want you," she huffed, letting her hands travel below his belt line so that he knew she wanted him. "I need you."

Kesh needed her too. "Dira," he gasped. "I need you more than you could ever know, Queen." He didn't want to feed off her blood. He wanted to feed off her passion. He'd been holding on to these feelings for her since the first day he met her. She'd drawn him in, like he usually did to others.

Kesh moved back up and whispered in her ear, "You feel so fucking good, Dira." Then he gently bit her lobe. A hot tingling feeling ran through his body. He had to fight the urge. He wanted her to be all his forever. But he knew turning her would change his feelings toward her. Kesh wanted her just the way she was.

"Are you ready?" Kesh asked softly, hovering above her so that she had to look right into his eyes.

Adirah moved her head up and down in the affirmative. She seemed lost in lust, mesmerized. Kesh knew this was because she had fed from him. He knew it would've been hard to get her to this point if he hadn't given her his blood and saved her life. Still, he felt her on so many deep levels that he didn't care why or how it had happened. He was in love for the first time since Adie.

Kesh stood up next to the bed, and Adirah lay there, watching, as he slid out of his fitted black

T-shirt, exposing his six-pack abs and sculpted muscular chest. His smooth brown skin seemed to glow against the faint beam from the sunlight coming through the slats in her blinds.

"Are you sure you're ready for me?" Kesh asked as he continued to undress.

Adirah shook her head and bit down on her bottom lip, but he could see her trembling like a lone leaf in a wild storm. Kesh smiled at her as he slowly unhooked his belt, unbuttoned his black jeans, and let them fall to the floor. He eased his boxers down and freed his long dick. It was standing up stiff as a roll of quarters.

Adirah smiled back, her eyes bulging slightly at the sight of him. "You're like a warrior . . . a black king," she said sexily. "I want you. I want to feel all of you," she demanded.

Kesh looked at her, amusement and shock rippling across his features. He knew it was him inside of her that had given her this new sexy prowess. She surely wasn't the shy, reserved, focused girl he'd met on the first day of class.

Adirah made the first blatant move and slid her hand down to Kesh's manhood. She took his girth in her hand and stroked it, letting him know she didn't want to wait another minute. She seemed to be saying that she needed him, she wanted him, and she was demanding him.

Kesh took her cue. "Your wish is my command," he said.

"What's happening to me?" she huffed. "You're so perfect. But . . . I . . . I . . . never."

"Shh. No, I'm not the one that's perfect. You're all I've ever wanted in a queen, Dira," Kesh replied, his voice gruff with lust.

Adirah's thighs trembled, but she didn't let that stop her from taking control. "Lie down with me," she commanded. "I want you now, please." Adirah seemed to let her inhibitions fall away; she wanted Kesh to understand that she was his now. All his.

"You're my queen, Dira. You'll be with me forever," he whispered. It was the second time he'd said it. Proclaiming it aloud, Kesh knew his clan would understand that Adirah was their new queen. That was exactly the message he wanted to send.

Kesh felt Adirah's stomach quiver at the sound of those words. "Your queen, Kesh," she repeated. "I'm yours forever."

That was it. She'd accepted him. He didn't have to bite her; she had accepted him in earnest. Kesh felt a serenity come over her that he knew meant it was real. Her previous fear and reservation were all tossed away at that moment.

Without another word, Adirah climbed onto
Kesh and straddled him. She leaned over his face
and looked right into his eyes. "I'm yours, Kesh."
Something exploded inside of him. Instinctively,
his canines extended. Adirah had her eyes closed
and didn't see it. She began licking his neck,
then moved a little farther down, trailing her
tongue down to his pecs and gently biting each
one.

"Argh," Kesh cried out heartily, his voice thick,
taking on a deep, monstrous tone.

With every noise he made, Adirah gained
more confidence. "I want you to feel good. I want
you to feel good," she chanted as she continued
down his abdomen, taking special care to run
her tongue over every ridge on his sexy, firm
six-pack.

Kesh groaned. Now he was the one trembling.
No woman had ever taken him. He'd always
been the taker.

When Adirah got to his manhood, she looked
up at his face. She gave a mischievous smile
and bit her bottom lip seductively. She grabbed
his dick, and with the skill of a professional, she
opened her lips and took him inside her hot
mouth. She let her saliva drip down his pulsing tool and spill down her own chin. Adirah
bobbed her head up and down over it, letting it hit the back of her throat a few times.

The sound of her gagging drove Kesh to the brink. He let out a long puff of air and grunted. Adirah could feel his muscles tense each time she bobbed her head up and down. She ran her hand up and down him as she moved her head at the same time.

Kesh was making noises that sounded like growling. He couldn't take it any longer. "I fucking need to feel you. I want to feel you now." He sat up abruptly and flipped Adirah over onto her back before she could even react or protest.

"Take it," she whispered. "Take me. I am yours forever." A pang of anticipation flitted through Kesh's chest. Adirah was on her back, watching him now. She put her hands on the top of his head. "Taste me first."

Kesh did not protest. He kissed her stomach as he inched down. "Mmm," he moaned.

Her scent and her essence were so overpowering, he felt like she had charmed him, instead of the other way around. Adirah's chest rose and fell in anticipation of what was coming. Kesh moved back up and kissed her, while at the same time he used his knee to part her legs gently. Adirah lifted her knees willingly to help him. He slowly guided his manhood into her deep, wet center. Adirah let out a song of soft moans and groans as he ground into her.

"Dira," he growled, his eyes closed and his nostrils open wide. He planted his hands on the bed, on either side of Adirah's head, for leverage.

"Oh, God," she cooed. "Kesh, you feel so good."

Kesh didn't know how much longer he could resist his urge to bite her. They were a perfect match. He filled her up just right. He'd never had that happen before, either . . . not even with Vila.

"Oh, God! Oh, God!" Kesh belted out, picking up speed from the excitement of feeling Adirah's pulsing, gripping insides. Adirah had tears in her eyes. Kesh opened his eyes wide. "Dira? Are you okay?"

She shook her head vigorously. "It's just that . . . it's . . . it's so good."

Kesh smiled at her and kissed her lips as he swirled his hips between her legs.

"Can I get on top?" she panted. "I want to see you." Before Kesh could protest or say anything, Adirah had him on his back. She climbed over his stiff tool and lowered herself down on it slowly. "Oh," she cried out as Kesh penetrated her insides. He looked up and saw the streaks of pain and pleasure ripple across her face.

He put his hands on her waist and guided her up and down. He could barely control his breathing. He felt every single vein in his body cording against his skin. Within minutes, Adirah picked up on his rhythm and began bouncing on him with each pump of his hips. Kesh could hear the old drumbeat he had listened to as a child whenever the slaves had their celebration of old lands, old lives. Kesh felt renewed. For the first time in a hundred years, he felt like a king—without having to kill anyone or force his clan to do his bidding. He felt like a king!

"Ahh!" Adirah yelled. "Y-you, I . . . I . . . ," Adirah stuttered. Even that, her sexy loss for words, made Kesh feel fireworks exploding in his loins. He quickly figured out that she was having an orgasm. Her eyes rolled up, and she threw her head back like she was having an out-of-body experience. Adirah started to chant in another language and in another voice. It was as if a spirit had taken over her body. She leaned down, planted her hands on Kesh's chest, and bucked against him hard. She bounced up and down on Kesh harder and faster.

Kesh lost control. His body shook from her efforts. He knew the consequences of letting himself go inside of her, but he also knew there was no stopping her. "You feel so *good*," he growled, clutching two handfuls of Adirah's ass cheeks.

Adirah chanted some more, moving like her life depended on it. She rocked back and forth and then swirled her hips, grinding harder and harder. "Ohhh! Ahhh!" she screamed out. She fell down onto Kesh's chest, letting her breasts brush against his pecs.

A light show exploded in his head, and sparks of light filled his eyesight. Adirah leaned down enough for Kesh to be able to urge her mouth to cover his. He sucked on her tongue. Another explosion erupted in his loins.

"Kesh!" Adirah belted out. Her entire body shook like she was at the center of an earthquake, and all of a sudden she was weak. Her legs trembled fiercely, and she went completely still, seemingly unable to move. It was only a few seconds later that Kesh's body tensed up and he had his climax, holding on to Adirah's ass as he let himself go inside of her. He poured his soul into his new queen. He didn't care about what that meant. He didn't care about the rules. He didn't care that she was a mortal.

Adirah collapsed on top of Kesh, and they both tried to calm their rapid breathing. He stroked her hair gently.

"Promise me that you'll stay with me forever as my queen," he said. "Promise me that you're mine forever and that you'll defend our love."

Adirah closed her eyes. "I promise," she said softly. "Now you."

"On the name of my clan, I swear aloud that you are my queen, now and forever. I promise I'll always be yours, Dira. Let's drop the Adirah and just call you Dira."

Adirah slid off him and lay next to him. She put her head on his chest and listened for the beat of his heart. At that moment, she decided it was there that she wanted to be. Forever.

"Dira. I like that. That is what my family used to call me," she said.

"I know, and now your new family will call you that. It is the name of the queen now. Queen Dira," Kesh said. He gently nudged her head up from his chest and kissed her deeply again. "My queen, Dira."

Chapter 7

Adirah held on to Kesh's hand as he led her down a narrow winding staircase that descended into the belly of the earth. They had entered from a hidden door that was barely visible on the side of Freeman building. There was no door handle, and the brick that the door was made of matched the building's facade perfectly. If Kesh had not shown it to her, Adirah would never have known it was there.

The acrid scent of cold dirt and mold, mixed with the sweet aroma of burning marijuana, connected with her senses before she reached the bottom of the staircase.

"What is this place?" she asked. The feel of it was that of an old dungeon. The walls of the staircase were made of piled stones that resembled those in the ancient caves in Africa she'd read about during her studies.

When they reached the bottom step, Kesh pulled her to his side and wrapped his arm around her shoulders. "These are my people. This is our place," he said, looking out into the dimly lit underground hideout.

Adirah's eye roved around the large cavernous room, but she was barely able to focus, thanks to the thick gray fog of smoke hanging in the air in perfect clouds that almost resembled helium balloons. It wasn't a heavenly feeling that Adirah was getting, but it was definitely otherworldly.

"Your people?" Adirah asked, looking up at Kesh.

"For some reason, you don't believe me when I say I am a king." Kesh laughed. "So I decided to show you." He shrugged.

Adirah laughed nervously. He had certainly told her he was a king, but she hadn't exactly got what he was saying. Between Lina drilling the undead, vampire stuff in her head and Kesh having a hold on her, Adirah was starting to feel like she was walking through one big dream. If not for the deep feelings she had for Kesh, she wouldn't believe she was even alive.

As they moved farther into the belly of the hideout, which Adirah decided was like some obscure club, she could feel all eyes on them. The people, who looked like partygoers, didn't hide their bright-eyed stares. Some of them even whispered and pointed right at her. Adirah did notice that even in the dark, their eyes and skin seemed to glow. There were a few people, girls mostly, standing around who didn't have that glow. Their eyes had an emptiness to them. Adirah had seen this look on the drug addicts back in Brooklyn. The hairs on Adirah's arms stood up, and a chill shot down her back. An eerie feeling and a voice invaded her ears again.

You're among the evil. You're in danger. Run fast. They don't want you here. You're not one of them, a silent voice said to her. It sounded like Adolphis.

Heat flared up in Adirah's belly. She waved her hand near her ear. *Not now! I told you I was fine. Stop doing this*, she screamed inside her head, telling the spirit that often spoke to her and haunted her to go away.

"You okay?" Kesh asked.

"Yeah, I'm fine," Adirah lied, stumbling a little bit. She couldn't shake the dark foreboding that had suddenly come over her. She felt like someone had thrown a dark hood over her head. The fairy tale she was creating in her mind with Kesh was being challenged by the voice and was causing her to doubt her actions.

As she and Kesh moved forward, Adirah looked to her left and suddenly froze. She squinted, thinking her eyes were deceiving her. She

opened her mouth to say something and lifted
her hand to point at a man with fangs who was
about to bite the neck of a young girl whose skirt
was hitched up around her waist and whose legs
were locked around the man's torso. *Does he
have vampire fangs?* she thought.

"Are those—" Adirah didn't get a chance to get
the rest of her words out.

"Let's go over here." Kesh tugged her to the
right, turning her away from what she thought
she saw.

"What was . . . ," Adirah began, but she trailed
off. She knew what she had seen. She kept trying
to look over her shoulder to confirm what she
had seen, but Kesh kept pulling her in the opposite direction

"Ahh, my people," Kesh announced. He
stopped in front of a group of men and women
who were in various stages of drinking, smoking,
and laughing.

Adirah crumpled her brow, thinking that
some of the faces were familiar, but she couldn't
remember from where. She waved off the
thought, deciding that Billet had a big campus
and chances were that she'd seen these people
around.

"Tiev," Kesh sang. "This is my new love, Dira,"
Kesh said, introducing Adirah and squeezing her
closer to him.

Adirah blushed. She had never had a man claim her like that. She lifted her hand, spread a goofy smile over her lips, and waved. Tiev stepped forward with his hand extended, but before he could connect with Adirah's hand, he was pushed aside.

"New love, huh?" A familiar girl stepped in front of Tiev, Kesh, and Adirah.

"Ah, another one of my closest friends," Kesh said and smiled. "Vila, this is—"

"I've met her," the girl rudely interjected, cutting Kesh off.

Adirah squinted. "Um . . . uh . . . ," she stammered, her pointer finger waggling. "I think you're . . ."Adirah knew for sure the girl was familiar.

"Vila," the girl said and thrust her hand in Adirah's face. "I am Vila. Another one of *Kesh's* loyal friends, as he said." She looked at Kesh directly when she spoke, almost through her teeth.

"Yes, Vila. Lina's friend. I think, um . . . Did we go out?" Adirah mused, rubbing her chin.

"Yes. I was the one who introduced you two," Vila muttered, looking up into Kesh's face again and rolling her eyes.

"Really? Didn't we meet in class?" Adirah asked, looking at Kesh, confused.

Kesh glared at Vila. "Why don't you go get us all a drink, Vila?" he demanded more so than asked.

Vila rolled her eyes, turned, and stormed off.

"What's with her?" Adirah asked. "Did you do something to her? She seemed pretty ticked."

"She's just a little testy," Kesh replied. "Let's dance." He pulled her away from his clan. Adirah could feel the heat of all their gazes on her. She shrugged off their apparent shock and dismay at her presence there as her being the new girl.

Kesh wiggled his hips to the music as he smiled at Adirah and pulled her. "C'mon. Move that body like I know you can," he said, encouraging her.

Adirah laughed and tried to resist being pulled into the center of the room. "I . . . I . . . don't know how," she said, her feet moving forward despite her playful protest.

"Just move your body to the rhythm. It doesn't have to be perfect. You're already perfect. I know. I've seen you and those thick round hips in action," Kesh told her, moving his body against hers. He let go of her hands, stepped forward, grabbed her back, splayed his hands over it, and pulled her so close, she had no choice but to inhale his intoxicating scent. Her body instantly fell into a rhythm with his.

"Dancing is not my thing," she said breathlessly. Adirah melted against his muscular chest and swayed with him. They were moving too slow for the thumping rap music. Adirah wasn't listening to the music; she was focused on her beating heart. "Oh, goodness," she panted, feeling her clitoris swell and her insides throb with lust. No man had ever affected her like this. Adirah was feeling helpless before Kesh's lust. "Kiss me," Adirah said, looking up into Kesh's face.

He smiled and lowered his mouth over hers, his dreads falling around their faces and creating a privacy blanket. Adirah opened her lips and allowed his tongue into her mouth. She was drowning in ecstasy and passion. His saliva was a sweet nectar. Bees could use it to make honey.

"Your drinks, *King*."

Adirah jumped apart from Kesh at the sound of Vila's voice. Kesh turned and accepted both drinks from Vila. He nodded at her like she was a servant, and handed one of the drinks to Adirah. Vila's eyes were hooded, and her fists were curled at her sides. She shot Kesh a look that could launch a thousand bullets, and then she stormed off.

"Thank you," Adirah called out before Vila got too far away.

"Don't thank me. Thank your *king*," Vila snarled, halting her movement to turn and glare at Adirah.

Adirah's eyebrows dipped. She looked from Kesh to Vila and back at Kesh. She was trying to figure out the dynamic between the two. Adirah had no idea what she could have done to upset this girl.

"Let me speak to you for a moment, Vila," Kesh said and then walked over in a fury and grabbed her arm. He pulled her farther away and out of Adirah's earshot.

"Wonder what that's all about," Adirah grumbled under her breath. She lifted her drink to her mouth, thought for a minute, and lowered it. She didn't like the way Vila had looked at her. A sinking feeling went through Adirah's stomach.

She turned around and watched the seemingly heated exchange between Kesh and Vila. Kesh had his face very close to Vila's, and he was scowling. Vila's mouth was pursed, and she was clearly angry. She moved her hands to emphasize whatever she was telling him. They were arguing. Adirah concluded that perhaps they were former lovers and Vila was jealous. She hoped to have a chance to smooth everything over at some point, but for now she would try to steer clear of the woman.

Adirah set the drink on a table. She certainly wasn't going to drink something Vila had given her. She just didn't trust something about Vila, especially now.

"You are being disobedient." Kesh gritted his teeth and squeezed Vila's arm, which he had in a death grip.

"*You* are being disrespectful," Vila growled back, wrestling her arm away.

Her defiance shocked Kesh. He looked around to see who was watching. Flames flashed in his eyes, and he breathed fast and hard.

"I am nothing more to you than a slave now? An obedient little servant?" Vila snapped. "I'm not good enough? You'd rather flaunt your little precious mortal girl? Why bring her here of all places? I had to deal with her in the outside world, but this place . . . this place is supposed to be for *us*, our kind. Only."

Kesh couldn't control his breathing, and he felt like steam was coming out of his ears. How dare Vila question him? "I am the king of this clan. I do whatever I want, especially when it is in the best interest of this clan. If you want to remain part of this clan, you will stop this blatant insolence," he said through clenched teeth. "If you keep it up . . ."

"You brought her here to hurt me," Vila interjected, her voice cracking. "She didn't need to come and break the sanctity of our place. We come here to live as our true selves. How will you explain it to her when these mortal girls in here never show back up to class because one of us has fed on them? How do you explain bar tops lined with glasses full of blood to feed us? If you want to reveal yourself to her and break every rule of the Council . . . go ahead. But we, the entire Sefu Clan, we don't want our existence in danger all the time. Bad enough we keep running and running from the Malum. Now you'll have vampire hunters and everything else coming after us," Vila said with feeling.

Kesh released his hold on her and softened his face. The one thing he could always say about Vila was that she was fiercely protective of the clan. Kesh understood her fury. She was doing it out of loyalty to the clan, to him. "Vila, I've been your king for decades. I have always done the right thing. I have chosen the queen that I know will be best for us all. Things will reveal themselves to her in time. . . . She has me inside of her," he said, his tone firm but softer. "She won't betray us. I assure you. This is what's best for us."

Vila swallowed hard and shook her head. "She's a mortal, Kesh. No matter what, she is not one of us. I could've been your queen. I've served you in every way. Correction . . . I have served you in every way. I continue to serve you and the clan in every way. Just because you *think* you love her doesn't mean we all have to accept her. I'll never accept her as my queen, even if that means disregarding you as my king."

Kesh balked, reacting like Vila had dashed a bucket of cold water in his face. "Listen to me, and listen closely, Vila. You can't survive without me. I am your maker and your king. I will destroy you right here and now." Kesh grunted out each word with feeling.

Vila looked in his eyes, and for the first time, he saw glimpses of her hurt and pain behind his decisions. He saw the innocent girl he had turned way back when. He also saw a jealous, defiant, and determined vampire whom he now had to watch out for.

"You will do whatever I tell you to do," Kesh demanded. "You will do whatever is best for this clan. Right now, me taking Dira as my queen is what is best. Besides, I love her. Get it through your head, I've never loved you." After the last words slipped from his lips, he knew he had gone too far. He knew they would be

like a wooden stake to Vila's heart. He instantly
wanted to take them back.

Vila threw her hands up to her face, and her
cries rushed out of her mouth like an alarm
sounding. "You don't have to worry about me
ever again. Love whomever you want," Vila cried,
then ran away, pushing people out of her path as
she moved.

"Vila," he called out, but it was too late. The
damage was done, and there was no way Vila
was turning around in that moment. Kesh's
shoulders slumped, and he sighed. He had
wanted to be firm, but he had never wanted to
hurt Vila like that. She was one of his most loyal
members.

Kesh turned to find Tiev standing right behind
him. Kesh was startled. He squinted. "Stop
following me," he barked. "I've already told you
this."

"This won't end well with Vila. You turned
her, Kesh. You can't just hurt her and leave it
like that. You could've handled that better. And,
she's right. It might not have been a great idea
bringing the girl here. Just look at her, staring
in shock at the things going on here," Tiev said,
jerking his chin in the direction of Dira's seat.
They both looked over and watched Dira move
her head from activity to activity. There were

things that she was witnessing that Kesh wasn't ready to reveal.

Kesh pointed in Tiev's face. "I am the king, and I do what I want. I'll fix this," Kesh said, his jaw stiff.

Tiev threw his hands up in surrender. "You're right. You are the king, and you'll have to deal with every single bit of fallout from your decisions. Vila . . . Tulum, and the Malum Clan. Oh, and the mortal girl's friend—Lina, I think her name is—I hear she's been snooping around our sacred grounds," Tiev noted. "Good luck, King Kesh. Good luck."

Kesh blew out a windstorm of breath as he watched Tiev storm away to find Vila. Kesh wanted to go make things right, but then he looked over at his sweetest love, Dira. He started toward her. "She's the only one who can make things right for me," he mumbled under his breath. "She has charmed me, instead of the other way around."

"You're so beautiful," Kesh moaned the words into Adirah's mouth as his hands worked furiously to unzip her pants.

"Oh, Kesh," she breathed heavily, her words hot on his lips, her hands snaking down to the bulge in his pants.

"I've wanted you for so long," he panted.

Adirah closed her eyes as her pants fell down around her ankles. "Me too."

She was so glad finally to be alone with Kesh. Away from his weird group of friends, particularly Vila. Adirah didn't have a good feeling about Vila, but she hadn't said anything to Kesh. It was obvious that there was more to their relationship than Adirah could understand from just watching them. She shook off the thoughts now, trying to stay in the moment. She didn't know what this new sexual confidence was about, but she seemed to have no control over it. Adirah felt like something or someone new lived inside of her now.

"Oh, God," she groaned, throwing her head back as Kesh trailed his tongue down the ladder of her throat. Adirah inhaled his scent; it had done something to her since day one, but now it was so much more pungent. Her sense of smell seemed more acute, causing her to be even more turned on by his scent. She embraced the fine sheen of sweat on his face as it dampened her own skin. She loved the feeling of his dreads sweeping across her skin. The friction sent sparks up and down her body. She was flushed with heat.

Adirah winced and blew out a breath when Kesh stopped at her weak spot—her breasts. He carefully lowered his hot mouth over the dark, rigid skin of her erect nipples. Adirah gasped. Just like the first time they made love, Kesh suckled her breasts, at first gently, then slightly rougher. He walked her backward a few steps. She fell back on his bed and grabbed on to the back of his head.

"You . . . I . . . we," she stammered, unable to find the words to express how she was feeling.

"Us," Kesh said breathlessly. "It's us now, Dira."

He dropped to his knees and wedged himself between her legs. He moved his tongue from her breasts down the curve of her abdomen to her inner thighs. He kissed the insides of each thigh gently. Adirah moved her thighs apart wider, giving him full access. The anticipation of what was to come made her mouth water. She planted her hands on the top of his head, then guided him to where she wanted him to be. Adirah felt and acted like a pro. All kinds of thoughts and voices swirled around in her head. How did all of this happen? Who was she all of a sudden? Where did this passion come from?

"Oh," Adirah belted out, arching her back as he blew on her gently. "Oh, my God, Kesh," she huffed, her voice gruff with lust. Electricity pulsed through her entire body. She panted through her slightly open lips. Her heart was racing, and her thighs trembled.

If you say you love him, he will leave you. He will betray you. You can't say it.

Adirah shook her head, trying to get rid of the spirit voices. She was in the moment; she didn't want to hear anything negative about Kesh.

"Do you feel good?" Kesh asked.

Adirah let out a small gasp as her body became engulfed in the heat of desire. She reached down and pinched her erect nipples, sending an even stronger electric sensation flooding all over her body. The combination of what was going on below her belly button and the pressure she was putting on her nipples was almost too much to handle.

"Yes," she whispered lustfully, lifting her hips slightly toward his mouth.

Kesh thrust his long, wet tongue deeper into her warm, gushy center. He used his hands to gently part the petals of her flower, carefully lapping up every bit of her nectar.

"I want to feel you again," Adirah whispered. "All of you." Kesh stood up and took off his pants. Adirah shivered just looking at his washboard abs and muscular legs. Kesh lowered himself down in front of her.

"You ready for me?" he teased, licking his lips like he was starving for her love. Adirah shook her head and licked her lips too. Kesh pulled her closer to him, until her hips were hanging off the edge of the bed.

"Ah." Adirah winced as Kesh used his steel-hard member to fill her up. Adirah's body was on fire. She lifted her pelvis in response to Kesh's rhythmic thrusts. Their bodies moved in sync, each feeling the buildup in their loins. Adirah's hands splayed across Kesh's back like a pair wings.

"Oh, oh, oh!" Adirah crooned. Her inner thighs vibrated from the explosion of pleasure filling her body. Just on the verge of climaxing, she could feel the pressure building. Her screams urged Kesh on. He ground into her pelvis with longer, deeper strokes. Her slippery walls responded immediately, pulsating and squeezing him tight. Kesh growled as his body picked up speed; he was at a tipping point.

"Are you mine forever?" he huffed in Adirah's ear. The heat of his breath sent sparks down her spine.

"Yes. Yes." Adirah gasped, losing her breath, as Kesh slowed down and began grinding into her slowly again.

"Are you sure?" he huffed.

"Yes!" she screamed out, tightening her legs around his waist as her walls pulsed in and out. Kesh followed with a stomach-clenching climax of his own. He collapsed on Adirah's chest. She reached down and stroked his head gently.

"You don't know what you've just committed to, huh?" he huffed.

"Whatever it is, as long as I can be with you, I don't care."

Chapter 8

Two months passed, and Kesh finally had her—his queen. He smiled as he watched her sleep. He'd been watching her for hours. He loved to look at the rise and fall of her breasts and the quiver of her flat stomach. Her hair spilled over the pillow in thick tufts, disheveled from a night of wild passion. Kesh had never seen anything look as divine. He knew Dira's passion for him was partly because of his blood, but the way she held him and looked into his eyes when she told him she loved him couldn't all be from the blood bonding. She had to be feeling it.

With each passing day, Kesh loved Dira a little bit more. With her, he felt like he had a deeper purpose, something more than just running from state to state to protect his clan. He knew that some members of the clan were unhappy with his choice in Dira, but he was following his heart.

Kesh reached over and touched Dira's thick lips, her nose, and ran his hands over the tiny cleft in her chin. He hadn't known this type of joy since Adie. He understood that after giving Dira his blood, there were things about her that would never be the same. Still, he didn't want to turn her. Kesh realized that Dira had her own gifts—she could speak to and hear the spirits—and those would disappear if he turned her. He'd seen her talking with the spirits. He knew that she was a spirit walker and that even if he couldn't be there, the spirits of her ancestors would protect her.

"Kesh, tell me the truth," Adirah whispered. His soft petting had woken her.

"About what?" He was leaning on his elbow, looking into her eyes.

"What happened the night we met? I keep having a dream of a fire and being burned."

"I've told you we met in class."

"Yes, I know. But that's not really where we officially met. You see, ever since I was a little girl, my dreams have always told me the truth. But this dream seems fuzzy. Like something is blocking that truth."

"Maybe it's just a dream and nothing more."

"No. My dreams are never just dreams." Adirah sighed and looked away from Kesh. "I'm going to confess something. Do you promise to take me seriously?" She turned back to Kesh for his answer.

"I promise, my queen."

"It might sound crazy, but I want you to know that I'm not crazy."

"I know you're not crazy." He kissed her forehead for reassurance.

Adirah took a deep breath, then began. "Spirits talk to me." She waited for his answer with wide, anticipatory eyes.

He smiled. "I know."

"What? How? Can you hear spirits too?" Adirah was shocked.

"No. I have seen you speaking to the spirits. I understand that some people have the gift. You have the gift, and that is just one more thing I love about you."

"So, you don't think I'm crazy?"

"Crazy in love with me, but not 'lock you up in an institution' crazy."

Adirah wrapped her arms around Kesh and kissed him passionately. When they parted, she said, "You're right."

Kesh smiled, showing his beautiful white teeth. "Now I have a confession."

"What?"

Kesh hesitated before saying another word. He needed to word this just right. He couldn't give her all the answers, but enough to make her understand what she was getting into with him. "That night we met. At the party," he began.

"Uh-huh." Adirah nodded.

"There was a fire, you're dream is right, and you were burnt. Bad."

"But what happened? Why can't I see it in my dream?"

"Maybe your dream is trying to protect you. I don't know. But after I got out of the house, I realized you were still trapped inside. I ran back in to search for you. You were barely breathing when I found you. I needed to do something, or you would have died."

"What? What did you do?" Adirah asked, urging Kesh to continue.

"You were hanging on by a thread. It needed to be done." Kesh closed his eyes. "I cut my wrist and fed you some of my blood."

Kesh kept his eyes closed, waiting for Adirah to respond. Her silence was killing him. He couldn't handle it. He opened his eyes, and Adirah was staring at him with a puzzled look on her face.

"But . . . that's not how a blood transfusion works," Adirah said, confused.

Kesh shook his head.

"Then . . ." Adirah's eyes darted around. She was trying to comprehend what she was just told and to make sense of it all. "What happened?"

"You drank my blood."

"And that was enough to save my life. To heal my wounds?"

"Yes."

"That means . . ."

"Don't say anymore." Kesh put his hand over Adirah's mouth. "My blood has healing powers. That's all you need to know."

Adirah nodded, and Kesh removed his hand.

"Are you hungry?" Kesh asked.

She smiled, knowing that she wasn't getting the full story. She didn't care, but she did have a few questions.

Kesh fielded all of Dira's questions after she realized the benefits of having his blood. She was equally shocked and amused when she learned that if she even got a simple scratch, she would heal faster than normal. She also realized that her senses had been heightened almost five times, which was why she could hear everyone's blood rushing through their veins or and stomachs processing food in class. She looked wide-eyed at Kesh, and he smiled and chuckled at her. Still, he didn't come right out and reveal himself. It was the one thing that Tiev and Vila had said that Kesh listened to—vampires couldn't reveal themselves to a mortal without killing the person afterward. Kesh knew once Dira figured it out on her own, she would be protected.

Kesh knew more questions would come, but until then, his focus was on keeping her happy and keeping her safe. It was a marvelous feeling, being in love, and he couldn't have met her at a more perfect time. The two were almost inseparable. The only thing that could break them apart most days was their classes—oh, and Lina. Other than that, if you saw one, you saw the other.

Adirah smiled at Kesh. His dreads hung loosely around his shoulders, and she reached up to move the few that were dangling in his face.

"There. Much better. That's the handsome face I fell asleep to," she said, smiling. "And now I *am* starving. You made me work up quite an appetite. You're so *nasty*." She giggled.

Kesh leaned down, placed a hand behind her head, and lifted it gently so their lips could meet. He kissed her deeply and then rested his lips on her forehead.

"With you, I feel that I have met my match. You fill me up in every way. Forgive me if I want to do the same to you," he said, planting light kisses after every word.

"I lo—" Dira began, but Kesh froze suddenly, and Dira cut her words short.

He moved to look at her, his face crinkled. He knew what she was about to say and could tell that she had caught herself. Dira's eyes were wide, and her nostrils were open. She looked like a guilty child who'd been caught just when she was about to say a bad word.

"What is it? What's wrong?" he asked.

"Nothing. It's just . . ." Dira sighed.

"Tell me. We've already been confessing to each other this morning," he told her, grabbing her hand and forcing her to sit up like him.

"Everything—and I mean *everything* that I have ever loved—has left me. And every time that happens, I lose a piece of myself in the process. That's a pain that I don't think I can handle having again. I feel things for you, Kesh, and it is crazy, because we only just met. But I know how I feel. I feel it in my core . . . and that makes me scared of you."

"Dira, my queen, since the first day I saw you, I have known that you belong to me. My soul has been gone for a long time, but you have made me whole again. If I could take every pain inside of you and replace it with an ounce of happiness, I would. My queen, don't be afraid of what you feel, because now that I have you, I will never let you go. I am yours forever."

"Promise me."

"I promise," Kesh replied, then leaned in to kiss her once more, but her rumbling stomach suddenly ruined the moment. "Let's go feed the monster inside of you."

They both laughed. He threw the fresh satin sheets off the bed, exposing their naked bodies and causing Dira to squeal.

"Kesh! It's freezing!"

"The faster you'll get dressed, then."

"Beat you to the shower!"

Dira took off for the bathroom inside Kesh's spacious room, but before she knew it, he'd scooped her up into his arms, with one arm under her knees and the other firm against her back.

"I will never let a girl defeat me," he said, and for a split second, his mind fell on Tulum and his evil queen, Calum.

A dark glaze rippled over his eyes, and it didn't go unnoticed by Dira. She placed a cool palm on his cheek and forced him to look at her. This was a look that she had never seen in him. It concerned her and scared her as well.

"You okay?" she asked.

"Yes." He blinked and forced the dark thoughts to the back of his mind. "Yes. I was just thinking about how hard it is going to be to keep my hands off of you when I see the water dripping from your body in the shower."

With that, he was telling the truth. The moment the hot water hit Dira's body, he had to fight with himself inwardly not to pin her to the wall and spread her legs open. He wanted nothing more than to dig his manhood deeper inside of her than anyone ever had and to listen to her love cries in his ears. Instead, he helped her wash her body, making sure that every crease was squeaky clean. When it came time for her to wash him, she got behind him. He heard her suck her breath in. His first instinct was to hide, but he wanted her to see it.

"I feel these all the time during our lovemaking, but I've never looked," Dira said, running her hands gently over every lash scar on his back. "What happened?" she whispered, kissing each jagged line of raised skin.

Kesh planted his hands on the wall and lowered his head until the water beat down on the center of it and his dreads hung around him like a cloak of shame, dripping with water.

"I want to take all your past hurt and pain away," Dira whispered, still kissing the scars.

Kesh let the water mix with his tears. The lash marks were the one thing that hadn't disappeared when he was turned. They were the

one imperfection that remained from his real
past. They were a sign of who he was. They
were a reminder that the Malum Clan had to
be defeated in order for Kesh to vindicate his
ancestors.

Kesh finally turned toward Adirah and embraced
her. "And I will take away all your past hurt and
pain too."

Kesh and Dira descended his stairs, laughing
and giggling together.

"Where are you two off to on this lovely day?"
said a voice.

Kesh turned his head to see Vila striding
toward them. Instantly, he felt Dira's hand
clutch his arm, not fearfully but possessively.
Vila smirked but kept her attention on Kesh.

"You have things to do. *Important* things,"
Vila said, staring at Kesh.

"They can wait. I will be back after I take Dira
to get some food."

"They can wait?" Vila asked incredulously,
looking at Kesh as if he had lost his mind. "So
your people can wait? We have waited long
enough, Kesh. You have been gallivanting
through the city day and night with *her* for the
past two months. It is time that you assume your
duties. We've been buying time, but . . ."

Kesh's eyes flashed with anger, but Vila did not back down. She stared back just as fiercely as he was gazing at her.

"Dira, my love. Will you wait for me outside? I will be right out," he said.

Dira hesitated. Kesh nodded at her to let her know he could handle it. After about ten seconds, Dira finally took her leave, but not before shooting Vila a scathing look. When she was gone, Kesh whipped his head back to Vila.

"I understand that part of your destiny is to find a mate, Kesh, but you were to find a mate *for* your clan!" Vila's tone was icy, malicious.

"Do you forget who you're speaking to? I understand my duties as the king of this clan, a responsibility that you or anyone else is not strong enough to take on. Had it not been for me, we would have lost more than what we did."

"And if you keep neglecting your duties, then we will lose the rest," Vila declared. "They are getting comfortable again, Kesh, as are you, apparently. The Malum will never stop coming for us, and we cannot afford to be caught off guard again. They know where we are. It doesn't bother you that they have not struck again in two months? That means they're planning an even bigger attack this time."

She went on. "They know your precious, *queen*," Vila said, doing air quotes at the word *queen*, "is a mortal. They know they can destroy her, and ultimately, that means destroying you. Thousands of years of vampire history show that when a king is this enamored with his queen, he can easily be destroyed. The others need to learn to fight again. This life that they have been living has made them forget our true ways. . . . Some have even tried to follow you and walk in the light. They don't even understand that that ring is the only thing making you able." Vila nodded toward Kesh's hand.

"Okay." Kesh waved his hand at Vila, letting her know that he was done with the conversation. "That is why I am putting you, Tiev, and Tiba in charge of training the others for a battle that is sure to come."

"It is your job to lead," Vila said, raising her voice.

Kesh was done. He turned his back to her and started to the front door. Just as he was about to exit, he turned his head so that he could speak over his shoulder.

"And it is your job to follow. Do as I say, Vila. You are starting to question me so much, I am beginning to wonder if you are turning into a Malum. I am wondering if you've already betrayed the Sefu."

Right before he was completely out the door, he heard Vila's voice again.

"She'll have to keep drinking from you, you know that, right? That is the only way she will survive without you turning her completely. The state that she was in? Not even your blood has the power to bring that back one hundred percent. You need to make a choice! Either she's one of us or she's one of them. You cannot have both!"

"I know," Kesh whispered to himself.

Adirah sat on the step outside of Kesh's temporary frat house, with her cheeks resting on her fists and her elbows resting on her knees. Her day had felt long, and she was feeling sluggish. The normal energy she had been feeling since meeting Kesh wasn't there. She hoped she wasn't coming down with a cold. Without warning, the leaves on the trees began to blow like a tornado was whipping through. She sat up, alarmed.

Adirah. Adirah. Dira. Dira. Dira.

She heard her name being called. Adirah shook her head, but she couldn't stop herself from getting up and following the sound. Her eyes wouldn't blink, and her entire body was freezing cold. It felt like her body was being controlled by someone else. No matter how much Adirah fought to gain control, she was helpless. She walked like a zombie a few paces, and then she saw him—her brother Adolphis.

He was standing at the edge of a field, waving her forward with his hands. *I have to show you something. Follow me.* He was smiling like he did when they'd play hide-and-seek as kids.

Adirah couldn't help herself; she kept walking toward him. He led her into a small thicket of woods at the back of the frat house. Adirah followed like an obedient dog.

Look at the tree. She will reveal the danger. She will tell you what you need to know, Dira. Watch it. . . .

Adirah did as she was told. She stood in front of the tree, watching and waiting to see what it revealed. Then, as if a movie projector were playing against the tree trunk, she saw two strange people, and she could hear them speaking clearly.

"We cannot let the blood ritual happen. If it does, then Kesh will rise to full power. Even with his clan cut in half, he will be unstoppable. Why haven't we attacked? They are sitting ducks."

The dark-haired white woman, dressed in an all-black, tight-fitting leather jumpsuit and shiny black thigh-high boots, stood beside a tall, pale-faced blond man dressed in a sweeping long black leather trench coat and pointed-toe black boots. They watched four others fight with swords. The woman's arms were behind her back as her eyes traveled along what appeared to be a makeshift battleground.

"You have trained them well, Calum," the man said, rubbing the bottom hairs of his blond goatee.

"Thank you, my love," the woman said, accepting the compliment. "I have been working with them day in and day out. While Kesh is letting his clan live like they are normal humans, I am training ours for war. A war that they are anticipating and wish to engage in once you give the order. Why are we waiting so long?"

"Because the time is not right," the man told her calmly.

"It has been two months, Tulum. If not now, then when? Kesh could very well be planning to uproot today. If he does that, we will waste another six months trying to find him."

"He will not leave. I see how in love he is with the mortal girl. He hasn't told her the truth. Therefore, she will not go with him. So, he will not leave."

"How can you be so sure?"

"He is in love," Tulum answered matter-of-factly. "He will not leave her behind."

"Love means nothing!"

"Calum." Tulum turned his head to look down at her. The struggle between admiration and anger rippled across his features. "Do you know why I chose you as my queen?" he asked.

She shook her head.

"Because you were always the only one who was ever bold enough to question my motives. And not only that, but you were the only woman in my whole life ever to catch my heart," he mused.

Calum blushed and took his hand in hers. "Yes, my king. I remember. When you found me, I was barely clinging to life. My clan was barely surviving against the witches and the werewolves. An entire clan of women would never fare so well alone . . . with no king," Calum remembered, the tiniest smile easing over her mouth. "I talked them into following me, with no real game plan. We were starving and living in the woods, drinking from animals, when you made your appearance."

"Yes, and I was rogue, on a mission to avenge my maker's death. A drifter vampire, with no purpose in life except the murder of all black vampires," he said. He snatched his hand from Calum and cracked his knuckles. His face turned red. "The moment I looked at you, with those beautiful brown eyes and that genuine soul, I had to have you," he said, his voice drifting.

She lowered her head. "I know it took a little persuasion to follow your lead, but that was because of my fears. Not only did we have many of the same beliefs, but we also had a common enemy. The Sefu," she said, her jaw rocking.

"Yes . . . the Sefu. I remember like it was yesterday the day they became my enemies for life," Tulum said through clenched teeth.

Calum looked up at him, stuck on his words.

He went on. "Buckets of blood were brought to us, the Malum Clan. It was a peace offering, the Sefu said. A way to end the old ways and open the door to new ways, a new law. We were thirsty and naive, so we believed the Sefu, and all gathered to toast to a new beginning. I was young, but I still didn't trust the Sefu, not even one bit. I did not drink an ounce of blood from the goblet. Shortly after, the members of my clan began dropping like flies, dead. I knew how hard it was to destroy us. It didn't take me long to figure out that the buckets of blood that the Sefu had brought in offering did not contain blood from the living. It was blood from the dead." Anger registered on his face.

"I lost everything and fled before it was found out that I had survived the act of genocide. For years I wandered aimlessly, until I finally found a young beautiful woman thirsty for revenge, much like me," he added, looking into Calum's eyes. "My beautiful queen, Calum," he said lovingly. "Do you trust me?"

"Of course I do, Tulum, but—"

"If you trusted me, there would never be a but," Tulum said and stepped out of the way as a young man flew by him, hit a wall, and landed with a thud.

Tulum addressed the young man without turning to face him. "Narum! You leave your guard down after every hit you land. If you celebrate victory too soon, then your defeat will be great."

Narum struggled to his feet behind Tulum and nodded his head, his face bright red, as he was clearly embarrassed. It seemed as if everyone had stopped fighting to stare his way, and some of the other vampires were snickering.

"Quiet!" Calum shouted at the others. "Of all the Malum, Narum is the youngest, yet he is still built like a warrior, better than some of you."

"Yes. We could all use some of Narum's speed and passion," Tulum said, then stepped forward to address his clan. "She says that you are ready for battle." Tulum's voice boomed as he raised his arm straight out, with his thumb folded in and his four fingers pointing straight out.

The members of the Malum cheered and followed their leader's move.

"But the way Narum fights shows me that you are not! All it takes is one of you to fail for us all to fail!" Tulum shouted, quickly changing his mood.

The others glared at Narum. He had made them all look bad.

"Do not look at him in contempt. It is not his fault. It is your fault. You are all so keen on standing out to Calum and me that you fight alone, instead of as one," Tulum told them.

With the speed of a cheetah and the strength of ten men, Tulum ran toward another one of his clan members. Before the huge man could react, Tulum's palm was at his chest and he was blasting him back with a powerful force.

"Ugh!" The unsuspecting victim's groan was loud.

As the huge man flew back in the air, Tulum moved so fast, it seemed like he teleported him-

self behind the man. Tulum caught the man in mid-flight and stood him upright, helping him to get his footing. The man's face was caught between an expression of shock and one of embarrassment, and he stepped quickly away from Tulum, but not before looking down at the burn marks Tulum had left in the center of his chest.

"As you can see, I was both Arlum's foe and comrade in that moment of sneak attack." Tulum nodded for Narum and Arlum to continue sparring. "You spar with one another to make the other better, not to outdo one another. We will not attack until I see that this clan is a family. If we attack together but fight separately, we are as good as dead. Understood?"

"Yes, King Tulum," they all said in unison.

Tulum walked back toward Calum. They could hear the fighting continue. He stopped when they were both side by side again, this time facing opposite ways.

"Kesh will not leave. Unlike us, the Sefu follow some of the vampire laws . . . with some expectations," Tulum said. "She is still a mortal, which means she does not know of his true nature. If he truly loves her, he will tell her who he is only when he is ready to turn her."

"How do you know this?"

"*Because that is what I would have done for you if you weren't already one of us. You don't want to live for all eternity with someone who resents you for not giving them a choice. This gift we have is both a blessing and a curse. A curse to those who don't want it, but a blessing to those who welcome it. We still have time. When it comes to love, time is, well, timeless.*"

Calum seemed to contemplate this. She looked like she wanted to argue with Tulum, but maybe she knew that his mind was made up.

"*I'm starting to think you are growing hasty,*" *Tulum said to her.* "*If you had waited last time, instead of sending your own set of troops, we would have had Kesh right where we wanted him. He would not have left so soon and found his soul mate, either. I'm starting to think that your personal feelings for him, the jealousy you harbor for him, are getting in the way of your judgment. Will they continue to be a problem?*" *he said.*

"*No, they will not,*" *Calum said.* "*I will keep myself in check from now on, my king.*"

"*Good. Do not fret. Once we have him where we want him, you will destroy him and take all the power from him, which you have always deserved.*"

Tulum walked away before he could see the smile crop up on Calum's face.

The tree went dark, and Adirah could no longer see the strange people. Her eyes rolled back into place, and she collapsed on the ground, too weak to stay on her feet. The vision had zapped all her energy. She heard Kesh calling out to her, but she couldn't respond.

"Dira! Are you all right?" Kesh wheezed as he approached her limp body.

Adirah groaned, still unable to speak. Kesh picked her up from the ground. Her head pounded, and her stomach swirled with nausea. She held on to him but quickly recoiled when she remembered what she'd seen.

"Kesh, who are you? What are you? Who are the Malum . . . Calum and Tulum? Am I in danger? Are you in danger? Are they real?" She shot these questions at him rapid fire.

Kesh pulled her into his chest. He was breathing like he was still running, and his body was rigid. He, too, had sensed the wind change, and by the time he came outside, Adirah had disappeared. He had had his clan spread out and search. Luckily, he had found her in time, and nothing had harmed Adirah.

"There are many questions and just as many answers. Right now, you need to trust me. But know this, my queen. In due time, Dira. I'll tell you everything in due time."

"Take me home," she whispered. "I need some time away. I need to leave. Now." Adirah was exhausted, confused, and scared.

Chapter 9

"My God, I feel like I haven't seen you in centuries," Lina squealed, meeting Adirah at the door.

Adirah had barely turned the key to her dorm-room door. "Dang. What were you doing? Standing in front of the door?" Adirah joked. She reached out and hugged Lina. They both moved inside. Adirah breathed out and looked around. It did feel like forever since she had been in her own dorm room. She had been spending so much time with Kesh that she had even begun to bring clothes to his place.

The first thing Adirah noticed was the pile of laundry on her bed, which was not hers, and the second thing that stood out to Adirah was the sheepish expression on Lina's face.

"Doesn't look like you missed me that much, since your clothes have found a new closet," she smirked, pointing at the pile of black garments covering her bed and the floor on her side of the room. She couldn't be mad at Lina; she probably would have done the same thing. Besides, who knew how long the clothes had been there? She might have just put them on the bed, although it looked like the clothes had been there for quite some time.

"I didn't think you'd mind, since you're never here," Lina replied, one eyebrow up.

"You're not about to let me live this down, huh? Between classes and him, I just . . . It's just easier," Adirah said, tripping over her explanation. It was the first time she realized how much time she had been dedicating to Kesh.

Adirah walked over to her side of the room, removed the duffel bag from her shoulder, and sat it on the part of her bed that wasn't occupied. After turning to Lina, she smiled at her. "I see nothing has really changed that much with you." Adirah motioned to the pile of black clothing.

Lina wore a pair of black leggings and a black-and-white Angry Birds T-shirt. Her hair hung wet, like she'd just washed it, and her face was clear and clean of her usual coat of makeup. "Can't say the same for you," she replied, giving Adirah a once-over. Lina walked over and put her hands on the sides of Adirah's hips. "Looks like you're spreading and getting a little booty to add to it."

Adirah swiped Lina's hands away, her face growing hot. "Spreading where?" Adirah quickly turned to the full-length mirror hanging on the wall. "Nah. As usual, you see things from those little skewed eyes of yours."

"I hope so," Lina shot back skeptically. "You know what they say about spreading." Lina made a mound gesture in front of her stomach and smirked.

Adirah waved her off. "Oh, please, Lina."

Adirah began taking her clothes out of the duffel bag. She hoped that Lina wasn't right. She had been feeling tired lately. When was the last time I had a period? Adirah thought. She couldn't remember. The sex had been amazing, but how careful had they been? Adirah couldn't keep dwelling on this; she needed to get her mind away from such thoughts. "Anyway, what have you been up to? How are classes?" she asked Lina.

"Don't 'how are classes' me. Where have you been?"

"I've been"—Adirah thought of Kesh, bit her lip, and smiled deeply—"around." She chuckled.

"I bet you have been," Lina said, still studying Adirah. "I can't lie, though. He is one of the finest dudes on campus. If you didn't snag him, I might've tried."

"Oh, now you would've tried? I thought you hated all the popular kids?"

"Hate, smate," Lina mocked. "I can make exceptions."

They both laughed.

Adirah said, "You're too much, girl."

Grinning, Adirah flopped down on top of Lina's clothes and sighed. She'd been spending so much time with Kesh that she could hardly stand the thought of not waking up to his voice or being with him every minute of every day. But there was something going on, and he wasn't saying. She'd asked for some time alone. Adirah knew that what she'd seen in her vision had to be real, as her visions usually were.

Adirah could feel Lina studying her. "Just ask," Adirah told her, without looking at her roommate.

"It's just . . . just . . . something is different about you, Adirah," Lina said. She folded her arms across her chest and walked over. "You just seem so . . . so . . . much more confident and sure of yourself. When you got here, you were so naive and innocent. The glow you have had since the fire is just, honestly, amazing, freaky, and scary at the same time." Lina blinked and stared.

Adirah sat up and faced Lina.

"See! Look at how your eyes glow, Adirah," Lina pointed out.

Adirah stared deeper into Lina than she ever had before, and it kind of gave her the creeps. She heard Lina's blood flowing and her heart beating. Adirah even picked up a subtle pulse in Lina's jugular.

She's one of them. I know it! Lina thought.

Adirah could hear Lina's thoughts as clearly as if Lina had actually said the words to her.

"One of who?" Adirah blurted before she had time to stop herself.

Lina took a few steps backward, away from Adirah. "Wha . . . what?"

"You said I was one of them. One of who?"

"H-how did you hear that?" Lina asked, her eyes wide.

It was then that Adirah realized that Lina's mouth hadn't moved. Lina's mouth hung open, and although Adirah's heart rate seemed to quicken, she knew she had to calm herself and convince Lina that she'd spoken out loud.

"W-what do you mean? You just said, 'She's one of them.'"

"No I didn't," Lina said, shaking her head. "I definitely didn't say it out loud. I said it in my head."

"Lina," Adirah said, making her voice sound as soothing and self-assured as possible. She even forced a grin. "You said it out loud. What do you think I am? Some sort of mind reader? I hope you're not getting back to the crazy talk again. You make me worry about you."

"I swear, I said it in my head. I was thinking it. I didn't say it," Lina argued. "I know for sure I was thinking it." She shook her head adamantly.

Wasn't I?

Adirah heard Lina's voice again but didn't see her lips move. Adirah's heart raced. She had to get out of there. What was happening? She had always been able to hear spirits, but she had never been able to read people's thoughts. Something was different. She couldn't have Lina questioning her and spreading rumors. If this started to circulate, then it could lead back to Kesh, and Adirah would not let that happen.

"Listen, Lina, I'll be back." She restuffed her duffel bag, zipped it back up, and threw it over her shoulder. "In the meantime, can you please get this stuff off my bed, just in case I might want to sleep here?"

Without waiting for Lina's response, Adirah told her good-bye and made her way back out of the door. It slammed shut. Adirah stood outside of the door and listened for a few minutes, knowing that Lina was probably in the same spot, staring at the door.

"I said that in my head," Lina mumbled to herself. "I know I did."

Adirah chuckled. "You definitely did."

Kesh had entered Adirah's dorm by using his gift. He'd used his speed and beaten her there. He'd entered like a gust of wind when Adirah opened the door, and he'd hovered above them in the room, almost invisible. Kesh hadn't left when Adirah exited the dorm. He wanted to see what Lina would do after the encounter with Adirah.

After Adirah left, Lina stood frozen, staring at the door. Kesh entered her mind to listen in on her thoughts. She was trying to make sense of what had just transpired. Adirah had done a good job of planting a seed of doubt in Lina's mind, causing her to wonder if maybe she had given voice to that thought. Kesh was pleased with his queen, but Lina would still need to be watched.

Lina was so mentally transfixed by what had just happened with Adirah that she jumped violently and gasped at the loud, resounding knock that shook her dorm door.

"C-come in! It should be open!" she shouted.

She knew the door was open, because she hadn't locked it after Adirah made her quick getaway. The door swung open.

"Hey, Lina," said a male voice.

Kesh had to keep himself from growling and giving away his position on the ceiling when he saw and smelled the source of the voice—a young member of the Malum Clan. He had been concentrating so much on Lina, he had not been able to smell his enemy until it was too late and he was in the room. Kesh was mad at himself, but this was not the time for any of that. He needed to be sharp in this moment. If he could pick up the scent of his enemy, his enemy could pick up the scent of Kesh. This was a delicate situation, and if there were more of the Malum Clan on their way, it could be disastrous.

Kesh noticed the five-point star symbol branded on the guy's arm right away.

"What's up, Narum?" Lina greeted. "You kind of caught me off guard there. You didn't say you were coming by my dorm today." Still, she grinned at the handsome olive-skinned boy as he shut the door. He was wearing a white short-sleeve button-up and a pair of khaki shorts that stopped just over his knees, exposing his hairy legs. A tan fedora was sitting neatly on his head.

Kesh shook his head at the outfit. They'd do anything to fit in with the crowds. They had never had their own identity. Another reason Kesh wanted no part of the Malum Clan.

But how was Narum walking in the light? Kesh suddenly felt a swirl of anger and nausea. There were only a few vampires who had the rings that allowed day walking, and they were all Sefu, not Malum.

Who in my clan has betrayed me? Kesh was seething at the thought. Above all else, Kesh cherished loyalty to the clan, and now someone had broken that sacred bond.

"Yeah, you really shouldn't leave your door unlocked like that. You never know what could get you. I could have come in here and tied you up," Narum joked.

"You?" Lina laughed. "Narum, I don't think you could hurt a fly if you wanted to."

Narum smiled at Lina, but he didn't say anything. Kesh saw the struggle to stay normal play across Narum's face. Kesh knew from the pulsing vein in the boy's neck that he wanted to throw Lina down and feed on her. Kesh could also tell, Narum was there for a purpose. The struggle between want and need flickered in the boy's features. Kesh figured that Tulum had to be the one who sent Narum.

"Was that your roommate?" Narum nodded toward the door. "She doesn't seem to be here often. I never knew you had a roommate."

Lina shrugged. "Yeah, I guess you could call her my roommate. She's been spending so much time with Kesh and his fraternity and sorority friends, I barely see her these days," Lina replied and sat on her bed. She was hoping that Narum would get the hint.

Kesh could see the interest rise on Narum's face. He moved closer to Lina, smiling. Kesh easily figured out that Narum was there to collect information so he could go back home to Tulum and tell him where Dira rested her head.

Lina looked at Narum suspiciously. "How did I go from the awkward girl who sat next to you in calculus class to this?" She grinned and reached out and grabbed his hand. "The girl who spends all these countless hours with you. You're doing something to me," she said, flirting.

Kesh heard Narum's heartbeat speed up. He could tell Narum really liked Lina. If he didn't, he would have already turned her. It was probably the one thing Tulum and Narum had not counted on when they decided to use him to infiltrate.

Narum exhaled loudly. Kesh could see the lust rising in the boy's chest. He could smell the musk and pheromones Narum was releasing. The boy had to be so fixated on Lina, he didn't pick up the presence of Kesh in the room. "Too . . . um, me too," Narum said, his protruding Adam's apple bobbing up and down his throat. "There's something about how you are so passionate about everything, and the way your green eyes pierce me when you look at me," he said, finally finding his man voice.

Lina reached out and grabbed Narum's arm and began pulling him over to the bed, and he winced. "I'm sorry." Lina drew back, alarmed. "Did I pull too hard?"

"No." Narum quickly changed his expression.

"Are you sure?" Lina looked flustered.

"Yes. I take a boxing class some mornings, and my body is a little sore."

"You? Boxing?" Lina chuckled and flopped on her bed.

"Yes!" Narum said playfully, climbing onto the bed with her and lying on the side nearest to the wall. "Is that so hard to believe?" He flexed the muscles in his arm, making her burst into a fit of giggles before she lay down and rested her head next to his on her pillow.

"You're so stupid," she said, hitting his arm.

"I just told you my body is sore, and then you go and hit me." Narum tickled her, making her

ball up into the fetal position and clamp her
arms down tight so that he would no longer have
access to her armpits.

"I'm sorry! I'm sorry!" She roared with laughter.

She turned her back to him and used her butt
to push him away from her. Finally, he stopped
trying to tickle her, but instantly, the grin left
his face. They were facing Adirah's bed. Kesh
watched Narum's eyes narrow. He must've
suddenly remembered why he'd been sent here.

She was here. Kesh read Narum's thoughts.

Narum grabbed Lina's face and turned it so
that she faced him. As she lay on her side, losing herself in his gaze, she seemed to get dazed.
Kesh knew Narum was reading Lina's thoughts,
watching what had happened with her and
Adirah in replay. Kesh almost revealed himself,
but he thought better of it. Instead, he probed
Narum's thoughts and watched what he was seeing. Kesh saw the entire exchange between Lina
and Adirah, including when Adirah read Lina's
mind and then left the room, leaving Lina to
think she might be going crazy.

The sound of Lina clearing her throat made
Narum blink. That broke Kesh's connection.
Kesh cursed silently to himself. Now he was
regretting staying hidden. He should have

attacked Narum. The more information the Malum Clan got on Adirah, the more danger she would be in. Kesh needed to protect Adirah, not leave her exposed.

"I'm sorry," Narum said, noticing Lina was looking at him as if he had spiders crawling on his face.

"Why are you looking like that?" she asked.

"Like what?"

"Like you saw a ghost . . . like you're out of it."

"Oh, I just got so caught up in what I'm going to do to you," he joked.

Kesh keyed in on Narum's thoughts now. He heard the boy questioning how Adirah had read Lina's mind if she was still a mortal.

Narum blinked a few times and then shook his head. He needed to focus. Tulum was counting on him. "Your roommate, did she make you mad?" he asked.

"Yeah," Lina answered, removing his hand from her face. "She just came to get some more clothes. You know she's been staying in the house with *them*."

"Yes. I remember you telling me."

Lina got an attitude. She pulled away from him and rolled her eyes. "I know you think I'm crazy. Everybody does when I tell them that I think the popular ones are . . . are . . ."

"Vampires?" Narum said, finishing for her, and laughed. "You've told me all about it. The undead, right? That is what you call them?"

"It's not funny! Something strange is going on with them. Their house is already rebuilt, *completely rebuilt*, after that fire. I just can't fathom it. And I know the only reason you sit and listen to me talk all day is that you're trying to game me into giving you my panties."

"I listen to you talk all day because I believe you."

"R-really?" Lina sat up.

"Yes. I want to prove who they really are too," Narum said, seeming to think fast. "How many students have gone missing? Especially after their parties. Somebody has to expose them. Have you ever thought about sneaking into their house?"

"Yes," she admitted. "But I'm afraid. What if I'm right? What would I do with that information? How would I tell Adirah that her boyfriend is . . . you know . . . ?"

"So many people think you're wrong. You'll never know the truth until you try."

"Will you come with me?"

Kesh saw that Lina's question had caught Narum off guard. Kesh knew that Tulum and Calum had probably warned the boy never to set foot in the Sefu Clan's home until Tulum gave the order. In school it was easy for Narum to hide his true identity, because he was able to blend in with the others, but to walk into a clan of vampires would surely blow his cover.

Lina gazed at Narum with her doe eyes, begging him. He rubbed his chin, deep in thought.

If she figures out who they truly are and exposes them to the school, then it will leave the Sefu vulnerable. That would be the perfect time to attack! Narum thought.

Kesh almost reacted to the boy's sinister thoughts. His body trembled. He couldn't risk exposing himself in front of Lina. For some reason, she was not as susceptible to the vampires' mind games as the rest on campus. He had to get out of there quick.

Narum smiled down at Lina and nodded his head. The happiness showed instantly on her face when he said, "Okay. We can go tonight." Then he focused on her lips. "But I must say, you were right about one thing."

"What?" she asked.

With a speed she'd never experienced, he gripped her wrists and pinned her arms by her head before lowering his face to hers. "I do want to get in your panties," he breathed sexily before placing his lips on hers.

Lina didn't even try to fight him off. Her legs instinctively opened, welcoming his body to press on hers, and she wrapped her thighs around his waist. The thin fabric of her leggings allowed her to feel the bulge forming through his khaki shorts.

Narum let go of her wrists and let his hands travel down her arms and then to her chest. His hands touched her erect nipples, and it pleased him to see that she wasn't wearing a bra. His fingers gripped the V cut of her T-shirt. He started to yank her shirt gently to expose her firm breasts, but his excitement got the best of him. and he ripped the shirt completely off.

"That was my favorite shirt," Lina told him, breaking the kiss.

"Sorry. I'll buy you a new one." Narum grinned down at her and threw the fabric on the floor.

Lina smiled back. "I like you a lot, Narum," she whispered. Then she pushed him away from her slightly with her palms. "And I need you to know something about me."

"Are you a virgin?" Narum was slightly alarmed.

"No, silly." Lina tilted her head up and licked his bottom lip. "But I don't give myself away too often. But when I do . . . I'm *nasty*."

"Nasty?" He smirked. He began gyrating his hips.

"Yes," she huffed, moving her hands from his chest and placing her fingers on her own nipples. She began circling them with her pointer fingers and thumbs. Her legs quivered. "Nasty. Everything that you've ever wanted to do to a woman, do it to me, okay? I promise I won't scream . . . unless you want me to."

"Are you sure you're ready for all that, Lina? I mean, I don't want to hurt you. You're so beautiful. . . . I don't want to bring you pain."

In response, Lina unhooked her legs from his waist, spread them, and brought them up on his shoulders. She did this all without moving her hands or removing her eyes from his. Hooking her ankles around his neck, she brought his face to hers again and slipped her tongue between his soft lips. The moment their tongues touched again, she moaned into his mouth, letting him know she wanted him in every way. He nodded his head in submission. He was going to give her what she wanted. The thing he didn't know was if he would be able to let her go afterward.

Kesh had seen enough. He quietly escaped. He had to meet up with Adirah. He had to protect her. He had so many things to do now that the Malum were planting their people too close to home.

***

Fall was descending upon the university. The leaves were changing, the temperature was dropping, and the days were getting shorter. Adirah was in deep thought during the entire walk across campus to meet Kesh. The vision she had had was still nagging her. She wanted to take some time away from Kesh to figure it out, but no matter what she tried, she couldn't resist him anymore when he wanted to be with her. All he needed to do was say the word, and she would be at his whim. Adirah couldn't understand it. Who were those people on the tree in the vision? Why were they after Kesh? What did she have to do with any of their conflict? If being with Kesh was going to cause him harm, then maybe it was best if she ended it with him. She didn't want to, but she loved him and wanted to protect him.

The sound of leaves and gravel crunching under her feet was louder than ever to Adirah now. She knew Kesh could feel the change in her mood. All she could think about was that vision, coupled with the fact that she'd heard Lina's thoughts. How had she done it? Ever since the fire, Adirah had noticed small changes in herself, but this, this was almost superhuman. It wasn't like hearing the spirits; that had been happening to her since she was very young. This time, she had actually heard a live person's inner thoughts. Adirah had also noticed that she had more strength than she had before, and she was even faster.

It also tripped her out that she could hear people talking dozens of feet away. Not just the sound of their voices, either, but full conversations. Her sense of smell was so sensitive that lately she hadn't had much of an appetite. Her vision was so clear that she was sure that she could count the stitching in the fabric of her shirt if she wanted to. At first she had chalked it up to some type of trauma caused by the incident. But the new senses had never gone away. Until today, with Lina, Adirah had pushed her new abilities to the back of her mind. Kesh had told her his blood had healing powers, but all this other sensory amplification was causing her anxiety. It was too much for her to handle. But now she couldn't ignore this anymore. She closed her eyes and sighed, trying to make sense of it all.

"What is wrong, Dira? Is something bothering you?" Kesh asked. He had appeared seemingly out of nowhere.

Adirah was startled from her thoughts. At first she contemplated lying and tell Kesh, no. She wanted to pretend that everything was fine. But she knew her mood would just change again.

She looked into his eyes. Kesh could see the tension and burden on her face.

"I'm not the same," she said, just above a whisper. "Kesh, I'm different. I can feel it. Things about me I can't explain. It seems to be getting deeper and deeper. Even this . . . with us. It's just been so fast. I can't even explain who I am anymore. This girl all in love with the guy she had tried her best to avoid. It just doesn't make sense. It is like I have knowledge beyond my years and abilities above human capability. Lately, it always feel like I'm caught in a dream. I don't know if I can go on like this."

Kesh was silent as he listened to her speak. "I want to take you somewhere," he said, taking her face in his hands. "Will you come with me?"

"Kesh, didn't you hear anything I just said? I pour my heart out to you, and you're talking about running off? Probably to some bed somewhere." She rolled her eyes and sighed.

"Will you come with me?" he repeated. "You said you were all mine, right? Well, I'm asking you to trust me." He tried to sound as comforting as possible.

Adirah couldn't resist. She twisted her lips. "Okay, but I want you to answer my questions when we get there, or else I am going to leave."

"Promise," Kesh agreed.

"You had better," Adirah joked. *Ugh! Why can't I stay mad at him*! she thought.

Kesh seemed to switch their usual route, and he turned onto a path that Adirah had never taken.

"Where?" she said.

"Shh."

"Oh, boy. I knew I shouldn't have agreed to this."

They walked and walked. After what felt like a few miles, which had taken them to the edge of a thick forest, Adirah stopped. "Okay." She folded her arms and tapped her foot. "Where are you taking me?" she asked. "You haven't said a word this entire walk, and we seem to be walking to nowhere."

"Ah, sweet Dira, don't be like that. You said you trust me," Kesh joked.

That made Adirah more aggravated. This time she was digging in and holding her ground. She wasn't going to let Kesh have his way until he answered her questions. Kesh tried to lead her off the road and into the thicket of forest. Adirah held firm; she wouldn't move any farther.

"Kesh, where are you taking me?" she demanded. "You need to tell me. Or else I will not move another inch."

"We're almost there." Kesh smiled at her. "Come on."

She tried to protest, but he tugged her forward by the hands, leading her with his sexy smile. Adirah couldn't resist that beautiful smile. She looked around at the tall, looming trees. They were so big that the sun rays could barely sneak through. If Adirah didn't know that it was still daytime, she would have assumed night had fallen.

"Kesh," she whispered. "It's eerie back here. We should head back to the road . . . to campus. I don't think it's safe here. There could be poisonous snakes and . . . and . . ." Her heart revved up.

"Werewolves. And lions and tigers and bears," Kesh added jokingly as he turned suddenly, with his hands up, like an animal ready to attack with its claws. Adirah damn near peed her pants.

"Not funny!" she said and hit him on the arm. "You're becoming so annoying. I've heard that boyfriends do that . . . become annoying."

"I'm sorry, my love," Kesh said, grinning. He grabbed her hand again and urged her on. "Come with me. You'll see that you have nothing to fear. This is a special place that I come to when I need to clear my head. It's a place I never share with anyone . . . but you. I want to share every single thing about myself with you, Dira."

Adirah looked around as they walked over mud, leaves, rocks, and crunching tree bark. "Ah!" Adirah jumped as a large snake slithered onto a tree trunk right in front of her. She moved closer to Kesh, squeezing his hand tight.

Her squeal had made him chuckle. "You're not scared of that little snake, are you? You're a big, tough girl from the city," he joked.

"Yeah, and in the city we don't have slimy, scary, venomous snakes," Adirah snapped back. The closest thing to nature that Adirah had ever experienced was the Bronx Zoo. And at the moment that was about all she ever cared to experience of nature.

They continued on, with Adirah desperately clutching Kesh. Every little sound spooked Adirah. She kept seeing things out of the corners of her eyes. Each time she would jump, Kesh would chuckle.

"We're here," Kesh announced. "This is my secret place. Now our secret place. Just you and me, one with nature . . . the world excluded."

"Um, what?" Adirah gasped, staring straight ahead, confused.

There was a stone wall covered in bright green moss. Adirah estimated that it was about five stories high. Odd that it was in the middle of this thick, scary forest.

"Kesh, are you playing a joke on me? What's supposed to be special about this nasty thing?"

Kesh didn't say anything; instead, he reached his hand out, pressed it into the thick moss, and stood back. The wall groaned and creaked and began to part where Kesh had just pushed. Thick clumps of moss fell to the earth, and water dripped from somewhere up above.

Adirah sucked in her breath. "How did you do that? What is this?"

Kesh laughed. "It's magic," he chimed.

Adirah blinked at what was beyond the wall of slimy moss. It was something so beautiful, it made her heart lurch. She inhaled, just to make sure she was still breathing. Her eyes darted around. She couldn't decide what to look at first. If she didn't know any better, she would've thought she'd been transported to some place other than North Carolina. It looked like a magical world pulled straight from a fairy tale.

Adirah blinked to make sure that she wasn't seeing things. But the sound of the water flowing in front of her let her know that she was definitely still awake and was actually standing in this enchanted place. In front of her was a pond, with a waterfall feeding into it. The grass surrounding them was so vibrantly green and lush, it almost hurt her eyes to look at it. The land was so vast, Adirah figured her entire Brooklyn neighborhood could fit in it. She craned her neck to look up at the trees. They were all so tall. Like the ones she'd seen in the Save the Rainforest ads around campus. The air was different; it felt pure and clean. The light inside this dreamlike forest was sparkling. Beams of bright diamond-white light were streaming through the trees.

"Kesh," she panted, barely able to speak. "This is so beautiful. I've never seen anything . . ."

A flock of beautiful pink and blue birds soared through the sky overhead as she spoke. She'd never seen birds as colorful or majestic as these. Adirah watched them glide through the beams of light and disappear into the canopy.

"It's all about what you believe in, Dira. If you believe in beauty, you'll be around beautiful things," he said.

Adirah closed her eyes for a few seconds and felt the warmth of the sun on her skin. She inhaled the scent of the flowers and the air. The air smelled so marvelous, she could stand there and inhale it all day. She could taste the sweetness on her tongue. If she had to imagine the Garden of Eden from the Bible, this would be it.

"Is that honeydew?" she asked, sniffing again.

"It is whatever you want it to be," Kesh told her.

A butterfly zigzagged its way up to Adirah. She reached out her hand, and the butterfly gently landed on her open palm. "Kesh," she said, holding the butterfly up to her face to get a closer look. "Kesh, this . . . this is so beautiful. How did you know it was here?"

"My people found this place a long time ago," he told her, motioning for her to take his hand again. "It's hidden back here, and because the world has become too cold and callous to stop and see the beauty, it is one of the most overlooked places in the world."

Adirah shook her hand softly, motioning for the butterfly to take flight, before she took Kesh's hand. He took her to the edge of the pond and allowed her to peer in it. The water was so clear that she could see the bottom thirty feet down. She was almost certain that she could drink the water and not get any type of sickness. She dipped her hand into the crystal clear pond. The cool crispness of the water felt therapeutic. Adirah watched the ripples she had created fan out in rings until they disappeared.

"But how did this get here?" she asked. "There's a waterfall, a fresh pond, untouched trees, and beautiful birds and flowers. It's like an enchanted garden. It can't be real."

"It's real. It's real for anyone who wants to believe. Not everyone has the capability to witness this place. But I stopped asking those questions a *long* time ago." Kesh chuckled while facing her. "Don't you realize yet that everything happens for a reason? And there is a reason you are here."

"Why did you bring me here?"

"So that you can know yourself." He rubbed her cheek softly. "Now, what is it that you were telling me? Well, complaining about on the long walk here?"

"I'm just different," she said, furrowing her brows and looking into his face. "Kesh, I'm so different now. Like stronger . . . wiser . . . I don't know. It's kind of strange."

"Strong? How strong?" he asked, teasing her.

"Like really strong. Stronger than I would've ever imagined myself being."

"Show me."

"What?"

"Show. Me." He released her. "Look at this." He pointed at a rock the size of a small boulder. "You think you're so strong you can pick that up?"

"Kesh, come on." Adirah rolled her eyes at him. "Now you're trying to make fun of me. You missed my point."

"No. No. I'm serious," he said, waving her over. "You said you are strong, and I want to see."

Adirah hated to be challenged. From the first day in class until now, she had never let Kesh win another argument. She walked over to where he stood, and looked at the huge rock. She bit the inside of her cheek, highly doubting that she would even be able to make it budge.

"Go on. Lift it. I bet you can do it," he urged.

"You think I can't do it, huh?" she said, slightly annoyed. "You know what? I don't have anything to prove to you, anyways." She folded her arms across her chest. "You're a bully."

He nodded at her and then at the rock, ignoring her little tantrum. Then he also folded his arms across his chest expectantly.

"You're so lucky I hate to lose," Adirah grumbled.

She sucked her teeth, bent down, and closed her arms around the rock. She tugged gently at first, not expecting to move the rock even an inch. Her eyes shot open and her jaw fell when the rock flew up easily, like it was as light as a piece of soft cotton. "What the . . ." Adirah was shocked. She knew that rock had to weigh at least a hundred pounds, but there in her arms, it felt like almost nothing.

Kesh laughed raucously. "Throw it," he instructed.

Adirah looked from him to the rock and then back again. "Whew," she said under her breath. "Okay. This is really happening. Okay."

"Throw it!"

Adirah tossed the rock with all her might and sent it soaring through the air and across the pond. When she heard the loud thud of it landing on the other side, her mouth hung open. She turned to Kesh with wide eyes to make sure he'd seen what she had done. He didn't look surprised at all.

Instead, he pointed to where the rock was and said, "Now go and get it."

Adirah, pumped and ready to throw the rock again, started to head around the pond, but Kesh stopped her.

"Not that way," he said and nodded his head toward the body of water. "That way."

Adirah crinkled her face. "Are you saying to . . ." She looked back at the water. She shook her head, feeling Kesh's gaze and pondering his challenge. "My clothes. I don't want them to get wet. Besides, I can't swim." As soon as the words were out of her mouth, she wished she could take them back. The sneaky smile that came to Kesh's handsome face was too much for her.

He shrugged his shoulders. "If you don't want to get wet, jump."

"Jump?"

"You heard me. Jump over it."

"Kesh, that's crazy!" Adirah waved her arms toward the pond. "Do you see how big that pond is? This is crazy. You're being ridiculous now."

"Almost as crazy as you throwing that rock all the way over there? Well, you thought you couldn't do that, and look how easily it happened." He shrugged. "You never know what you can do until you actually try."

Adirah opened her mouth to say something, but then she shut it. Nothing in her life was making sense anymore, and maybe it was because she was trying so hard to understand it. Nodding her head, she backed up a little farther from the pond and studied the water. She figured she would be jumping the length of a city block to make it across the pond. If she jumped and nothing was different and she didn't make it, then she would probably be only a few feet from shore. Either she would be able to get herself back on land somehow or she had to trust that Kesh would save her from drowning. He had saved her once from burning to death, so Adirah figured he would save her again if she went into the pond.

Okay, Adirah, you can do this. She took a deep breath while she coached herself. *Go!*

She took off, running full speed, focusing only on the other end of the pond. Her legs were moving faster than they ever had in her life, and right when her feet would have touched the water, she leaped high into the air and over the water. She looked under her and saw the ripples of water passing by as her legs did a running motion in the air. The entire jump lasted only a few seconds, but it felt like things were going in slow motion around her. Suddenly, she was terrified; it felt like all the wind had left her chest. She lost control and felt her body dropping. When she had almost made it completely across, she fell. But not before she saw a blurry figure moving even faster than she had. It landed in the water before her. It wasn't until she was in his arms that she realized it had been Kesh. He looked down at her as she looked up, frightened, at him. His complete torso was submerged in the water, but he had made sure not even a drop touched her.

"Kesh, what am I? What are you? What did you do to me? This is insane."

He didn't answer. Instead, he held her as he walked out of the water.

"Kesh? Tell me," Adirah demanded.

He put her down gently in the grass and sat beside her. Kesh stared out at the pond. He pulled at the grass between his legs. There was something on his mind. Adirah could feel a shift in his energy.

"You're going to give me the silent treatment now? I have to know what is happening to me . . . to us," she said.

Kesh looked into the water. Adirah studied the troubled expression on his creased face. She couldn't say she was dreaming, because she knew she was awake. Still how could she explain what had just happened? That kind of thing happened only in movies, and even then they had props to help them pull off the stunts. A ray of sun engulfed the two lovers as they sat side by side. Kesh was lost in thought and was playing with the ring on his finger, spinning it around and around with his thumb. With a shaky hand, she grabbed his wrist, making him stop the spinning.

"Are you nervous? What's the—" She stopped mid-sentence. She had been about to keep pressing him with questions when a glint from the ring hit her eyes. Adirah had to blink and throw her hand up to her face because it hurt her eyes to look at the ring while the sun beamed down on it. Adirah grabbed Kesh's hand and brought the ring closer, to where she could get a better look at it. She examined it closely, running her fingers over the markings. She'd seen the symbol before. It was the fraternity's symbol and was branded on Kesh's chest.

"What does it mean?" she asked, sliding the ring down his finger to the tip.

Kesh grimaced. "Dira . . ." There was a warning in his tone, but he didn't stop her. She held the ring tightly and brought it back up to the light. Kesh fell back and began trembling. His hand began smoking, and he cried out in pain. He was writhing in complete agony. His hand was charred to a crisp.

His reaction almost made Adirah's heart stop. "Kesh! What's the matter?"

He held up a weak hand. "The ring," he wheezed.

She quickly slid the ring back on his finger. Kesh choked and coughed and labored for breath. He lay there on the grass, grimacing in pain, battling to regain his normal breathing. As his breathing began to normalize, Adirah watched in amazement as his hand slowly healed, returning to perfection. She witnessed it go from burnt to a crisp to smooth and beautifully manicured in a matter of seconds.

Adirah's eyes were stretched so wide, they watered at the edges. "I don't understand. . . ."

"The light . . . it's one of the many things that can hurt my kind," he told her. "This . . . this makes it possible for us to walk in the light," he continued, holding his hand up. "That is why we wear these and never take them off. They allow us to walk in the light. They allow us to live and love."

"Y-y-y-you're a vampire?" Adirah gasped, jumping to her feet. "Lina was right?" Adirah started backing away from him. It was beginning to make sense now. Her heightened powers and senses, the hold he had on her. It wasn't just that his blood had healing powers; he was a vampire. How could she be so gullible? Of course he was a vampire. Adirah felt like she should have known, and maybe she had, and she had chosen to ignore it. Adirah was even more confused now.

"Yes," he answered honestly. "Now you know what I am . . . what I will always be. I, Kesh, am the king of my clan. The Sefu Clan of vampires. You figured it out on your own, but if I had told you, I would have had to turn you."

Adirah pinched the bridge of her nose and shook her head. "Wait . . . the other . . . all the others?"

Kesh nodded. "They're my people, Dira. And you're my queen."

Adirah couldn't grasp what he was saying. "And Vila?" Adirah asked, thinking about how protective she was of Kesh.

"She is a vampire too. I am her maker."

"Oh, my God! Why didn't you tell me? You can't just have me fall in love with you and then tell me you're not real!" Tears began rolling down her cheeks. She couldn't keep track of each emotion she was feeling. They were coming in such fast waves, there was no way for her to process any of them.

"I kept it from you to protect you."

Adirah shook her head no. "It was dishonest." She began to sob.

"It is against our law to tell a mortal of our true nature. But you are different now, Dira. You've always had gifts . . . even before me. You're a spirit walker. That is why I was so attracted to you . . . your gift. The voices . . . the visions . . . they're not a mistake. You are here to save our clan. There is a greater purpose for you."

"But I'm not a human anymore? You changed me? Did something to make me different?" She stopped at a realization. "Oh, my God . . . I'm a vampire! That's why I can . . . I can—"

"No, my beautiful Dira," Kesh said, grabbing her to calm her down. "Just as I expected, you're freaked out. I wish that I had had a little bit more time before I revealed this to you, but that would be selfish of me. Everything you were saying, I already had taken notice of. You didn't know it, but whenever I fed you food or drink, I fed you some of me . . . my blood," Kesh confessed. "I had to do it."

Adirah pulled away from him. "You liar! You wanted to make me a monster," she boomed.

"Dira. Listen to me," he begged. "It's not what you think."

"No!" She pounded his chest and backed away from him.

Kesh put his hands out in front of him, pleading. "Hear me out. I knew that if I didn't give you some of my blood, you would get too weak. Vila was right. When I saved you, you were on the brink of death. There were only two things that could save you. The permanent fix would have been to turn you into one of us, but I knew I wouldn't be able to live with myself if I took away your chance to decide whether you wanted to live for decades, unable ever to rest in peace. So instead, I used the healing powers of my blood to save you."

Adirah, mortified, covered her face with her hands. She fell down on her knees and sobbed. "You've turned me into a monster."

"Dira." Kesh tried to tug her hands away so he could look at her, but to no avail. "You looked so mortified about the new gifts that I had to set things straight. It crushed me to know how sickened you were by what you thought you'd become. I did not change you, but allowing you to drink my blood was the only way to save you. You almost died. I had just found you, and it might have been selfish, but I loved you already. I couldn't lose you so soon. But . . ."

"But what, Kesh?" She ripped her hands from her face and stared straight into his eyes, challenging him.

"You must drink from me, or else you will grow too weak to live. You will succumb to your original wounds and . . ."

"Die?"

"Yes."

Adirah went silent. Her body shook all over. She looked at the ground, at the pond, even at the ladybugs crawling on the grass around her. Anything to keep her from looking into his eyes. The juxtaposition of the beauty of their surroundings with the ugliness of their truth was not lost on Adirah.

"So, I'm at your mercy forever?" she said defeated.

Kesh's silence gave her the answer that she didn't even need.

"Why didn't you just turn me? And make me like you?" she asked.

"Living for decades and decades, roaming and feeding, is not something that should just be given. It can be a curse, a long, lonely curse. I would never do that to you, not unless you wanted it. I can keep you alive just like this if you choose," Kesh said.

"But then I would grow old . . . and you wouldn't, right?" Adirah thought about everything he was telling her. She was trying to make sense of it all. Her views on fact and fiction were forever altered. "If you had turned me, then . . ."

"I wouldn't have been able to live with myself if you were unhappy with me after that," Kesh said. "Like Vila. She'll never really forgive me. She has gone through decades, unfulfilled. Unable to find love. She hates it, but she is loyal and will not leave my side."

"*If* you had turned me," Adirah said, "then I wouldn't have been lonely for eternity, though. I would have had you forever."

She finally turned back to Kesh. He was gazing at her with his mesmerizing eyes, a look of hurt on his face. Adirah could see that his decisions had weighed heavily on him. The love he had for her seemed to ooze from his skin. Looking at him, she realized that it wasn't Kesh whom she was frightened of. She could never be afraid of him. Rather it was the knowledge that was staring her in the face that she was scared of. She'd been feeling the presence of spirits since before her brother died. In the deepest part of her mind, she had always known that there were supernatural forces in the world. But now she was being forced to acknowledge that they were real and that she couldn't ignore them any longer.

They sat in silence as they both wrestled with their inner demons. All the cards were on the table, and decisions needed to be made. Kesh hoped that his decision finally to reveal his true self didn't backfire and destroy the only true love he had ever experienced. Adirah needed time to untangle her emotions and make a clear decision about the rest of her life.

"Kesh." Adirah broke the silence.

"Yes?"

She turned her head to look at him. "I love you."

He picked his head up from staring at the grass and looked into Adirah's sparkling eyes.

"If I sat here, mad at you, that would be the most awful thank-you known to mankind. You saved my life, and for that I should be grateful," she said.

Relief washed over his face. Kesh pulled her on top of him and pressed his lips against hers. Her fingers got tangled in his dreads, and she felt his clothes drenching hers, but she didn't care. If his clothes didn't do it, the ocean between her legs soon would.

"I have to tell you something," Adirah said.

"What is it?" Kesh pulled away from her and stared into her face.

"That day . . . the day you found me in the woods when I collapsed, I saw something. It was a vision," she said apprehensively.

"Tell me," Kesh said, pressing.

"Those people I asked you about—Tulum and Calum—they're coming. They're training their people to attack you. I heard them say stuff," Adirah confessed.

"What kind of stuff?"

"They said that they cannot let some blood ritual happen, and that if it did, you'd rise to full power," Adirah said.

"What else did they say?" Kesh asked urgently.

"What does that mean, blood ritual?"

"Dira, you must tell me what else was said." Kesh watched her and hung on her every word.

"The female, Calum, wanted to know why they haven't attacked. She's training all their people, making them fight each other viciously.

She's got a vendetta against you, and she said she wouldn't rest until it is fulfilled."

Kesh ran his hands through his dreads, a nervous reaction.

Adirah went on. "She said that while you're letting your people live like they are normal *humans*, she is training theirs for war. A war that they are anticipating once the man—I guess their leader—gives the order."

"And what did he say?" Kesh asked, pressing. Adirah could see concern rippling over his features.

"He doesn't think the time is right. No matter how impatient the woman got, he kept saying no. He seems to believe you're in love . . . I guess with me," Adirah said, her words catching in her throat.

Kesh watched her closely. "Of course it's you whom I love."

"The man thinks you'll stay here, afraid to leave me behind. But she . . . she thinks love means nothing to you. . . ." Adirah's voice trailed off when she said the words.

"Love means *everything* to me, Dira. He's right. I won't run. I won't leave you behind. I have no choice now but to stand and fight. I'm tired of running from them."

Adirah shook her head. "You can't stay around here for me and let them destroy you, Kesh. They are really making serious plans of attack. They're training . . . seriously training. I thought it was all a dream, something fake. You wouldn't tell me who they were when I asked. . . . Time is probably running out now."

"I know," Kesh said quietly.

Adirah continued. "The man says you're his enemy for life. Something about your clan feeding him some poisonous blood. He was so angry, he picked up one of his own men and threw him. It was like he had the power to teleport himself too. He's pretty powerful. Kesh, I couldn't stand it if anything happened to you on account of me."

Kesh sighed. "We are all powerful, Dira. Don't worry. Nothing will happen to me, and I won't let anything happen to you. I swear it."

"Well, he thinks because I am, as he called me, a mortal, I don't know who you really are. He said he would've done the same for her if she weren't already one of you."

"He was right about that, Dira. I told you . . . it could be a gift and a curse."

"Tulum told Calum that her personal feelings of jealousy toward you are getting in the way of her sound judgment. Why does she hate you so much? Was she once someone you had or loved?" Adirah inquired.

Kesh shook his head. "Calum blames me for the same reason Tulum blames me. They don't think it's right for me, a black man, a vampire, to have the things I have. They can't handle that I am powerful and strong. There were wars over the decades. It has always been about one race versus the other. They couldn't let it go. Revenge is in their blood, while peace is in mine. They come from a very racist ancestry. Their hatred for me is based on no more than the color of my skin . . . the color of your skin." Kesh's jaw rocked as he spoke. He clenched his fists and lowered his head. "Their attacks are based on no more than that . . . just pure inbred hatred."

"I'm worried about you, Kesh," Adirah said, touching his face.

"Don't," he said, pulling her to him. "All you have to worry about is staying with me and being my queen. I'll never let them touch a hair on your head. I swear it, Dira. There's a reason we were drawn together. It might be up to us to save an entire race of people."

Later, still in that magical world beyond the stone wall covered in bright green moss, Adirah and Kesh were entangled in each other's arms.

They work fiercely to strip each other out of their clothes. Adirah felt the cold grassy plain on her naked body and let the goose bumps remind her to be in the moment. She ran her fingers on every part of Kesh's body, while he did the same thing to her with his tongue. He then laid her on her back; her erect nipples pointed up at the sky. Kesh positioned his face so that he was staring at her other set of lips.

"What do you see?" Adirah asked breathlessly.

"I see the jewel of my life. Your juices are seeping from this sweet opening, and I am going to lap them all up," he answered, his voice raspy. Kesh did just as he had promised. His tongue hit against her swollen clit to a beautiful beat, and her cries of pleasure were the perfect background music. Kesh licked up every drop of her sweet nectar. Adirah's body shook every time she came inside of his mouth.

"Tell me if it's too much for you. I'll stop if it is," Kesh said between licks, teasing her.

"No!" Adirah cried out. "Please don't stop! Don't ever stop!"

By the way her voice quivered, Adirah knew she was nearing her next climax. He took her clit into his mouth and sucked, while licking the tip of it at the same time.

"I love how you squirm," he said. "I love everything about you, Dira."

Adirah felt him bringing her to the brink of absolute submission. Just as she felt the gush of juice escape her body, Kesh released her from his mouth and put his hips between her legs. Her head was tossed back, as she was trying to control the intensity of her orgasm, but Kesh would not let her rest. He thrust inside her pulsating love cave and instantly felt her walls contract on his shaft.

"Kesh!" Adirah screamed, her arms outstretched, calling him to her. He fell down on top of her, and she wrapped her arms around him.

"You told me not to stop," Kesh moaned. "And I won't. Not until you tell me to. I am at your mercy."

Adirah moved her body and matched Kesh thrust for thrust. She opened her legs wider for him, giving him complete access to her. "Kesh! Oh, Kesh!"

"Will you submit to me?" he asked, pounding harder.

Adirah clawed his shoulders. It was all she could do to keep from screaming at the top of her lungs.

"I said, do you submit to me, Dira?"

"Yes! Ah! Ah! Ah! I submit to you, Kesh! Come with me, Kesh! Please! I want to feel it inside of me!"

His moans drove her crazy. He pumped a few more times before his body finally bucked. Adirah tightened her legs around him once more as her body quaked under him. She felt him empty himself inside of her. She welcomed all his essence into her.

"Ah!" they shouted together as they came in unison.

It took a few minutes and some effort for Kesh to catch his breath. He removed himself from her and slid to the side. He rolled onto his back. Adirah snuggled up to him in the grass and kissed his cheek, feeling very sleepy.

"I guess this really does make me a queen. Queen of the Sefu Clan of vampires." Her voice was soft, and her eyes were becoming too heavy to keep open. She smiled faintly before allowing sleep to consume her.

Chapter 10

The cameras set up in the Sigma Rho fraternity house had been rolling constantly since the fire and the rebuild. Kesh had them connected to his phone. At any moment he could look in on the house. If someone approached the front door, he was alerted. There was a feature that he could set that alerted him if anyone was moving about in the house. Kesh rarely had this feature turned on, because it would always go off. There was usually someone in the house, and Kesh didn't feel like getting alerts all day.

Kesh and Adirah were on their way back to the house when he felt a tiny vibration from his phone. He removed his phone from his pocket and took a look at it. The alert that was on the screen warned him of someone approaching the house. He swiped right to unlock the phone, and as he touched the security camera icon, his phone went dead.

"Damn," Kesh said. "The battery sucks on this thing." He put the phone in his pocket, figuring it was probably just one of the clan who needed to retrieve something they'd forgotten at the house.

The cameras, however, were still recording. Their lenses caught two intruders sneaking about the house. The cameras could record their movements, not their motives.

A loud crashing sound caused Lina to spin around.

"Shhh!" She glared at Narum, her face curled into a scowl. "How do you bump into a table during a break-in?" she whispered harshly. The huge porcelain vase that was resting on the wood-top table had toppled over, but Narum had rushed to catch it before it shattered on the floor. Lina shook her head at him. "Careful. And be quiet."

"Sorry," Narum said sheepishly and carefully placed the vase back in its spot. The ring on his finger had slipped to his knuckle, and he pushed it back down quickly. "I didn't see the table there. I was making sure no one was behind us."

"*Sorry* won't be enough if the popular ones find us in here, snooping around," Lina said, continuing her gripe. "And try to keep your voice down please."

The two of them had done exactly what they had said they would: they'd snuck into the Sigma Rho frat house. They'd gotten in through a window at the back of the house that led to the basement. Narum had used a rock to break a small pane of glass, had pushed his hand through the broken window, and had unlatched the lock on the other side.

Once inside, Lina had turned left, right, and left again. She'd looked like a lost child in a store at the moment when the child realized that his or her mother was nowhere to be seen. She hadn't seemed to know what to look for. "You think they have coffins in here? Dead corpses? And stuff like that?" she'd whispered as she crept around.

"No. Now let's go upstairs and see what we can find. There's nothing down here but construction supplies, if you ask me," Narum had said.

Narum and Lina tiptoed their way through the dimly lit house, listening for any sound of life.

"It is way too quiet," Lina mouthed to Narum.

He waved his hand at her and shook his head. "It's Friday night, so this doesn't surprise me.

Lina got close to Narum and whispered, "This quiet must mean they're all out having the time of their lives, sucking innocent people's blood."

"I thought you said to be quiet?" Narum chastised. "You're whisper is louder than your regular voice."

Lina rolled her eyes at him.

When Narum and Lina found the living area, Lina's eyes went wide and her jaw hung slack. She appeared blown away. So much so, she stopped and took the time to actually look around. "This can't be the same house," she said. "It's not just different. It's *better* than it was the night of the fire. This place doesn't even feel like it belongs on campus. It is really like some luxury mansion in here. Who are these people? Not only do they look like perfect models, but they also live like celebrities too," she said, whirling around in awe.

Narum motioned her to move along, but she was too busy ogling the high ceilings, the crystal chandeliers, the plush furnishings, and the museum-quality art. Lina stamped her feet. The carpet beneath her shoes was so soft, this motion didn't create a bit of sound.

"And who decorated in here?" Lina mused. "Look at how the furniture is situated so precisely around the room. These beautiful burgundy couches look like if you sit on them, the plush fabric will have you feeling like you're sitting on a cloud—"

"Where do you want to look first?" Narum interrupted her. "We can't stand here, looking around like we're museum spectators."

"Umm." Lina turned in a circle until finally her eyes fell on the grand staircase. "Up there. Let's find *his* room."

Narum agreed, took the first steps, and halted. His legs nearly buckled as he lifted his head and sniffed the air. By the look on his face, it was apparent that Narum knew there were vampires on the second level of the house.

"Just stay as quiet as possible," Narum warned Lina. "I think someone is here. Maybe they're asleep."

"There," Lina rasped, pointing.

"Shh," Narum chastised. He put his hand up to his lips and pointed to the same spot she had pointed to. Then he led the way up the rest of the steps. Once they were on the second level, he stopped and directed Lina's attention to the tall dark brown double doors at the end of the hallway. "Come," Narum said and then placed his hands on Lina's shoulders. "But tread softly."

"I want to know what is on the other side of those double doors," Lina whispered.

"Me too," he agreed.

Lina nodded her head and followed closely behind Narum. They passed six doors before they reached the tall set, which was so far from the rest. Narum stopped in front of the double doors and ran his hand over the Sefu Clan's four-point symbol on one of the door panels. He cracked a sly smile. He grasped the golden handle on the door and turned it. Surprise registered on his face at how easily the door handle turned.

"It isn't locked," he said, his eyebrows arched.

"Well, isn't that a good thing?" Lina said. She pushed him to the side and hastily entered the room. "Whoa," she gasped once she crossed the doorsill. "Something is definitely different about this guy, Kesh. I feel like I've taken a step into the royal quarters of a real king," Lina said in awe. She walked over and examined the bed in the middle of the room. It had messy sheets, like someone had just laid in them.

Narum shut the door behind them. Lina noticed him turning his head and looking around the room. He looked like he was sniffing the air again.

"What are you? A bloodhound?" she asked. "Why do you keep sniffing the air?"

"Don't worry about me," he replied as he moved around slowly and methodically.

"I came here for a purpose," she whispered. "I'm not about to stand around here and lose the chance to get what I came for. Get to work." Taking her own advice, Lina got to work rummaging through the dressers around the room. After a few minutes, her shoulders slumped.

"Shit. I don't see anything suspicious. Just normal things a man his age would have. Clothes, jewelry, lots of cologne, but not even one porn picture or anything dirty I could hold over his head," Lina said, flustered. "And look at this shit. Even a few of Adirah's things are here." Lina held up a T-shirt that she recognized. "She's practically living here. I guess it's only right."

"There has got to be more here," Lina said. She walked over to the closet door and gripped the handle, expecting it to turn as easily as the bedroom door handle had, but it didn't. "Who locks their closet door?" she grumbled.

Narum heard her and came up behind her. He leaned down to examine the lock. In his hand he had a key that he'd found in one of the drawers in the room. He inserted the key into the lock, looked at Lina, told her with his eyes to keep quiet, then turned the key. It didn't budge. The key was not cut for that door.

"Can you look and see if you can find a safety pin?" he whispered.

Lina did what he asked, figuring that he was going to pick the lock, but after she had taken a few steps back to one of the dressers, she heard a popping sound behind her.

"Never mind," Narum told her, shrugging his shoulders, when she turned back toward him. "I had one in my pocket."

He pushed the door open and flicked on the light switch. They both stood at the threshold, looking inside a normal walk-in closet. Neat rows of clothes hung on every bar, folded stacks of sweaters were stuffed department store–style in wooden cubby slots, and shoe boxes were stacked like blocks against the walls.

Lina squinted and stepped inside the closet. "There is something that Kesh is hiding in here, I'm sure. Otherwise it wouldn't have been locked up and off-limits," she said, moving the clothes around in a hurry.

"We've got to hurry. We've already been in here too long," Narum warned her.

"There has to be something in here," she said, frustration lacing her words. After kneeling down, she hastily moved the stacks of shoes out of her way. "There has to be *something*. Ouch!" Lina winced when her hand hit something behind some of the shoe boxes. "What the hell was that?"

She moved her hand again and dug around. "Ah. I found something." She bent farther over to get a better view of what she was feeling. Her face was resting on the carpet in order for her to see all the way to the back of the closet. "Its . . . it's like an old treasure chest." After grabbing it with both hands, she tugged on the chest. She tried to pull it away from the wall, but it didn't budge. "Narum, ugh!" Lina groaned, trying to pull it again. "Narum, I think I found something. Help me pull it out. It's heavy as hell."

"Watch out," Narum said, nudging her aside. With little to no effort at all, he lifted the chest up and stood to his feet.

"My goodness," Lina said, her eyes bulging at his strength. "Maybe you do take boxing classes."

Narum shot her a look. His focus was on the chest in his arms. His eyes widened as he studied it, seemingly amazed. "I can't believe these still exist," he blurted. Immediately, his eyes went wide, a sign that he knew he'd said too much.

"What? What is it?" Lina asked, pressing.

"It's a vampire box," Narum revealed.

Lina threw her hands up to her mouth. "See? I was right," she said, letting her hands fall slack at her sides. "I knew that dude was one of them. I'm never wrong. But what if Adirah—" Lina's face iced with concern.

"Shh," Narum said, stopping her from saying any more. "Let's just see if that's what it really is." Narum set the chest down in front of them. "I heard vampire boxes hold enchantments cast by original vampires . . . the first of their kind. It is where vampires of old kept their most prized possessions, but these babies were thought to be long lost with the originals. Obviously not, because here we are, with one right in front of us."

"How do you know so much?"

"Maybe you're not the only one who does research," Narum replied.

Narum tried to open the chest. It was locked.

"The key. Try the key you found," Lina said.

Narum removed the key from his pocket. This time the key smoothly opened the lock. Narum opened the chest, gasping at the sight of its content. "The elixir," he whispered under his breath. His eyes were transfixed by the vial of liquid in front of him.

"What is that?" Lina asked with a wrinkled brow as she peered inside the chest.

"Um . . . ," Narum said, turning his head away from her. "Um, nothing. It's just some cologne. My favorite actually."

"That's it? He has cologne locked in a chest hidden in his locked closet?"

"I guess." He shrugged his shoulders. "Did you hear that?" he suddenly said, trying to draw Lina's attention away from the elixir.

Lina turned her head to listen. While she did so, Narum grabbed the elixir and pocketed it, then quickly closed the chest.

"We better get out of here. I think someone is here." Narum pushed the chest back into place and replaced the boxes of shoes. "Let's go," he whispered for effect.

They both exited the closet. Then they quietly snuck out of the room, holding hands.

"I guess I am just crazy, after all," Lina whispered once they were halfway down the hallway. "I could have sworn we were going to find something that screamed 'vampire' in the chest. Not some dumb cologne in a bottle so small it could fit in your pocket."

"We can still watch him . . . them. Maybe something else will be revealed," Narum said, squeezing Lina's hand.

"I guess you're right. Not exactly worth bringing this stupid wooden stake out of the dorm, now, was it?" she said, gesturing to the pouch hanging by her hip.

Lina headed for the stairs, but Narum grabbed her arm to stop her. "Wait. I think they are downstairs. We can't go down there." He was playing it up to the fullest.

"How do we get out, then?"

"There." He pointed to a window at the end of the hall. Narum ran to the window, with Lina following.

"I'm not jumping out of that window," Lina protested in a whisper.

"I'll jump first, and then I'll catch you."

She looked at him like he was crazy.

"Come on. We have to go." Narum had urgency in his words. He needed to get back to his clan with the elixir. He opened the window. "You can either jump or not. Come on. You can do it."

Fear was on her face. She didn't trust that Narum would catch her. He was wimpy. Yeah, maybe he had made that chest look easy to move, but she'd never seen him show any strength besides that.

"Let's jump. I'll catch you. I promise," he told her when he saw that she was debating what to do.

"I'm not going out that window," she asserted.

"Well, then, we need to get back to the basement." Narum yanked her toward the stairs.

Chapter 11

Kesh could have held Adirah for a few more hours or days, but he'd already been gone from his clan for too long. Kesh could already picture Vila and Tiev discussing his absence and what they needed to do to reel him back in. Admittedly, Kesh hadn't planned to be missing for that much time, but he had needed Dira to understand that there was nothing wrong with her. He had wanted her to embrace herself, even if that had meant letting her figure out who he really was.

On the way back to the house, Kesh finished telling her everything she needed to know about the Sefu and their sworn enemies, the Malum. Although Kesh didn't want the others to know that Dira knew about them, he was elated that he was no longer keeping any secrets from her.

"This is still unbelievable," Dira told Kesh when they approached his house. "I can't believe you are *real*. I've heard stories and watched movies, like everyone else, but I never, ever believed it."

"Was that lovemaking real enough for you?" Kesh joked. He shimmied his shoulders just thinking about it. "It was very real for me. I think so real, I could use more and more and more."

"Oh, my goodness. Stop it. You're making me blush." She giggled.

Kesh stopped at the front door and turned to her, his smile faded. He grabbed her shoulders and looked at her seriously. "Dira, listen to me. The others cannot know that you know about me yet." Although he had already told her, Kesh told her again. "They won't understand or believe that you came into the knowledge on your own. They have a hard time listening and understanding things. Especially Vila. I took you to that place because I knew Tiev wouldn't be able to pick up my scent there. He wouldn't be able to follow me, like he usually does. I'm telling you this for your own safety. They have to see it being revealed to you in another way, or else they'll want me to turn you . . . t-to kill you." The words seemed to catch in Kesh's throat.

"I understand. I won't say anything. I know they don't really like me. I can feel the way they all look at me, especially Vila," Dira said. "She really hates me."

Kesh pulled her to him and squeezed. "She does not hate you. She just doesn't trust you. Most of them . . . well . . . us . . . don't trust mortals. We've always been trained not to trust mortals, and for good reason. They've hunted us, destroyed us, banished us, and made decades of living hell for us."

"Then why live like them . . . I mean . . . *us*?"

"It just makes life easier," Kesh replied, opening the door. "We've lived like animals before, in hiding. Not wanting to be seen. Hunting down prey in the thick of the night. Murdering so that our prey wouldn't expose us. Walking in the light makes this eternal life a little more bearable. We get to live as mortals do . . . learn new things, participate in the culture and, most importantly, fall in love." Kesh kissed Dira on her forehead.

She smiled and nodded. "Yes, that's the most important."

Kesh stepped inside the frat house, then held the door open for Adirah and let her go ahead of him. She looked around her and was surprised at how quiet it was inside the house. It had never been this quiet at the house the times she'd been there before. Usually, many members of the clan were involved in lots of activities at the house.

"Where is everyone? I have never seen this house so empty. It's kind of eerie," she said.

Kesh looked around, seemingly puzzled too. He didn't have a good feeling. Suddenly, the alert from his phone came back to his mind. He had got an alert that someone was approaching the house, and now no one was at home, so it didn't add up. He didn't want to alert Adirah that something might be out of the ordinary, so he played it off. "I guess they're all busy. Vila and Tiba probably trained all day. Those two," Kesh replied. He craned his neck, still looking around. "My guess is everyone is out doing something constructive with their time. Tiev and the others should be out getting strong. At nightfall, we rest and build up."

"You mean out feeding?" Dira blurted. "That's what Lina told me vampires do at night. They feed on humans . . . for their blood."

Kesh saw the look on her face but could not discern if it was disgust or sorrow. "Yes," he answered honestly. "Feeding. It keeps them . . . us strong."

"You let your people murder them . . . I mean *us*?" Dira asked, catching herself again.

"No!" Kesh snapped, his face getting serious. He grabbed Dira by the shoulders so that he could look her in the eyes. "My clan does not drink to kill. They drink enough to survive, and they never leave their host too weak to function. It does not take much to charm a mortal to bend to your will. When we realized that, we stopped killing. Unless we absolutely have to. Understand? The Sefu Clan does not kill . . . unless we have to. Unless we absolutely have to."

Dira shook her head up and down; her eyes glazed over. Kesh saw the relief wash over her face, and just like that, she was back to normal. She grabbed Kesh's hand. "Let's go to bed," she said seductively. She tugged him toward the stairs. Kesh got set to follow his beautiful queen but stopped suddenly.

"What's wrong?" Dira asked. "Are you okay?"

Kesh hushed her by putting a hand up. He took a few steps away from her and turned his nose to the air. He sniffed around and noticed a change in the atmosphere inside of the house. Kesh's heart sped up as he moved around like a bloodhound. The scent of fresh human blood was so strong that it alarmed him. There was another familiar scent. One he'd smelled before, and one that wasn't mortal.

"Somebody is here," he hissed, and then his upper lip rose and he snarled, exposing his long fangs. "You need to go, Dira. Go hide."

"No. I'm not leaving you." She turned around to face him and looked at him strangely. "I don't understand what you see or hear."

"Don't ask me any questions. Just go," Kesh whispered harshly.

Just as the last word was out of his mouth, he heard the sound of two whispering voices. If it was anyone from his clan, they wouldn't have to whisper. Kesh knew right away he had unwelcome company. He froze and listened.

"Well, then, we need to get back to the basement," said a male voice.

Kesh growled low in his throat and dropped down into a fighting stance and waited.

When Lina and Narum rounded the corner into the living area, Kesh was so angry, the veins in his neck pulsed visibly under his skin. Lina and Narum both froze, like deer caught in headlights. Narum made the mistake of looking Kesh directly in the eyes. Kesh focused hard and read Narum's most recent memories.

"Malum boy! How dare you enter the sanctity of another vampire's home unwelcomed?" Kesh barked. He raised his upper lip and bared his teeth like an attack wolf. He took off toward Narum so fast that he was on top of the young man before he could react. Kesh wrapped his hands around the younger vampire's neck. "Spy! They sent you to spy on me? Huh? Was your leader too much of a coward to come himself again?" Kesh spoke in a voice that was otherworldly. He sounded like a cross between an old-world king and a werewolf. "Where's Tulum now? Where is the cowardly king now?"

Kesh tightened his grip on Narum's neck. Saliva seeped from the corners of Narum's lips, and his tongue protruded from his mouth. Kesh squeezed harder and harder. Narum struggled against Kesh, but to no avail.

"What are you doing? Get off of him!" Lina screamed. She took off running and barreled into Kesh's back with all the strength she had. She pounded her fists on Kesh's back. "Get the hell off of him. You're a vampire! You're evil! Leave him alone!" Lina screeched. She reached up and dug her nails into Kesh's hands, fighting to pry Kesh's hands from around Narum's neck. In a knee-jerk reaction, Kesh took his left hand and backhanded Lina with a force so strong that she flew backward into the air.

"Lina!" Dira cried out, terror etched on her face. Using her newfound speed, Dira jumped in front of Lina and caught her before she slammed into the wall. Kesh turned his head and was shocked as he watched Dira use her gift to catch Lina.

"Back to you," Kesh growled, turning his attention back to the younger man. "You will not get away with this."

Kesh swung a powerful fist and hit Narum in the face. The force from Kesh's punch was not powerful enough. Narum had absorbed so many powerful blows during training that his ability to withstand punishment was great. Narum laughed, and the instant Kesh loosened his grip to punch him, Narum jerked out of his grasp and jumped backward. Kesh planted his feet, preparing for battle.

"You will not get away with being in my house," Kesh hissed, moving in. "Your death will be a slow and painful one, as it says in the laws. You have violated a king!" Kesh boomed.

Narum moved from side to side on his legs, weighing his options. Kesh could see the fear glinting in Narum's glowing eyes, but he also knew that the young vampire had nothing to lose. Narum slowly drew a wooden stake from his pocket and clutched it.

Kesh growled. "You think you can use that folklore weapon on me?"

Narum swallowed hard, then thrust the stake in Kesh's direction, still buying time. "I know that if Tulum and Calum find out I have come here, I risk punishment," Narum panted, his mouth bloodied. He spat in Kesh's direction. "It will be a painful, dreadful punishment. Because they know if you and your weakling Sefu catch me here, you will most likely torture me for information about the Malum," Narum said, his voice shaking now. "Even you can't save me from that fate. I am doomed either way."

Kesh's chest heaved, and he set his jaw and began rounding on the young vampire. "That's right."

"Still, a part of me felt obligated to protect Lina from any harm, because I knew nothing would keep her away from this house, and no mortal is safe around an entire clan of vampires, especially when armed only with a wooden stake. She wouldn't even get close enough to use the thing," Narum said, jerking his head toward Lina.

"Get away from him!" Lina screamed.

"Stay still," Dira barked, trying her best to hold on to Lina.

Kesh turned his head toward Dira and Lina for a millisecond, and that was enough time. Narum leaped into the air and straight over Kesh's head. Kesh had thought of himself as the more powerful and faster one of the two, but he'd lost his focus. His concern for Dira had gotten him.

"And the contents of this vile . . . ," Narum said, holding up the elixir bottle.

Kesh's face immediately went pale. His body shook at the sight of his precious drink.

"This potion so powerful that it could take over the most powerful of minds, even yours. So my risk taking will be worth it when this potion is in the hands of my leaders," Narum said before racing out the door like a cheetah.

"No!" Kesh roared and then took off after Narum.

"Kesh!" Dira yelled after him, but her cries fell on deaf ears. This time he could not be distracted. He had to get his elixir back. That was a matter of life and death.

The world around Kesh was a blur as he chased Narum, barely able to keep up. Kesh thought he was faster, but Narum had put a lot of space between them. Kesh felt like he was stuck in slow motion. He knew that meant he needed to feed. The time he'd spent making love to Dira in their secret place had left him drained. Now his gift of speed wasn't working. His legs ached, and his chest felt like he'd swallowed a fire-lit sword. Still, he couldn't let Narum give the elixir to Tulum; that would certainly spell disaster for Kesh's clan. Tulum had no regard for rules and laws; he'd certainly use the elixir on Kesh and destroy him.

Narum ran off campus and into the street. Kesh dodged in and out of traffic, nearly causing car accidents. The drivers of the vehicles would never know what the blurs were that flashed past their vehicles. Horns honked in Kesh's wake.

"You don't know what you're doing . . . what you're causing for yourself!" Kesh yelled when he finally got close enough to reach for Narum's collar.

"Anything to destroy the Sefu!" Narum made a sharp right turn into the woods, causing Kesh to grab nothing but warm air.

Kesh felt like his entire body would explode. He needed to feed, and quickly, or he would be in trouble. He hadn't let his reserves get this low in decades. He didn't remember how disastrous it could be, either.

When Narum left the street and turned into the woods, Kesh was forced to jump up to avoid a head-on collision with a Toyota Corolla. Kesh landed hard on the hood of the car but did not care about the dent that he'd made. The car screeched to a halt, and Kesh hopped off the hood before the driver had time to get out and inspect the damage. Kesh struggled to move, to breathe. Everything hurt.

As weak as he felt, Kesh focused on the fact that he could not let Tulum and Calum get their hands on the elixir. They both already yearned for power too much. Kesh had made a promise long ago to keep his people safe. Maybe Vila was right. If Kesh had been home, instead of out with Dira, this wouldn't have happened. Once again, he and his clan had gotten comfortable, and they'd left their home vulnerable. Kesh willed his feet to go faster through the woods, because if he didn't do something to stop Narum, they could all be in grave danger. Again.

"Y-y-you're one of them!" Lina said, pushing Adirah away from her. "Don't touch me, vampire!" Lina backed away, her body trembling like a leaf in a wild storm.

"Lina, listen to me. It's not what you think." Adirah put her hands up, trying to calm her friend down. "If you just listen for a few minutes, I can explain everything to you. It'll all make perfect sense. I know now that you weren't wrong, but I'm telling you for sure that it's not what you think."

"How can it not be what I think, Adirah?" Lina exclaimed. "I just saw your boyfriend move at the freaking speed of light, and I saw you do the same thing. I saw his teeth. I saw his eyes turn yellow and glow like a cat's eyes. How do you explain that? Huh, Adirah? I knew it. I knew they were the undead, and now they have you too."

"Calm down, Lina," Adirah said and tried again to soothe her by placing her hands on Lina's shaky shoulders, but Lina jerked away from her, then stumbled back a few steps.

"No, I won't calm down," Lina snapped, pointing an accusing finger in Adirah's face. "I knew what they were from day one. I tried to tell you, but you didn't listen, and now they have got you too. Just look at you. Your skin is glowing. Your . . . your body looks like you had cosmetic surgery." Lina pointed at her chest.

Adirah looked down at herself, her eyebrows dipping low.

"Oh, you didn't think I noticed those breasts sitting up and how those hips rounded out? All the girl ones are perfect like that . . . just too beautiful to be real," Lina accused.

Adirah sighed and shook her head. "It's not like that," she said, exasperated. "Kesh is a man. He is a real man. He's not evil at all. I am not dead, Lina. I'm alive—and no thanks to you. You've got everything so wrong."

"Wrong? Wrong, Adirah? I am standing in the home of vampires. . . . They have frigging vampire boxes, or whatever you call them. I saw one with my own eyes. They kill people to live, for God's sake, Adirah," Lina said, shaking her head. She finally let the tears come down her face. "I

don't know what else to do, Adirah. You're lost
now. I knew if I came here, I would find something. After Narum and I found the chest with
just the cologne in it, I almost gave up. But now
I come to find out that it is some kind of elixir.
And *you two* show up, with your speed and
glowing skin, proving that I was right all along,"
Lina cried, hugging herself.

"Lina, listen. . . ." Adirah went to touch her.

"I said, don't touch me!" Lina boomed, slapping Adirah's hand away. Her mood was suddenly swinging like a pendulum, going from frail
to fierce. She squinted her eyes into dashes and
pointed again at Adirah's chest. "I swear, Adirah.
I will have every vampire hunter from here to
Transylvania on your ass and his too. If you even
think about harming a hair on my head, they will
find you and destroy you," Lina promised, her
tone venomous.

Adirah tried one more time to grab Lina, but
Lina ducked out of the way.

"Don't you touch me with your evil vampire
hands!" Lina exclaimed.

"Oh, my God," Adirah huffed. "I'm not a vampire. I swear to you, I'm not, Lina. We just need
to speak calmly about this. You're upset, and
that's understandable, but if you just hear me
out, you'll know that I am *not* a vampire."

"Then explain how you just caught me in the air! What normal college girl can do that?" Lina threw her hands up and shook her head. "Explain it. I'll wait." She tapped her foot.

"It's . . . I . . . ," Adirah stammered, the words stuck in her throat. There was no way that she could explain what she was, because *she* didn't even know. Was Lina right? Was she a full vampire? But wait, no. She was still alive. Adirah shook her head, unable to land on a firm answer for Lina.

"I didn't think so," Lina snorted.

"It's just complicated," Adirah said. It was the best she could come up with.

"Stay away from me, Adirah. I swear to the real God that I will scream it all over campus if you try to come near me again. I don't feel safe," Lina told her as she started to back up toward the door. "And another thing . . ." Lina pointed in Adirah's direction. "You purposely tried to make me feel crazy when I told you I had suspicions about all these students on campus suddenly needing blood transfusions. Remember that? You have always tried to make me seem crazy, and now I know why."

Lina went on. "I also did some research, and this . . . this so-called fraternity doesn't exist in any records of the school's history. It's like somebody just made it up and the school went along with it. But why? Did these evil ones use their mind-control tricks to make that happen? I know now that I was tricked. That . . . that girl, she tricked me that day. Oh, you have no idea, Adirah. I can't wait to tell the whole school what you all are. I can't wait to get every hunter available. I'll have my wooden stake, my crosses, my holy water, garlic—whatever it takes to keep you and them away from me." She glared at Adirah. "There's no way I'm living on campus with all this evil. I'm telling the whole story," Lina proclaimed, her hand curling around the wooden stake she'd pulled from her pocket.

"I don't think so," a voice boomed from behind them.

Lina jumped so hard, she almost fell over. When she turned around, Vila was standing there, snarling, with her fangs extended. Lina still had the wooden stake in her grasp. With shaky hands, she held it out in front of her.

Adirah's eyebrows shot up into arches, but she couldn't react fast enough. "Lina! No . . ."

"Argh!" Lina roared as she charged forward and into Vila, with the wooden stake leading the way. Vila grabbed Lina's wrist mid-lunge and pulled forcefully until she and Lina were chest to chest.

"Please. Please. Oh, my God. Please," Lina begged. Adirah saw the stream of urine seep into Lina's pants, darkening the material.

"That was dumber than you coming to this house in the first place. This isn't a movie," Vila snarled. "Let me show you how real this is."

With a quick jerk of her thumb, she twisted Lina's wrist to the side. There was a loud cracking sound.

"Ahhh! Ahhh!" Lina screeched, her eyes snapping shut from the pain. "Please! Please I won't tell anyone, I swear! Just don't kill me!"

"Too late for all this begging now," Vila hissed. "I've been waiting to feed on one of you weak bitches since I got here. You thought that your stupid all-black clothing was going to protect you? You thought we'd never catch up to you with all your snooping? Huh, idiot? You're so lucky Kesh made me return your mind to normal, or else I would've made you a simple, babbling fool for life."

Just as Vila was about to bite down on Lina's carotid artery, Adirah's voice stopped her.

"No!" Adirah yelled. "Please, Vila, don't. She's really harmless." Adirah walked closer. "Kesh told me that you're good. . . . You don't just kill for no reason. You're not evil, Vila. I know everything. . . . I know all about you and him and the Sefu."

Vila twisted her neck and glared at Adirah with a look that could set the entire room on fire. "She knows too much, and so do you. This is against our law. The both of you will meet your fate. You're lucky I don't have you in this position right now," Vila retorted, her nostrils flaring wider than those of a bull on the charge. She turned her sights back to Lina.

Adirah had to think quickly. "Please, Vila. Listen to me. Kesh is in trouble. He's out there . . . alone. I think the boy . . . the boy vampire is leading him into a trap," Adirah yelled out frantically. Adirah knew exactly how Vila felt about Kesh. She knew that would work.

The crazed look on Vila's face faded, replaced with a furrowed brow look of concern. She did not loosen her grip on Lina, but she did focus her attention on Adirah. "What kind of trouble? What are you talking about? Is this a ploy to save this bitch?" Vila squinted.

"No. No. I swear. He's really in trouble," Adirah answered, her words rushing out. "Lina was here with a boy from the Malum—"

"Malum!" Vila twisted Lina's already broken wrist even more.

"Agh!" Lina screamed. "I . . . I didn't know who . . . what . . . he was."

"Yes," Adirah said, realizing the new information had not saved Lina and might even have signed her death certificate. "He was from the Malum, but I don't think Lina knew what or who he was. He said he took some elixir from a chest in Kesh's room or something like that. Kesh got so mad about it that he chased the boy out of the house, but . . . but I just don't have a good feeling about this. Kesh wasn't himself at all. The boy got away from him too easily."

Vila inhaled deeply. Her faced turned a darker shade, like someone had placed their hands around her throat and squeezed. "You better be telling the truth, mortal girl. Because if I find out you were lying just to save her"—Vila released Lina with a hard shove—"you'll be sorry, and so will she. I don't know who you think I am, but I will destroy you if I have to."

"I—I swear. I'm not lying," Adirah assured her. "Kesh is out there. He is not himself, and he may be running right into a trap."

"If you're right and it is the Malum, and they've taken what I suspect, Kesh is in more trouble than we think," Vila remarked, her words laced with concern. "We have to find him. Now!"

"Lock her up in the basement," Vila said breathlessly to two other Sefu Clan members. "I'll deal with her when I get back."

"No! Let me go! Please!" Lina screamed, but it was all for nothing. They weren't going to let her out of their sight now.

Adirah shot her a look that said, "Just be happy you're still alive . . . for now."

"Kesh's scent is still fresh. We have to go now, before it fades," Vila said. "You have abilities like us, don't you?" she asked Adirah.

Adirah nodded her head slowly. She wasn't sure if the answer was really yes or no. She was also shocked that Vila wanted to work with her. Adirah had only seen Vila look either angry or totally sure of herself. Seeing fear find a home on her gorgeous face was something Adirah had never anticipated. It made her scared too.

"I think so," Adirah finally managed to say.

"Good. Because you'll need them. Let's go."

Chapter 12

Kesh couldn't control his breathing. His chest rose and fell so rapidly, it almost hit his chin. He could feel his legs shaking, and it had taken all the strength he could muster to catch up to Narum. The wind whipped around them like a small tornado, and all the animals around had scurried into hiding. Kesh's body shook fiercely as he used the last of his might to hold on to Narum's throat. Kesh had the younger man pinned against the thick, rough trunk of an old tree, and he squeezed his neck until Narum's eyes bulged.

"Did you really think you could beat me? Huh, little boy? Do you know who I am?" Kesh snarled, spit flying from the sides of his mouth into Narum's face. Pain shot up Kesh's arms and down his back. He knew he had to act fast, or his life would be ending. "Where is my elixir?" Kesh growled, clamping down harder.

Narum's body shook; he couldn't speak.

"Where is it!" Kesh boomed, using his free hand to pat down Narum's pockets. Kesh's body ached all over, but he wouldn't let go. Finally, he felt what he was looking for and dug into Narum's pocket. Kesh fisted the bottle of elixir, a small explosion of relief bursting in his chest. His energy was so depleted, he wasn't sure how much longer he would have been able to overpower the young man.

"You're so lucky I got it back, or you'd be sorry. I'd take you back to my clan and let them torture you mercilessly, and then we'd leave you in the light to burn," Kesh hissed, releasing his grip on Narum's throat. "You're lucky that I am a changed man and that I really want peace. A final end to this war."

Narum slid down the tree trunk and collapsed on the ground, coughing and gagging. "You . . . you've made a grave mistake," he rasped between breaths. "You should've just killed me. They'll come. My leaders and my clan will come. They know that I am here." Narum finally got enough air into his lungs and started laughing hysterically. "They know I am here, and I'm going to watch them torture your mortal—"

A kick to the face sent Narum's words tumbling back down his throat.

"Don't you ever mention her! Do you hear me? Don't you ever," Kesh growled. He could barely keep himself up, as his energy was fading fast. He needed to feed. Sweat drenched his face and shirt.

"My clan will destroy you," Narum gasped, blood painting his teeth.

"I'm not scared of your clan. I won't run anymore," Kesh spat, staggering on his wiry legs. He felt close to passing out.

"Is that so?" a voice called out from behind Kesh.

In response to the voice, Kesh spun around, almost falling over. His eyes lowered into dashes at the sight of his enemy Tulum.

"You should be smarter than this, Tulum. Sending this . . . this baby's breath vampire to infiltrate me . . . ," Kesh said, kicking dirt in Narum's direction. "You thought you could send a mere amateur to steal from me?" Kesh was unsteady on his feet. He tried desperately to hide the fact from Tulum.

Tulum's face crinkled. He looked down at Narum. "What is he talking about? What did you steal from him?"

Narum bowed to Tulum. "It . . . it was the girl. Lina. She wanted to go to the Sefu's place. I . . . I . . . had to go along, or risk blowing my cover. Please, King. Please forgive me," Narum pleaded.

"Idiot!" Tulum growled just as his queen, Calum, and other members of the Malum Clan closed in behind him. "Get him out of here, out of my sight."

"Wait, King Tulum. Let me make it right. Listen to me. I had the elixir in my possession. He . . . Kesh took it back. It's here. He has it now," Narum shouted as he was being dragged off. "It's here! All because of me! I got it here! I got it here!"

It was no use. The other Malum were forcefully dragging him deeper into the woods. His protests grew quieter the farther away they got. Tulum had no patience for insubordination, and Narum had just committed the most blatant disrespect of the rules. He was going to pay the price.

Tulum turned back to Kesh. Fire flashed in Tulum's eyes, and Calum moved to his side, licking her lips.

"Finally. It's time to finish him off once and for all," she said, rubbing her hands together. "I've been waiting for this day for decades."

Tulum put his hand up to hold her back. "Hand the elixir over and you can hope to make it out of here in one piece," Tulum said as Calum hissed and growled, dying to get to Kesh.

Kesh swayed on his feet, barely able to stay upright. He shook his head no.

"You can make this easy or hard. Especially since it seems like your loyal followers haven't cared to find you. My queen would love nothing more than to take care of you once and for all. I never knew it was your people who pillaged and destroyed her home."

"You'll never take it. I will die first," Kesh retorted, dropping down into a weak defensive stance. He felt his entire body quake, and he wanted to throw up. His legs were about to give out. He needed to feed, but he couldn't let them know he was losing his power. "Never," he said, struggling.

Calum threw her head back, cackling. "You're so weak," she said, getting serious in an instant. "I can see the pallor of your skin. You haven't fed. There's no one around to feed on, weakling. You're finished."

Kesh coughed. Still, he didn't back down. He growled low in his throat, and his top lip quivered. He looked like a cornered dog in an alley, a dog that was about to get captured by the dogcatcher.

"Let me take him out. Please, King. I've been waiting for this day," Calum said, bending at the waist and moving from side to side like she was ready to pounce.

"I will fight my own battles," Tulum replied. He lifted both of his hands, his fingers splayed and the flats of his palms aimed at Kesh.

Kesh bore down, his knees bent, but his efforts were for nothing. He felt himself flying up in the air. Tulum had the upper hand this time.

"Argh!" Tulum roared, jerking his hands back and forth.

Kesh's body slammed into the same tree he'd pinned Narum against. Kesh made a howling noise as all the air was knocked out of his body through his mouth. He felt something crack between his shoulder blades. He slid to the ground in agonizing pain, a lump of flesh about to be pummeled by his mortal enemy. Tulum wasn't finished. He walked closer and stood over Kesh.

"You will never win this war," Tulum declared. "Now, hand over the elixir." With that, Kesh was hoisted into the air again. Tulum yanked his left hand sideways. The motion sent Kesh flying up into the air again. This time he landed face-first on the ground.

Dazed and confused, Kesh knew he needed to get up, and he struggled to do so. He was digging as deep down in his soul as he could for any strength he could find. He could hear Tulum's footsteps closing in on him. Kesh bit down on his lip and willed his weak body to cooperate. Kesh kept his head near the ground, but when he was sure Tulum was close enough, he turned swiftly and used every ounce of energy he had left to jump to his feet. "Argh!" Kesh yelled as he bulldozed into his enemy at the perfect time.

Caught off guard, Tulum fell backward. Kesh wasted no time in attacking. He straddled Tulum, but Tulum bucked his body and easily threw Kesh to the side. Kesh rolled out of the way in the nick of time just as Tulum tried to pounce on him again. Kesh struggled to his feet and charged into Tulum. They fell in a heap, their arms and legs tangled. Both men grunted as they scrapped to get the best of the other. Kesh slammed his fists into Tulum's face, busting his mouth and temporarily slowing Tulum's attack. Kesh continued to reign punches down on Tulum. Tulum blocked many of the blows and was able to reach up and push Kesh's chin up. He then gripped Kesh's chin and turned his head, trying to snap his neck. The battle was intense, each king fighting for dominance, neither one giving an inch.

"Get off of him!" Calum shrieked, grabbing Kesh's collar and yanking it.

"No, you let go of *him*!" Vila stood with both of her hands out. "Don't touch my king, you bitch!"

Calum turned around slowly at the sound of Vila's voice. She laughed. She'd been waiting for the day when she could finally tear Vila's throat out of her neck.

"Well, if it isn't the little black slave of the Sefu Clan," Calum taunted, still holding on to Kesh's collar.

Vila charged over and grabbed Calum by the hair. "I said, let go of my king, you piece of white trash," Vila demanded. She dragged Calum down to the ground and away from Kesh. "I've been waiting to kick your ass for years!"

Calum raised her hands and dug her nails into the top of Vila's hands. But Vila wouldn't loosen her grasp on Calum's hair. "Agh!" Calum yelled as she struggled against Vila's death grip. Vila started twisting her hair at the roots. Calum could hear some of her hair being pulled right out at the roots.

Calum struggled to gain a solid footing as Vila continued to drag her. At one point Calum was able to plant her feet on the root of a tree and come to a stop. She bucked her body and flipped over so fast, Vila lost her grip on her hair. Vila looked at her own hands, surprised at how swiftly Calum was able to break free. Taking advantage of Vila's confusion, Calum swung her leg and kicked Vila across the face.

Vila flew up into the air and landed with a crunch. Dust flew up in her wake. The impact knocked the wind out of her. Temporarily weakened and struggling to regain her breath, Vila was vulnerable. Calum wasted no time attacking again, this time grabbing Vila by the hair. She was going to give Vila a taste of her own medicine.

"How does it feel to be dragged by your hair?" Calum snarled.

A shrill scream cut through the air just then and halted all the fighting. "Kesh! Help me!"

Kesh let go of Tulum and struggled to his knees. "Dira," he shouted, then fell down onto his chest at the sight of her. "Dira! No!" He reached out a weak hand.

Vila and Calum had paused in their fight too. They both turned in the direction of Dira's shrieks. Calum smiled at the sight of her. Vila was alarmed.

"Let her go," Kesh wheezed, barely able to get enough power behind his words. His strength was all but gone.

Two Malum Clan members were dragging Dira away. Kesh tried to move forward, but Tulum grabbed him and easily threw him back down on the ground. Vila tried to race forward too, but Calum jumped in front of her and blocked her path. Calum slammed Vila to the ground again and pounced on top of her immediately.

"Don't let them take me!" Dira cried out, stretching her arms toward Kesh as she was being dragged away. "Please!"

"You'll never save her. I told you, I'll never let you have a queen. Especially *her*," Tulum growled. With that, he used his power and blasted Kesh in the chest. Kesh lay flat on his back, barely breathing. He had no more strength. His body was finally giving out. Tulum kicked Kesh in the ribs. Kesh wheezed and gagged. He flipped himself over and tried to get on his knees, but Tulum kicked him again.

"Kesh!" Dira squealed.

Kesh felt his heart crumbling. He hadn't felt pain like that since he lost Adie. He inched forward, trying desperately to get to his love. He wouldn't make it if he didn't feed soon. He reached out a shaky hand toward Dira, but he was helpless. "Dira," he rasped. It was the last thing he said. He collapsed, and the world went dark.

"Get off of me," Adirah demanded, tugging her arms away from the two rival clan members who were dragging her. Tears ran down her face at the sight of Kesh, weakened and reduced to almost nothing.

Dira, dig down deep. You have the power inside of you to defeat them. Just dig down deep. He needs you. You can win this. You have gifts. He saved you. Now it is up to you. Dig down deep.

Adirah heard the voice, but she didn't know what it meant. . . . *Dig down deep?* she thought. She kicked and bucked her body, but still she was no match for her captors.

Whatever you think you can do, you will be able to do. Whatever you think you can do, you will be able to do.

"Shut up! Just tell me what to do!" Adirah screamed at the spirit that was speaking to her. "Just tell me!"

With her anger at the spirit welling up in her like a ripe geyser, Adirah squeezed her eyes shut and yanked her arms inward, toward her chest, with a power she didn't know existed in her five-foot-three-inch tall body. Suddenly, she fell forward, and the pressure on her arms had disappeared. She opened her eyes and was shocked when she realized she had broken away from the two strapping Malum Clan vampires.

"Wait? What?" Adirah looked at her hands, still amazed at herself. Then she looked at the two men, who were now trying to scramble up from the ground. "I did that?" she gasped, squeezing her hands and then relaxing them, as if she thought lightning bolts would shoot out of them. She inspected the rest of her body to see if there were any physical changes. Had she always had this strength and never knew?

"*Dira!*" the spirit called to her.

Adirah lifted her head, spurred to action once again. She didn't have much time to contemplate her new strength, as she had to get back and help Kesh. This was no time to stand around waiting for the Malum men to regain their bearings.

"Get her!" one of her captors barked. He and his partner had finally gotten to their feet.

Adirah raced around both captors with a speed that she couldn't understand. She moved so fast, both vampires got dizzy and fell back down.

"This is like a cartoon," she mumbled to herself. "Unreal."

Kesh had saved Adirah's life, and now it was time for Adirah to repay him for that deed. The tables had turned, and Adirah wasn't going to let her man down. Her little escape had bought her enough time to get back to Kesh without the Malum men interfering.

Adirah came bursting through the trees in time to see Calum pummeling Vila. "Argh!" Adirah yelled as she charged forward and dragged Calum off Vila. "Queen to queen," Adirah shouted as she punched Calum in her face.

Calum stumbled backward, holding her mouth. She was surprised by Adirah's attack. Calum looked at Adirah, wiped her mouth, and smiled. She might have underestimated the mortal. Adirah had escaped from the Malum men, so perhaps she would be a formidable foe. But not for long. Calum lifted her head, squinted her eyes into dashes, and ran straight for Adirah.

Adirah took off straight for Calum. They were on a collision course. They both jumped at the same time and slammed into each other. The impact shook the surrounding trees. The queens crashed into the earth with a violent thud. Both women lay on the ground, stunned. Adirah slowly rolled over and crawled toward Calum. When she got to Calum's side, Calum was moaning in agony. Adirah held her fist in the air, ready to unleash her full strength into Calum's face, but an unknown force stopped her.

"I got this now. Go look for Kesh," Vila shouted from a few feet away. She was holding out her hand in the direction of Adirah's fist. When Vila dropped her hand, Adirah felt a release of the tension surrounding her fist.

It took Adirah a few seconds to react. She couldn't believe that Vila wanted to work with her. The women made eye contact, and there was a moment of recognition by both women. A truce had been offered. The tiniest grin spread over Vila's lips.

"Go help our king! He's very weak!" Vila demanded, her voice high pitched and frantic. Adirah wasted no more time. She took off running. She quickly found her man. Tulum had a hold on Kesh's head and was dragging him across the dirt clearing in the woods. His body looked lifeless, like a stuffed doll. She swallowed hard at Kesh's bloodied face.

"Let him go," Adirah said through clenched teeth.

Tulum turned around and flashed an evil smile at her. "Or what, mortal girl?" he snarled. "You think you are more powerful than me?" He laughed at her.

"Or you'll be sorry," Adirah retorted, her chest heaving. The sight of Kesh in such bad condition had turned her into someone she didn't recognize.

Tulum started slowly advancing toward her. He laughed and flashed his fangs. He was taunting Adirah and was absolutely enjoying it.

He's not more powerful than you, Dira. You are the one with the gifts. You are the one they fear. They know you are more powerful than all of them.

Adirah took a deep breath, squeezed her eyes, and ran straight for Tulum. Tulum's jaw dropped and his head jerked up as Adirah sailed over his head. He clearly didn't expect her to have the same powers as vampires. Had she been turned? No matter. He would still destroy her.

"Impressive," Tulum said, raising his eyebrows. "Let's see what else you can do." He thrust his hands toward Adirah and sent her flying backward. She crashed into the ground. As she scurried to her feet, Tulum calmly advanced toward her. She rushed Tulum and launched herself at his throat. He easily swatted her aside. The instant she landed on the ground, he was at her side, kicking her in the ribs.

"Tulum! Enough!" Tiev yelled out.

Tulum whirled around so fast, his coat swung and slapped his legs. His eyes were wide at the sight of Tiev and an army of the Sefu Clan behind him. "Ah, finally a real challenge." Tulum smiled, then let out a roar. Within seconds the trees started to rustle and branches were cracking all around them. Then it became apparent that Tulum's roar had summoned the Malum army.

As the Malum appeared from the depths of the forest, Tiev yelled, "Sefu!" The two armies raced toward one another, and a ferocious battle ensued.

Adirah rushed over to Kesh and threw herself down at his side. He was barely conscious. "No . . . Kesh. Wake up." Adirah took his head in her hands and shook him gently. "Wake up." The fighting raging all around them.

Kesh groaned and tried to speak, but he was too weak. There was no glow left to his skin. In fact, Adirah swore she could see wrinkles cropping up on his face with every passing minute. Her heart pounded against her sternum.

"Tell me what to do, Kesh," she cried helplessly.

Adirah looked out at the bloody battle happening between the Sefu and Malum Clans. There was no one else left to help her king. It was up to her and her alone.

Dira, you can do it. You can save him. You have to believe you can do it.

"How?" Adirah whispered through her tears. "Tell me how?"

It's within you, Dira. You have the power.

"Kesh." Adirah shook him. "Tell me what you need. Tell me what to do to help you get your strength back. I'll do anything for you . . . anything," she pleaded, tears running down her cheeks.

Kesh's eyes closed, and his head lulled to the side.

"Help me!" Adirah screamed. "Help me save him." There was so much death and destruction swirling around her, no one paid any attention. Adirah hadn't felt this helpless since she'd watched her brother die at her feet. Her head spun with a tornado's eye of thoughts. She couldn't let another person she loved die like that. Her soul couldn't handle the burden of another preventable death.

"Please," she sobbed. "You can't leave me like this."

Vila approached her from behind. "He needs to feed," Vila huffed, kneeling down next to Adirah. The blood on her face was a reminder of the fierce battle raging. "He needs to feed now. If he doesn't, he will become too weak to feed at all, and that will be the end of him. That would be the end of all of us," Vila announced gravely.

"Wh-what? How?" Adirah stuttered. She couldn't even think. "Tell me how to feed him. What can we do? Get a bird? A small animal? Help me to understand," Adirah begged. She held Kesh's head like it was a piece of precious crystal.

"You have to let him drink from you, or he will perish," Vila said. "You're the only one here with human blood. With him being this weak, an animal's blood won't work. Human blood is the only thing that will suffice. He will have to turn you. . . ."

Vila's words sounded like they were coming out in slow motion. Adirah looked up at her desperately. She was hoping that she had heard Vila wrong. Hoping that there was some other way that Vila wasn't remembering.

"Do it! If you really love him, you will do it!" Vila barked. "You claim you love him as much as I do, so then do it!"

Adirah looked down into Kesh's face. "I . . . I . . . How?"

Vila scooped Kesh out of Adirah's arms, got behind him, and put him into a sitting position. Kesh's head fell forward, and his arms fell limply over Vila's.

"Kesh, c'mon. You need to feed." Vila shook him. "His heart is barely pumping anymore. Get down here. Hurry up. The clan won't be able to keep the Malum away much longer," Vila yelled at Adirah. They both looked over at the fierce battle still raging between the clans. Bodies were flying, limbs were snapping, and corpses lay on the ground.

"You can show your allegiance to our king right now. A real queen would do it. A real queen needs to be of the same kind as her king. Prove that you are his queen," Vila said, pressing, shooting Adirah an evil glare.

Something hitched in Adirah's mind, and she got a sense that something was off with Vila. She couldn't decipher Vila's intentions at that moment.

"Are you going to save him or wait for the Malum to kill us all?" Vila said.

Adirah shook off her suspicious thoughts. She couldn't worry anymore about whether Vila was trying to walk her into a trap or not. She had to save Kesh's life.

"I'm going to save him. I'm going to save our king," Adirah proclaimed. With that, she moved closer to Kesh's face. Tears streamed her cheeks. She was about to leave the life she knew, and there was no way to return, but she refused to let him die.

Vila made her body move in a way Adirah couldn't understand, but it jolted Kesh awake. He sucked in his breath, his eyes popped open, and his canines extended. He reached out and grabbed Adirah roughly. He wasn't himself. In that moment, he was a monster possessed. He held on to her roughly and drew her to his mouth. He breathed like a huge beast lived inside of him.

"Ah!" Adirah screamed, instinctively trying to pull away.

"Stay still! He's in an animal state right now, and he needs to bite you," Vila barked. "You said you would save him. . . . Now save him."

Adirah shook all over, but she closed her eyes and finally went as still as she could given the circumstances. Kesh sunk his teeth into the soft flesh of her neck and sucked and sucked and sucked. Adirah felt a hot, searing pain engulf her entire body. Her chest felt like it would explode. Her arms and legs went stiff, and her eyes rolled into the back of her head. The sound of her own heart thumped in her ears so loudly, she couldn't hear anything else. Not even Kesh's animal noises. Her body bucked, and white foam spilled from the sides of her mouth.

There's no turning back now. You're one of them now. Your gifts are at stake. You can't turn back. You can't change back. Life eternal. Hell eternal. You're one of them now. Dira. Dira. Dira.

The spirit voices swirled in her head, and Kesh's howling screams filled her ears.

In that moment, Adirah saw her brother Adolphis. He was smiling and waving her on.

Her parents were there too. They were running in a field of flowers. They were also waving her on. Adirah giggled and turned. Addis was behind her, laughing and playing. She waved to him. He started following her, she followed her parents, and her parents followed Adolphis.

"Dira, we are all together again. You brought us all back together again," Adolphis said, turning and reaching for her. She finally grabbed his hand. The power inside of him jolted through her, and he laughed. His laugh turned from happy to sinister all within a few seconds. "I finally got you to follow me," Adolphis said, but he sounded just like her father.

"Dira! Dira! Dira!"

She heard her name being called from different directions. Then she fell into darkness. Adirah knew at that moment she was dead.

Chapter 13

"Lay her down," Kesh demanded, his voice high pitched and frantic. The Sefu Clan members who were carrying Dira rushed past him and into his room in a flurry. They gently placed her down on Kesh's bed. "Everybody out," Kesh demanded, pushing his way through his people. "I want to be alone with her."

"Kesh, let me—" Vila began, but Kesh threw his hand up in her face, halting her words.

"I don't know what was more important to you, Vila, saving me or making sure Dira turned. You know I love her and I didn't want to turn her. You were dying for the opportunity to make it so that I had to turn her. You let your own jealousy rule you, and I hate you for that. Now leave," Kesh spat cruelly.

A pin-drop silence fell over the room. Time seemed to stand still. Vila's head jerked back, as if Kesh had thrown holy water in her face.

"I saved you, King. I needed to—"

"Leave!" Kesh boomed, the vein at his temple visibly throbbing. Everyone in the room seemed shocked, and they stared at Kesh and Vila with wide eyes and agape mouths. "I said, leave!" Kesh bellowed, his upper lip raised and his fangs showing.

Vila's face reddened, and tears sprang to her eyes. She stumbled backward, with her hands up in surrender. "You don't know what you've done, *King*," she rasped. Black blood tears streaked down her cheeks. She turned swiftly and ran from the room, her cries trailing her.

"Everyone out, I said," Kesh mumbled, massaging his aching temples. He heard the disapproving grumbles and hushed murmurs from his clan, but he didn't care. Everything he wanted was lying on the bed behind him. He'd seen decades and decades of living fade away when he finally saw Dira lying on the ground, lifeless. Kesh didn't know what was worse—being on the brink of death or watching his greatest love fight for her life now.

Kesh knew better than anyone the pain of transitioning. It was another realm of being. The body fought the process as hard as it could. The vampire code was relentless in its attack on the mortal form. The converting of DNA from mortal to vampire was an agonizing process that caused physical as well as mental transformation. The person's instincts went from human to animalistic. The organs in the body needed to adjust to the new blood being pumped through the body. The red blood cells became black.

When the room was finally empty, Kesh went to the side of the bed. He looked down at Dira's stiff, pale body. Kesh's lips trembled, and a hard knot lodged in his throat. He kneeled at her side, took her limp hand into his, and pressed it against his forehead.

"God, why?" A sob bubbled to his lips as he felt the rigidity settling into her cold fingers. "Dira, my queen. Submit, please," Kesh cried. "I need you." He couldn't stand to see her blue lips and pale skin. It had been more than three hours, and there still hadn't been any change, no sign of the transition. Her mortal side was putting up a valiant fight. If the fight went on without a resolution, there would be a point of no return and the outcome was death.

"C'mon," he whispered, moving her hand to his lips and planting a kiss on top of it, like he had when they first met.

Kesh felt the dam of his resolve cracking with each passing minute. He moved up on the bed and laid his head on Dira's chest. He listened for any sign of life. Silence. Just like her hands, her chest was stiff.

"Agh!" The screams burst from Kesh like lava out of a volcano. For the first time in centuries, he wept openly, without regard for what anyone would think or say about him as a man or about his display of weakness. His shoulders vibrated with wracking sobs, and tears drenched his face. "Dira! I need you!"

Kesh had been through this type of grief centuries ago, when he lost Adie, and still he wasn't prepared to deal with it again. Kesh knew now why it had taken him so long to fall in love again. He hated to experience the pain of loss over and over. He felt like someone had stuck their hand into his chest and snatched his heart out . . . for good this time.

"Dira, please. I know you can do it." Kesh sniffled and closed his eyes. He hadn't prayed in decades. When he was still a slave, he believed in the white man's religion, but when he turned, Kesh never believed in a higher power again. He'd seen true evil in the dark world of vampirism. He'd been a leader in that world before, killing mortals with reckless regard for life. Kesh had lost faith in everything good. He didn't believe any God would allow that type of evil to exist. But now Kesh felt so helpless, he mumbled a silent prayer under his breath. He called on his old higher power. He'd given up being evil, so why couldn't his prayer matter?

Kesh opened his eyes and looked at his love again. No change. Kesh inhaled and exhaled, trying to gain some composure. He had to pull it together for her and his clan. The pain was so raw, he felt like he'd die for good if Dira didn't make it. *Maybe that would be best*, he thought.

Kesh heard the members of his clan abuzz outside of the room. He knew they were all worried about him. Kesh wanted to stay angry at Vila for making Dira sacrifice herself to save him, but he understood why Vila had done it. He couldn't remember everything, but Tiev had told him that his death was imminent before Dira let him feed on her.

Kesh looked at Dira's stiff form now and shook his head pitifully. His heart ached and his head pounded from the emotional roller coaster he was on. What would his life be like now if she didn't make the transition? He wished he could tell her how to accept her new fate, but he knew she was stuck somewhere in the crossover from life to eternal existence. In that stage, Kesh realized, she could easily choose final death. The line was that fine. The thought of that made his insides churn until he was sick. He leaned over the trash can next to the bed and threw up, purging all the emotion and guilt that he was storing deep in his soul.

After washing his mouth with mouthwash, he came back to Dira's side and took her hand. As he quietly wept, he gently stroked her forehead. She lay motionless. Even though he wasn't sure if she could hear him, he began speaking to her.

"Dira, I'm so sorry. I didn't want this for you," he said between the hiccups of his sobs. "This is all my fault. I was supposed to protect you from all harm. I was supposed to be your king. I wanted you to be able to live, to love, and to choose your own fate. I didn't want to force this life . . . this eternal existence on you like this." Kesh shook his head and swiped at the black blood tears running in jagged lines down his face. "Just come back to me. If you do, I promise, I'll never let anything happen to you for all eternity. We will be together forever, I promise."

"Has she turned yet?"

Kesh was startled. He hadn't heard anyone enter the room, and his instructions were for everyone to leave him alone. He turned to find Tiev approaching from behind, limping from his battle injuries. He was the one person whom Kesh needed to see at the moment. Tiev was his brother-in-arms, his confidant.

Kesh looked at Tiev through his red-rimmed and swollen eyes. "They should've let me die," Kesh croaked, shaking his head in despair. "I didn't want this for her. We can't control how this will turn out . . . what kind of vampire she will be. What if she doesn't transition? What if the evil ones get her on the other side? And, her gifts . . . She will lose her mortal gifts."

Tiev put his hand on Kesh's shoulder and squeezed it. "We've had to sacrifice mortals to save kings before, Kesh. This wasn't the first time, and it won't be the last time. It was unavoidable. We couldn't let you perish in the battle, or else the Malum would have won. The fate of the whole clan rested on Dira's shoulders. Therefore, no matter how it turns out, she will always be our queen. Just like you, she gave everything for the clan. And she will have a new set of gifts. The problem is, the Malum know that she has gifts. They've known all along. If she was a target then, she's more of a target now. We will spend the rest of eternity fighting to protect her and you. The running will never end."

Tiev went on. "I fear that the Sefu Clan is in a worse position now than we were before. Tulum and Calum were defeated this time, but they weren't destroyed. They'll heal, and they'll come back stronger than ever next time.

We've lost some key people, and they know that you're weakness is Dira. I'm afraid our hope of living in peace is all a fantasy now. There will never be peace," Tiev said and lowered his gaze to the floor solemnly.

"There's one thing I have to tell you, Tiev," Kesh said, letting go of Dira's hand and standing up.

Tiev looked at him and tilted his head. "What is it, Kesh?"

Kesh looked at Dira one last time and then turned back to Tiev. "Walk with me, friend."

Tiev followed Kesh to the other side of the room, away from the bedside. Kesh swallowed hard and shook his head.

"What is it, Kesh? You don't look good."

"When I fed from her, I . . . it . . . she's . . ." Kesh fumbled over his words. He closed his eyes, inhaled, and exhaled a windstorm of breath. He struggled to bring himself to tell Tiev what he knew. He didn't want to believe it himself.

"Tell me," Tiev insisted, his brows knitted together in confusion.

"Dira is—"

Suddenly a shrill scream cut through the air. Kesh spun around, unbalanced. His words went tumbling back down his throat like hard marbles, and his jaw dropped until his mouth hung open. Tiev's eyebrows shot up into arches, and he jerked around toward the piercing sound.

"Dira?" Kesh gasped, rushing over to the bed. "Tiev, help me!" Kesh called out.

Kesh tried to grab Dira, but her body twitched and bucked spasmodically. Kesh couldn't get a hold on her. He stepped back to get a clear picture and figure out how to help his love. His eyes went round and his hands shook as he watched Dira's head twist and jerk and her shoulders tremble like she was having a seizure.

"Dira!" Kesh gasped, reaching out to her again.

Tiev tried in vain to pull Kesh back. "No. Leave her be. You know she has to go through it," Tiev barked, holding Kesh in a bear hug.

"Let me go, Tiev. I have to help her!"

"You can't! You know this already," Tiev replied, holding Kesh even tighter.

"I can't stand to watch her in pain like this," Kesh whimpered, his muscles so tense, they felt like knotted balls of rope all over his body.

"We've all gone through it, Kesh. It's a natural process. At least you know she submitted to the transition and she will be back in your arms soon. You will have your queen, Kesh. Queen Dira will be good for all of us," Tiev said.

Dira made a guttural animal sound. Kesh turned his face away, but he could still hear her fighting the transition. She screamed again.

Then Kesh heard the vomit spewing from her mouth and hitting the floor. He gagged and doubled over. He could almost feel every ounce of her pain. Dira hissed and spit and beat her fists on the bed as everything inside of her changed. Kesh was happy she'd turned, but he was afraid of what she might become.

Adirah collapsed on the floor, exhausted. The violent shaking of her body had tossed her right off the bed and onto the floor. She shivered. She'd never felt so cold in her life. Her chest rose and fell heavily. Every inch of her ached, even her ears.

"Dira?" Kesh said.

Adirah's eyes shot open. She planted her palms on the floor and hoisted her body up. Her legs felt like two limp noodles. She growled low in her throat, and her eyes flashed with fire.

"Dira, it's okay. You're okay," Kesh said, reaching for her.

She recoiled from his touch.

"Tiev, leave us. Let me help her. Go tell the others that she has transitioned. We need to prepare things for her. She'll need to feed right away," Kesh huffed, his words rushing out in heavy, exasperated breaths. As he spoke, he never took his eyes off her.

"What happened to me?" Adirah asked, her voice hoarse. "What did you do to me? What did you do to me?" Her voice rose ten octaves with each question. Adirah's eyes were wild, feral. Her fingers were bent, resembling claws. She tried to straighten them, but they wouldn't move. Her muscles felt tight, and her insides felt like they'd been through a meat grinder. She was definitely different now. She felt a hunger inside that was animalistic.

"Let me explain, Dira. Let me help you," Kesh said, gently touching her arm.

Adirah jumped back from his touch so far, she flew into the wall behind her. She hit it and slid down to the floor, dazed. She groaned. She was confused as to how she had flown against the wall. Had Kesh pushed her? She felt that she had retreated from him and had been in control, but then how had she traveled so far? She hadn't put that much effort behind her retreat. She had begun to feel stronger before transitioning, but this was a new level.

Kesh rushed over and grabbed her. He pulled her into his arms. "Dira, you have to get used to your new existence," he said, rocking her. "It will take some time, and I will help you. I will teach you how to live this new life."

Adirah pushed him away. Kesh wasn't prepared and was unable to anchor himself. He
went flying. He was surprised. Adirah was stronger than any newly turned vampire he'd ever
encountered.

"Get off of me." She scrambled up from the
floor, her nostrils flaring. "What did you do
to me?" she screamed, the veins in her neck
cording against her skin. "You knew you'd do
this to me all along. You set me up."

Kesh got to his feet. "Listen to me. I'm trying
to explain to you what has happened. I would
never do anything to hurt you. I didn't want this
for you, Dira. I swear it."

"Want what, Kesh? What has happened?"
Adirah stared at him, waiting for him to say what
she already suspected. She looked down at her
breasts. She ran her hands over the flat of her stomach and over her hips. "Whose body is this?"
She shook her head.

"It's yours, Dira. Your new one. You've turned.
You're one of us now."

"No!" Adirah yelled. "Why did you do this
to me? You lied to me. You told me you would
protect me."

Kesh pulled her into his arms and held her
tight. "I didn't do it, Dira. You did it to save my
life, just like I saved yours. It was our fate. This
was meant to happen. From day one, it was

meant to be. You were always going to be my queen. Nothing about that has changed. You are Dira, queen of the Sefu Clan."

Adirah melted against him and sobbed. "So I'm . . . I'm dead?"

"No, Dira. You're more alive now than you've ever been," he whispered as he stroked her hair and planted kisses on top of her head. "You are my queen, and the child that you carry is the heir to our greatness. We will be fruitful, as it is written in the books," Kesh said.

Adirah pulled away and looked Kesh in his eyes. "What do you mean? What child? How do you know?"

Kesh put his finger on her lips. "Shh. When I fed on you, I tasted the freshness of the blood. It is coursing through your body. I can feel it. I can hear it. When you lay stiff and your own heart was frozen, the life you carry still lived. It is our way. There are only a few of us that can reproduce like mortals. This was written long ago. Dira, you will bring forth the life of a child born of a mortal and a vampire. That is one of the greatest gifts on earth. The child will be heir to everything great. But we have to protect you both, Dira. There will be many who won't be happy about this. Even many among us won't understand it. We will have to go away before they find out about this."

Adirah closed her eyes and touched her belly. She inhaled and exhaled, saddled with the weight of what she had just heard. She was a vampire, and she carried a vampire life inside of her.

Chapter 14

Kesh closed the door behind him and stepped into the hallway. Many of the clan members were milling about. Some were leaning against the wall, others were sitting on the floor, and a few were down the hall, in an intense discussion. The tension was thick.

When Tiev saw Kesh, he rushed over to him. Kesh held up his hand. "She's resting now. She will need to feed soon. I have so much work to do, Tiev."

"We have to talk, Kesh," Tiev said, pinching the bridge of his nose.

"What is it?"

"The mortal girl . . . the one who broke in with Narum. She escaped while the clan was gone at the battle," Tiev said gravely.

"Why would I be worried about one little girl?" Kesh shrugged. "Vila will find her."

Tiev sighed. "That's the other thing I wanted to tell you. Vila is gone. She has denounced our clan and run off."

Tiev's words exploded in Kesh's ears like tiny bombs. Kesh's eyes flashed with fire. His nails extended and his fangs came out—all the things that he couldn't control when he was furious. The disloyalty shown by Vila in a time of utmost importance was a treasonous act against the clan. Kesh sensed it could destroy the entire fabric of their universe.

"I made her," Kesh growled. "She can never escape from me. She is indebted to me. She can't just denounce our clan."

"If she turns on you, there are ways for her to be free from you, and she can pledge allegiance to someone else. Kesh, this could prove disastrous for us. Vila knows everything about us. Her betrayal could completely destroy us," Tiev said, hanging his head. "You should've done a better. . . ."

"What!" Kesh boomed, getting in Tiev's face. "I should've done a better what?" Kesh hissed.

Tiev stepped back a few paces. "Listen, King, I don't want to get into a battle with you. We are in enough crises right now. We need to stick together."

"You have the power to find Vila. Use it," Kesh demanded.

"Vila knows that we can connect with her. She's not stupid, Kesh. You know this better than anyone. She won't be somewhere where I can sniff her out or enter her thoughts. I'm telling you, Kesh. She's gone. We will have to be worried about Vila turning on us, worried about the Lina girl gathering up her vampire hunters, and worried about the Malum rebuilding their clan with more newly turned vampires. Kesh, you and Dira are in grave danger. We could be facing attacks from all sides. You'll have to go away now. We can't follow you. It'll bring too much attention. I'm afraid you will have to give up being king of the clan right now. You'll have to hide away . . . for the sake of us all."

"Argh!" Kesh slammed his fists through the wall. "When you find Vila, you bring her to me. I will be the one to handle her. And I'll decide if I want to go away. You concentrate on our enemies."

Adirah awoke to Kesh shaking her. She smiled up at him. She had been in and out of sleep and consciousness for two days. The transition had taken a toll on her body. She needed time to adjust and replenish her energy.

"Dira, we have to go away for a little while," he whispered gruffly.

Adirah sat up, still dazed from her deep sleep. "What's wrong, Kesh?"

"Something has come up, and we need to leave tonight."

"But I can't. My classes . . . school . . . my life." She fumbled over her words.

"All that has changed now, Dira. We have to protect you and the baby. There are others who don't want to see us together. They don't want you to bring this life into the world," Kesh said, his words rushing out in a string of breaths. "Now let's go."

Adirah couldn't think. She was being asked to make huge life decisions in a matter of seconds. It was all happening too fast. Everything around her had been upended. Two days ago, she had been a college freshman with big hopes and dreams. It seemed like overnight she'd been turned into a beast, a monster she didn't recognize. Now this.

The first night Kesh had taken her to feed, but Adirah couldn't bring herself to bite her victim—a young college guy who'd stumbled out of a well-known campus dive bar. It had taken some prodding from Kesh and her body getting weak for her finally to do it. At Kesh's urging, Adirah had walked right up to the guy, and she had immediately noticed his baby face and the peach-fuzz beard on his chin.

"You all right?" she'd asked, moving in front of the driver's side door of his car.

The guy's car keys jingled with every stagger-ing step he took. He laughed and scowled at her almost simultaneously. When his blurry eyes were finally able to focus on her, he sneered at her. "Who the hell are you? Don't come giving me no lecture about designated driving and that crap," the guy slurred. "Move . . . move out of my way. I'm driving my-myself."

"Now, Dira," Kesh whispered from a distance. "You have to strike now."

The guy staggered and turned around so fast, he wobbled sideways. "Who's there? Fu . . . fuck going on—" the guy began, barely able to keep his balance. Before he could finish, Adirah rushed into him and pushed him. The guy's reflexes were so impaired by the alcohol that he was unable to get his hands in front of him to absorb the impact, and he landed face-first on the ground. His cheek was split open by the impact.

"Wha . . . what are you . . . ?" the guy stammered as Adirah dragged him out of sight. "Help!" He struggled and tried to scream, but his efforts were short lived.

Adirah straddled him. The smell of blood leaking from his cheek flipped a switch inside of her, and she covered his mouth with her hands and sank her fangs into his neck. Just like Kesh had taught her. The guy's body thrashed. Adirah was able to keep him under control, and within seconds the loss of blood rendered him too weak to continue fighting. Adirah's eyes had rolled up in her head as she drank the guy's blood. Her insides had warmed up until she felt almost orgasmic. Kesh had warned her that feeding on mortals could become addictive. Every nerve ending in Adirah's body had come alive and tingled. This was how she imagined she would feel if a high-powered drug had been introduced into her nervous system. Adirah growled, and her heart pounded so hard, her head felt light. When she was finished, Adirah felt so powerful, she thought she could run a marathon and move mountains.

As she sat next to the lifeless body she had just fed from, Kesh approached his queen. "You okay?" he asked.

"This . . . this blood thirst . . . does it ever go away?" Adirah asked. She looked down at her hands, which were covered in blood, and wondered if she'd ever get used to the superhuman power she possessed now. It was greater than when she'd been saved by Kesh's blood after the fire.

Adirah snapped out of the memory of her first feed. "Where are we going?" she asked.

"I will find a safe place for us, Dira," Kesh huffed, slight frustration lacing his words. "We just have to go now. I have to make sure you're safe." He checked the lock on his vampire chest, which again held the elixir, hoisted it under his arm, and pulled the door open to let Adirah go out before him. He paused, a strangled look on his face. His body went stiff, and he raised his head, as if he were sniffing the air, sensing something.

"Kesh, what is it?" Adirah asked, but her words were short lived.

Kesh was snatched through the doorway before Adirah could react.

"Kesh!" Adirah screamed, but she did not get a chance to say anything else. Suddenly everything around her went black. She opened her mouth to scream, but the black hood that had been thrown over her head muffled the sound.

"You will not bring a pure vampire life into the world," a familiar voice said. "You will not have a legacy that doesn't belong to you. I will destroy all of you. I will have my revenge."

Adirah recognized the voice. She struggled to break free but couldn't overpower her captor. She realized that she needed to stay as calm as possible if she was going to escape. She tried to get her thoughts together and muster the strength she needed to save herself, Kesh, and their baby.

Adirah was slammed on the back of her head with what felt like a baseball bat, but it was probably just a vampire punching her. The wind was knocked out of her when her body landed with a thud. Adirah could smell that she was in the presence of other vampires.

"Let's go! We have to get her out of here," Adirah heard the familiar voice say. Before she could react, she was kicked in the head and her world went black.

Kesh's head was covered, and the strong scent of incense obscured his usual sharp sense of smell. He tried to move but realized his wrists were chained. The pure silver chains were attached to the wall that Kesh was leaning against. He winced with every movement, the silver burning into his flesh.

Kesh listened, and even in his weakened state, he felt his insides churning with rage. He recognized the voices around him, and if he could have gotten free, he would've killed them all with his bare hands. Some of his own clan had turned on him. Kesh listened to them, and with each passing moment, his heart broke and his anger grew deeper and deeper.

"But it is against the vampire laws to kill one of our own," a familiar male voice said. "The rest of the clan won't agree to this. They are loyal to our king."

"They will all have a change of heart once they realize the key to reproduction lies in his blood," a familiar female voice replied. "A fact that our so-called king hid from us. He wanted to be the only one who could procreate."

Kesh felt like his heart would burst through his chest. He couldn't believe this betrayal.

Vila! How could you? After all I've done for you. How could you?

"The key to our future is in his blood. He has to have known the whole time, but he didn't think enough of us to reveal it. Instead, he reproduced with a mortal. That is dangerous! She is dangerous! She will become so strong and so deadly that she will turn on us," Vila continued, trying to convince some of the other clan members to stay on her side. "That is why he has been searching for a mate for so long. We will have no choice but to drink from him. We could all gain the ability to reproduce without turning mortals. We won't need a king. He's shown us time and time again that he values power more than our lives. He let the Malum keep us on the run, and when the battle happened, where was he? Weak and unable to fight."

Hushed murmurs and grumbles of agreement resounded around Kesh. He listened as the others agreed with Vila, and he was enraged. Kesh bucked against the restraints, and pain rippled through his arms. He winced, and his entire body trembled.

"Ah, I think our king wants us to talk to him," Vila taunted. She finally snatched the hood from Kesh's head. She laughed in his face at the sight of the once powerful king unable to break free from his shackles. "Look at you . . . the almighty Kesh, king of the Sefu Clan," Vila spat. "You don't look so mighty now, do you?"

"You . . . you're making a big mistake," Kesh growled. "Vila, I . . . I am your maker. You can't do this to me."

"Shut up!" Vila boomed, throwing holy water on Kesh's bare chest. "Shut your mouth!"

"Aghh!" Kesh shrieked. His flesh burned where the holy water had made contact. Kesh could hear it sizzling like a strip steak on a hot plate at a steak house.

"All these years of being loyal to you, loving you, letting you fuck me whenever you wanted, you never looked at me like I was more than your *worker* . . . a little loyal slave. I've killed for you, and at one point I would've even died for you. But that never meant a thing to

you. *She* is the only thing that you care about.
A disgusting mortal girl who didn't even want
you. Now she will be the thing that destroys
you," Vila hissed, her words loaded like a cannon
ready to destroy its target.

"W-where is Dira?" Kesh managed to ask.
"Have you hurt her?"

Kesh screamed in agony when Vila tossed
more holy water on his body. He could feel his
skin melting away. He clenched his jaw and
absorbed the pain. He looked Vila in her eyes,
daring her to throw more holy water on him.
Pure hatred beamed from Vila's eyes. She flung
more holy water across his chest. Kesh tried
unsuccessfullly to mute his scream. As he flung
his head to the side, his eyes darted over to a
table covered with wooden stakes.

"Even now, in pain and about to die, the only
thing you care about is her," Vila said, hurt evident behind her words. "That's the only way to
hurt you, isn't it? After all this time, you finally
have a weakness. Well, prepare to be in a world
of hurt forever." Vila walked over to the table
and picked up the longest of the wooden stakes.

"You will not get away with this once the rest
of the clan finds me. Tiev will—"

Vila laughed hysterically. "Tiev? Oh yeah,
about him . . ."

Just then, two defectors dragged Tiev's limp body into Kesh's line of sight.

"No! Tiev!" Kesh growled so loud the room almost shook.

Vila let out a loud, evil cackle. "Oh, wait. But what about her?"

Adirah was dragged out, a knife to her throat and silver chains around her wrists and feet. The men holding her roughly pushed her down to the floor. Her lifeless body was splayed out at their feet. Kesh couldn't tell if she was dead or alive.

"Dira!" Kesh hollered. He turned his blazing gaze to Vila. "What do you want? I'll give you what you want. Just let them go."

"Well, King Kesh, you have something that the rest of us need. We have all looked to you as our leader for so long, thinking you were this great being. But in all actuality, we all could be great beings. All we have to do is drink your blood to be stronger. Isn't that right, Dira?" Vila spat. With that, she turned and kicked Dira in the ribs. "It was your best friend, Tiev, who told me about your ability to make pure vampires. He said that once the clan drinks from you, we'll all be just as powerful," Vila added.

"It's not true," Kesh rasped. "That's just a myth."

"Liar!" she snarled, and this time she took the wooden stake in her hand and put the pointy tip at the center of Kesh's chest. She pushed it just enough for Kesh to feel the pressure. Any harder and it would have penetrated his flesh. Kesh looked her in the eyes again. The betrayal he was experiencing was worse than any physical pain he would endure.

"Once I am done drinking from you, I will kill you with this stake, after it has been soaked in your own blood." Vila walked over to Dira and pointed the same wooden stake at her growing belly. "And then I will destroy your offspring," Vila said.

Through all Vila's taunting of Kesh, Adirah desperately tried to move. Something was keeping her paralyzed. Was it the silver handcuffs or some unknown force? She didn't have enough experience or knowledge as a vampire to understand any of it. As Vila pressed the wooden stake into her belly, Adirah looked at Kesh. Their eyes met for a second. No words needed to be said; their love was evident.

Vila raised the stake above her head.

"No!" Kesh screamed out.

Adirah closed her eyes. It was the only way her body could protect itself. Voices immediately filled her head. Tears danced down her face,

and her mind raced. Suddenly she was back at
Adolphis's funeral. She could smell the embalm-
ing fluid and the scent of dead roses. The funeral
home was packed, and most of the people there
had come from the media and the neighborhood
to see the little boy who'd been murdered by
his father. Adirah sat in the front row, huddled
between her mother and her baby brother, Addis.
Tears streamed down her face. A voice told her
to stand up and walk to Adol's casket. Within
seconds, Adirah felt like someone was standing
next to her. She heard her brother's voice loud
and clear.

*I never wanted to leave you. I just wanted
him to stop hurting her. But all that did was
hurt her more. You have to promise to protect
them all. You're the hope for our future, Dira.
Dira, you're our queen.*

With that, her brother was gone. At that moment, way back then, Adirah realized that the
worst thing that could ever happen to a mother
was to lose her child.

"But the king will die first, and then we will
publicly torture your queen for all the clan to
see." Vila's voice was like a foghorn wailing in
Adirah's ears. She snapped back to the present.
Her eyes shot wide open in time to see Vila, with
the stake over her head, spin around and rush

toward Kesh. Adirah instantly kicked the legs out from under the clan member standing next to her. The commotion didn't slow Vila. Adirah was able to launch herself at Vila. She slammed into her back, knocking the stake out of Vila's hand.

Vila skidded to the floor and landed right in front of Kesh. Kesh swung his legs out and caught Vila around the chest. He locked his ankles and squeezed his thighs.

"You bastard!" Vila screamed. "Get him off of me!" She called for the other clan members. They started to advance on Kesh.

"If you save us, I will spare your lives," Kesh promised them. "You cannot live a good life if you turn on your own king," he said.

The clan members stopped advancing. They contemplated his words and weighed their options. In an instant, they pounced on Vila like a lion pride on helpless prey.

Finally free, Adirah stumbled to Kesh. They became locked in an embrace but were barely strong enough to hold it.

"We have to go. We have to save the baby," Adirah told him.

"I can't leave Tiev," Kesh said.

"Your own clan has turned on you. You have no choice. You don't know whom to trust," Adirah said. "Think about us." She touched her belly.

Kesh took her hand. "We have to fight to survive."

Kesh ran over to Tiev, who was still splayed on the floor. The first thing Kesh did was check for a pulse. It was weak, but it was there. Kesh hoisted Tiev over his shoulder. Clan members were rushing about. "Gather what you can. Take care of the wounded." Kesh bellowed the command. A war was coming, the Malum Clan was regrouping, and now Kesh didn't know whom in his clan he could trust. His priority now was his queen and the baby she was carrying.

Kesh grabbed Adirah's hand and led her through the maze of hallways and doors in the underground lair. There was a flurry of activity all around. The signal had been given that it was time to move on to the next location. Kesh knew it was the right thing to do, but he also knew that eventually they would have to stand and fight the Malum. It would be the final battle between the two clans, and the winner would take all.

Just before they reached the exit, Kesh stopped one of the younger clan members, Edon. "Tell the others to meet in the forest. At the crest of the tallest mountain to the north. The elders will know the place."

"Yes, my king." Edon ran off to deliver the message.

Kesh and Adirah raced out of the lair and into the cover of the thick forest. Tiev was slumped over Kesh's shoulder. Adirah followed her king, trusting that he would lead her to safety. With each step, she was getting farther away from her old life, the life she had dreamed of and worked so hard for.

The deeper they got in the forest, the thicker the cover got and the stiller the air became. There was an eerie quietness to their surroundings, which made Adirah uncomfortable. Her senses were tingling on high alert. She was preparing for a sneak attack by the Malum at any moment. She heard a few branches snap off to her right.

"Kesh. Did you hear that? I'm afraid we're being followed."

"Don't worry, my queen. The Malum are too weak right now to mount an attack."

"But what if it's one of our clan who've turned on you?"

"They already know where we are headed."

Tiev made a quiet moaning noise.

"He doesn't look good, Kesh."

Kesh took Tiev off his shoulder and rested him against a tree trunk. His eyes were closed, and his head was slumped forward. The Malum had tortured him within an inch of his life.

"He needs to feed," Kesh said.

"Where will we find anyone all the way out here?"

"We won't. It's not the same or as potent, but we need to find him some animal blood."

"Like a squirrel? Gross." Adirah scrunched her nose.

"Not enough blood. Something bigger. Stay with Tiev. I'll go hunting."

"Okay." Adirah nodded.

Kesh kissed her forehead, then went running in the direction that Adirah had heard the branches breaking. She hoped he wasn't running into a group of waiting Malum. Once he was out of sight, Adirah sat beside Tiev and leaned her back against the same tree. The sun was emitting its last rays of light before tucking behind the horizon. The faint light was trying to shine through the trees. A few rays made it through and illuminated the forest floor.

Adirah looked around the lush forest. Not one sign of life—no insects, no birds, no critters. She wondered if Kesh would find anything to help feed Tiev. She looked at the failing man beside her.

"Tiev?" She waited for a response.

No sign of acknowledgment from Tiev.

"Tiev. Can you hear me?"

This time a faint sound came from Tiev.

"Tiev. Tiev." She gently took his head in her hands. "It's me. It's Dira." In an attempt to hear him, she raised his head. She was shocked at how gaunt he looked. "Can you hear me?" she asked.

His eyelids fluttered. He was trying to open his eyes. Again, he mumbled something inaudible.

"I don't understand. Just hold on. Kesh will be back with blood. Just hold on."

His eyes were unable to stay open, but he was still mumbling something.

Adirah put her ear close to his mouth. "Are you saying Vila? What about Vila?" she asked. "Can you open your eyes? Look at me, Tiev." She wanted to try to read his thoughts, but she needed to look into his eyes to do so.

As she was trying to get him to open his eyes, Kesh came dashing through the trees, dragging a deer by its antlers. The deer was badly wounded. The low guttural moan coming from the deer was painful for Adirah to hear.

"I think this is what you heard earlier," Kesh said. "Here. Let me put this deer next to Tiev." He motioned for Adirah to move from her spot. She gently let go of Tiev and then jumped up. Kesh laid the deer down, then positioned himself behind Tiev. He wrapped his arms around Tiev's chest. He then did some awkward movement.

This was the same movement that Vila had done when she got Kesh to turn so he could feed on Adirah. The same result happened with Tiev. His eyes burst open, his fangs came out, and he went right for the throat of the deer. He hungrily sucked on the deer's neck. The blood covered his mouth and cheeks, and he looked like a baby messily eating ice cream.

When he was done feeding, Tiev leaned his head back against the tree. A content, satisfied look appeared on his face. The lifeless deer lay next to him, its dark eyes wide open, staring into the abyss. Its neck fur was stained with its own blood.

"Thank you," Tiev said.

"How do you feel?" Kesh asked.

"Weak."

"The deer blood won't be enough to sustain you. We need to get you to the clan," Kesh said.

"I know."

"Do you think you have the strength to walk? I can still carry you, if you need."

"No, my king. I will walk. Help me up." Tiev reached out his hand.

Kesh grabbed his hand and helped him to stand. Tiev was unsteady on his feet. It took him a second to get his legs under him.

Tiev inhaled a deep breath, then said, "Lead the way, my king."

All three continued the trek north to meet the rest of the clan. It was slow going. Tiev needed to take numerous breaks during the hike. Adirah was growing impatient with each break. She would feel much better once they were surrounded by their own clan. Being in the forest with Kesh and a weakened Tiev made her feel vulnerable. She knew Kesh would put up a fight, but they'd just been through so much that everyone needed some time to recover.

"Tiev, is there any way you can go a little faster?" she asked during one of their breaks.

"Dira," Kesh scolded, "he is moving as fast as he can. The deer blood does not have the same effect as mortal blood."

"No, my king. She's right. I will pick up the pace for my queen." Tiev got to his feet from his sitting position. "No more breaks."

"This way," said Kesh as he stared straight at Adirah.

They made it to their destination sometime in the middle of the night. When they broke through the trees surrounding the camp, all the clan gathered around them. There were some members who were still too wounded to move, so they remained where they were.

Edon stepped forward. "My king, I gathered the clan, as you requested. Many are still wounded and need to recover."

"I see. Great work, Edon." Kesh bowed his head.

Edon, clearly pleased, smiled and bowed in reverence.

"Someone tend to Tiev," Kesh commanded. "He is in need of mortal blood."

Three clan members came over to carry Tiev to a designated area of the camp. It was a makeshift medic area. All the wounded were gathered in this corner.

Adirah was sensing an energy in the camp that didn't seem right. It was faint, but it was there. She looked around at the clan members. She was looking for any sign, perhaps an aura that was off or a clan member who looked out of place. Nothing seemed out of the ordinary. Kesh looked at his queen.

"What's wrong, Dira?"

"Something's not right." She looked at Kesh.

"I sense it too," Kesh answered, looking around the camp.

"Can you see any changes?"

"It is muddled with all the wounded. Everyone's aura is out of whack." She shook her head.

Kesh beckoned Edon with a nod of his head. "Edon, did you sense any hesitation from any of the clan members to come to the camp?"

"None, sir. But truthfully, I was focused on making it here to meet up with you."

"You weren't followed by any Malum, were you?" Kesh asked.

"Definitely not. I made sure of that."

"That is all." Kesh ended the inquiry.

Edon bowed and disappeared among the clan members in the camp.

"Come. We must speak with Tiev," Kesh said to Adirah.

There were eight clan members huddled around Tiev as Kesh and Adirah approached. They were all speaking in hushed tones. When one of them spotted Kesh and Adirah, he stood up, and the others followed his lead. The conversation abruptly stopped. The men parted to allow Kesh and Adirah through to Tiev. Tiev was sitting on a boulder.

"How are you feeling, my brother?" Kesh asked.

"Better. I was fed mortal blood. I can feel my strength regenerating already."

"Good news. We will need you in the coming war."

"We are not running anymore?" Tiev asked, surprised.

"No. We are standing and fighting. It is time," Kesh said with authority.

"When do we attack?" Tiev asked eagerly, looking at the eight clan members surrounding them.

"We will discuss our strategy in the morning. Right now we all need to rest and recover. The battle will not be easy, and we will all need to be at full strength," Kesh said to all the men.

Kesh and Adirah found a spot in the camp from whence they could easily view the entire camp. It was on the edge of the clearing, on top of a little rise. They settled themselves against some boulders and looked out over the camp. The camp began to quiet down.

"Why didn't you tell me we were going to fight? I don't like it, Kesh. I need to protect my baby," Adirah said.

"I don't need to get your permission, Dira. I am king." He shot her a daring look.

This was something Adirah had never seen. Before she started to make a scene and argue with Kesh, she realized that the clan could see them. She needed to keep up a strong appearance. Instead of challenging him, she turned away from him, clutched her belly, and closed her eyes.

A few hours later Adirah was awakened by Kesh. He was shaking her and whispering, "Dira, get up. We have to leave."

She rubbed her eyes groggily. "What?"

"We have to leave now," he whispered with command.

Adirah heard the urgency in his voice. She was instantly awake. She looked around the camp, expecting there to be a flurry of activity, but all she saw was the clan members all sleeping. "What's going on? No one is moving."

"We are leaving. No one else. We must go now." He took her by the arm and helped her up. She barely had time to get her feet under her before they were running through the forest.

"Kesh, where are we going?"

"I know who the traitor is," he said.

"Who?"

"I watched one of the clan members sneak off. I had my suspicions before, but this solidified them."

"I thought we were fighting?" she said as she tried to keep up with Kesh's rapid pace.

"I was never intending to fight right now. I said that to see their reactions."

"Why didn't you tell me?"

"I was afraid one of the clan members would read your mind and know I was lying. I needed you to believe me." Kesh pulled her as they made a sharp left down the side of the mountain. They got to the bottom of the incline, and Kesh stopped. He turned to her and grabbed her shoulders. "Dira, you have great powers. Maybe the greatest I have ever seen. I need to teach you to harness and control those powers. Right now you can't understand the awesome power you have."

Adirah was taking it all in. It seemed that every hour her life was taking a new turn and she was learning more and more about her new life. She nodded her understanding.

"We need to disappear so I can teach you and you can give birth to our baby. Our destiny is to be a royal family," Kesh told her.

As Kesh was explaining his plan, Tiev reentered the camp with four members of the Malum Clan. They quietly snuck over to the others and roused them from their slumber. They all followed Tiev as they snuck through camp then fanned out and converged on the sight where Kesh and Adirah had last been seen. Tiev was enraged when their sneak attack came up empty. He had come from the side, holding a wooden stake to plunge through Kesh's heart. He had jumped and come down with his full force, only to hit an empty mound of clothing. Kesh had bundled together some clothes and had made the bundle look like two bodies sleeping there.

With rage in his eyes, Tiev looked at the men with him and commanded, "Find them!"

All twelve men disappeared into the forest to hunt down their prey. Tiev stood in the spot where Kesh had been. His jaw was clenched, and his fists were tight. He vowed revenge for the death of Vila.

Adirah screamed in agony. Fear was etched on Kesh's face. Adirah had never seen this from him. He was always so strong, so sure of himself. She screamed out again. "Squeeze my hand!" she yelled.

Kesh followed her orders and took her hand. She did all the squeezing, practically breaking Kesh's hand. The baby was almost out. The local nurse was urging Adirah to push. Kesh would have to get inside the nurse's mind later to make her forget that she had ever seen them. The birth was happening in Kesh and Adirah's home somewhere in the hills of Virginia. Adirah had enrolled in classes at the local university, and Kesh was using the campus as his feeding ground.

One last push and the baby appeared. Kesh cried when he saw his son for the first time. The nurse cut the umbilical cord and then handed the baby boy to his mother. Adirah held on to her son, tears and sweat staining her face.

"Oh, my beautiful boy," she cooed. "My beautiful little Adis."

Kesh stroked Adirah's forehead and kissed the top of his son's tiny head. "We have fulfilled the first part of our destiny. We are a royal family," he declared.

The three of them were together for the first time. Adirah and Kesh were ready to do everything in their power to protect their newborn. Their journey was far from over, their return to the clan would come in due time, but for now Kesh and Adirah were content to stay where they were and raise their son.